Echoes
From the Heart

Echoes From the Heart

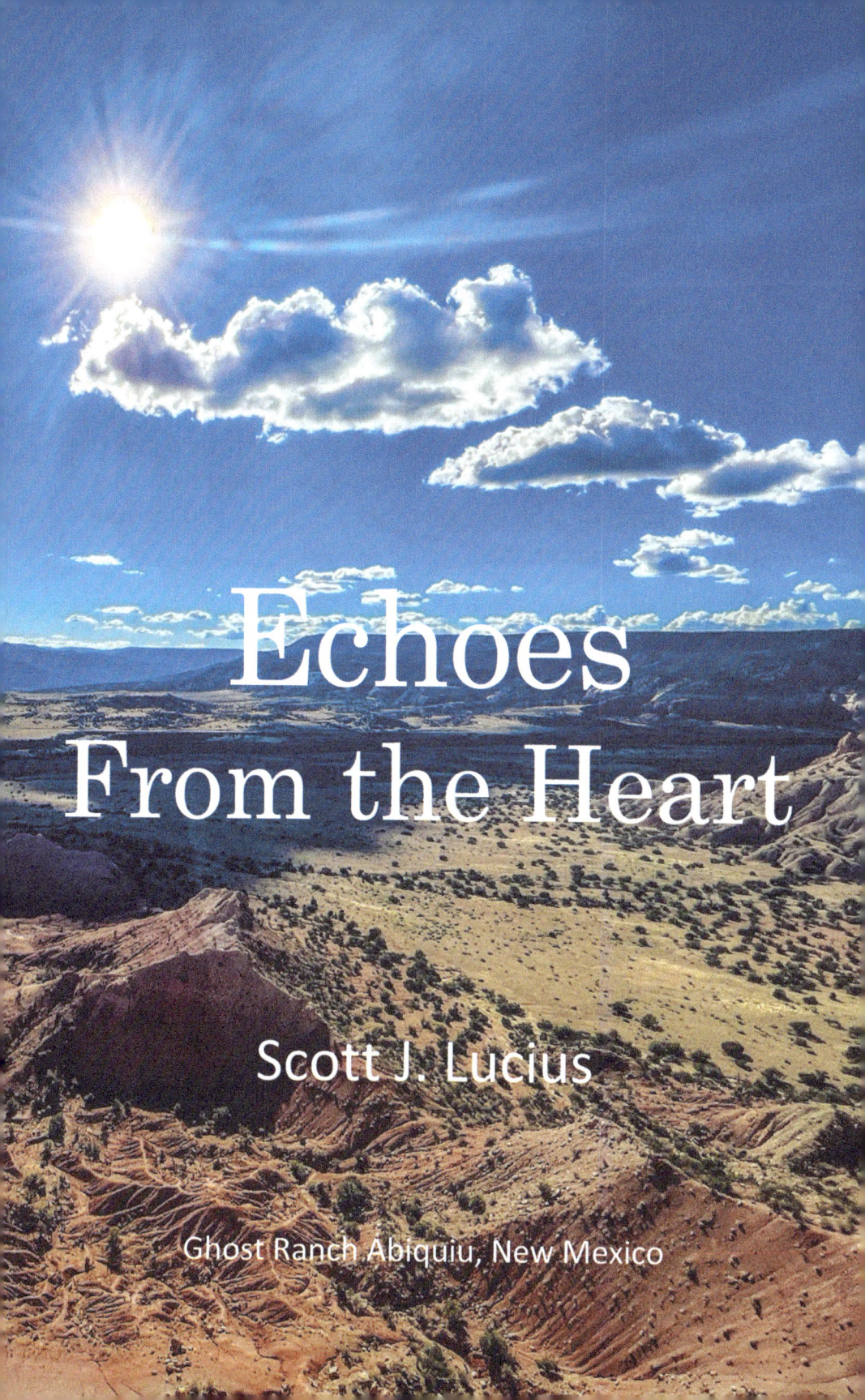

Scott J. Lucius

Ghost Ranch Abiquiu, New Mexico

© Copyright 2024 Scott J. Lucius, Poetic Expressions

All rights reserved. No part of this book, either photographs, images, or text, may be reproduced or transmitted in any form except reviews without permission in writing from the author.

All rights reserved by the U.S. Copyright Act of 1976. The scanning, uploading, and electronic sharing of any part of this book without the permission of the publisher and author constitutes unlawful piracy and theft of the author's intellectual property. If you would like to use material from this book (other than for review purposes), prior written permission must be obtained by contacting the publisher and author at sjlucius@gmail.com. Thank you for your support of the author's rights.

All photographs and text by Scott J. Lucius, unless otherwise stated.

Book design by Scott J. Lucius
Edited by Monique Stempowski

eBook ISBN: 978-1-965683-81-1
Paperback ISBN: 978-1-965683-82-8
Hardback ISBN: 978-1-965683-83-5

Front Cover: By Scott J. Lucius

To my father, Leo Joseph Lucius, whose unconditional love and steadfast faith in me made every challenge surmountable. He was more than a parent—he was a constant friend and a lifelong source of inspiration. He was my hero. His legacy lives within me, guiding me through every step of life.

ACKNOWLEDGMENTS

I want to express my deepest thanks to my family and friends, whose constant support has been my greatest strength. Special thanks to my sister, Cynthia Lucius, and my cousins, Laurie (Lucius) Clouse, Diane Lucius-Reedy, Lisa Pirwitz, and Diana Jackson. Your love and encouragement have given me hope through my hardest times.

A sincere thank you to my editor Monique Stempowski, for her valuable feedback and support.

I'm also incredibly grateful to the inspiring community of poets and readers. Your passion has motivated me to share my work with the world.

To all of you, I am deeply thankful for helping me on this journey of expression.

CONTENTS

PREFACE 2
INTRODUCTION 4
INSPIRATIONAL 7
   Dare to Dream 8
   Silver Threads in Shadowed Skies 10
   Embrace with Love 12
   Azure Hues 15
   Dreams Unleashed 16
   Guardians of the Mind's Realm 19
   Journey of Belonging 20
   To Be a Dog 23
   Unveiled 24
   Albatross 27
   Something Will Bloom Tomorrow 28
   Sunrise Serenade 31
   Whisper of Cascading Waters 32
   Journey of Life 35
   Everything Has Beauty 36
   Quilt of Life 39
   Dusk's Embrace 40
   Finding Gold 42
   The Karma Equation 44
   The Joy to Live 46
NATURE 49
   Stellar Symphony 50
   Sunset Serenity 53

The Seasons of My Resolve 54
Sunset's Tender Farewell 57
Whispers of the Night 58
Muddy Water's Edge 61
Echoes in the Gale 62
Whispers to the Wind 65
Rhapsody of the Storm 66
Garden of Thoughts 69
Fire Tree 70
Whispers of Ambergris Caye 73
Resilience's Gem 74
The Serenity of Reflection 77
Whispers by the Watermill 78
Sovereign of the Serengeti 81
Echoes in the Desert Homestead 82

SORROW *85*
Why Love Feels Like a Penitence 87
Why Does Love Hurt 88
Fragments of Serenity 91
Field of Valor 92
The Tears That Taught Me 95
Someday, I Hope to Forget 96
Never Let Me Down Again 99
The Eternal Knot 100
The Many Faces We Wear 102
Embers of Challenge 104
Harvesting Sorrow 107
In Chains 108

Jars of Dawn 110

Apology 112

Shards of Serenity 115

Tell Me the Darkness 116

Roaring Silhouettes 119

A Quiet Descent 120

LOVE *123*

The Loudest Way to Love 124

Special Moments 127

Through My Eyes 128

Echoes of Emotions 130

Unspoken Echoes 132

Embrace of the Abyss 135

Unclaimed Thoughts 136

A World of Whimsy 139

Embraced by Moments 140

In the Realm of Truth 143

Whispers of Departure 144

Guardian of the Key 146

Fragments of Solace 148

Matters of a Giddy Heart 151

Unyielding Hearts United 152

Hearts Adrift 155

FAITH *157*

Strength in Our Toughest Battles 158

Thorns of Serenity 161

Fire with Fire 162

Guiding Lights of Christmas 165

Sentinel of the Shore 166
Echoes of Harmony 169
Ephemeral Graces 170
The Quiet Spark Within 173
Guiding Light 174
Sunflowers Fleeting Sunlight 177
Light from the Shadows 178
Crown of Thorns 181
The Lord's Mantle 182
Faith Amidst the Fury 185
Always Believe 186
Build Your Own Testimony 188

ABOUT THE AUTHOR 190
PHOTOGRAPH & PAINTINGS COPYRIGHTS 191

Echoes from the Heart

PREFACE

As I sit down to pen this preface, I am shrouded in the journey that has led to the creation of "Echoes from the Heart." This collection is not merely a gathering of words; it represents a deep and resonant mosaic of feelings, experiences, and introspections. Each piece is a fragment of the life I've experienced and the dreams that have fueled my spirit.

My path to poetry began as a subdued echo, a medium to voice the plethora of emotions that sought expression beyond the confines of ordinary language. This echo gradually evolved into a symphony of verses, each line a step forward, each stanza a milestone in my odyssey of self-discovery and articulation. This book, born from a marriage of passion and introspection, is a testament to that journey.

The poems in "Echoes from the Heart" are imbued with the spirit of the natural world, the ebb and flow of the human heart, and the delicate interplay of light and shadow within us. They reflect upon love and loss, hope and despair, joy and sorrow – themes that touch each of us at different moments in our lives.

In writing these verses, I frequently journeyed through the corridors of memory, revisiting moments of bliss and periods of adversity. Each poem became a conduit through which I navigated the complex current of emotions, a guide leading me through the unexplored realms of my inner landscape.

This collection will share a part of my being and resonate with you, the reader. If these poems offer comfort, kindle understanding, or serve as a companion in reflective moments, then my purpose has been achieved.

Echoes from the Heart

My heartfelt thanks go to those who have stood by me on this path. To my family, for their unwavering faith in my vision; to my friends, for their enduring support; and to my mentors, for their wise counsel – this book is a tribute to your generosity and belief.

I invite you to immerse yourself in "Echoes from the Heart." May these pages find an echo within you, reflecting the universal emotions that weave us together in the intricate areas of human experience.

With heartfelt thanks and warmth,

Scott J. Lucius

INTRODUCTION

Welcome, dear reader, to a world woven with words, a realm where emotions take flight in the form of verse. "Echoes from the Heart" is more than a collection of poems; it is a journey through the landscapes of the heart and soul, a voyage into the depths of what it means to feel, to dream, and to live.

In these pages, you will find reflections of love in its myriad forms, from the first flush of youthful passion to the deep, abiding affection that stands the test of time. Some verses speak of loss, of the aching void left by departed dreams and vanished voices. Yet, amidst this tapestry of the heart, there are also threads of hope and strands of resilience that speak of the human spirit's indomitable will to endure and flourish.

This book features a distinctive collection of poetry where each poem is accompanied by an image specifically crafted to reflect its essence. The imagery is designed to mirror and deepen the poem's themes, drawing readers into a richer emotional and intellectual experience. Each piece of visual art amplifies the poem's mood, adding layers of meaning and encouraging thoughtful reflection. Together, the words and images form a harmonious artistic expression, inviting readers to engage with poetry in a visually immersive way.

Each poem is a snapshot of life, capturing moments that, though fleeting, leave imprints on our being. Like echoes, these experiences reverberate within us, shaping who we are and become. This collection is an ode to these echoes, a recognition of their power and presence in our lives.

As you journey through these poems, you are invited to pause, ponder, and find pieces of your own story reflected in these lines and imagery. May you find solace in knowing that you are not alone in your experiences and that the echoes of your emotions resonate in unison with those of others.

This book is a tribute to the beauty and complexity of human emotions. It is an invitation to explore the corners of your heart, to listen to the echoes of your own emotions, and perhaps, in doing so, to understand a little more about the intricate puzzle that is the human experience.

Step into this journey of verse and let "Echoes from the Heart" resonate with you. Life thrives on taking us out of our comfort zone. It's in these moments that we find our resilience, face new challenges, and are inspired to improve and excel.

2nd Book – "Echoes: Whispers of the Soul"

In the second installment of the Echoes poetry series, "Echoes: Whispers of the Soul," I continue to explore the intricate tapestries of human emotions and experiences. Building upon the foundation of 'Echoes from the Heart,' I have taken a unique approach to enrich your reading experience. Each poem is accompanied by its own carefully selected imagery and picture. These visuals have been thoughtfully curated to enhance and enlighten your journey through the verses. As you immerse yourself in the world of these poems, you'll find that the fusion of words and imagery creates a deeper connection, inviting you to explore the emotions and stories in a more profound way. I believe that this addition will not only resonate with seasoned poetry enthusiasts but also captivate new readers, making this collection a truly immersive and enriching experience.

Echoes from the Heart

INSPIRATIONAL

Dare to Dream

In the heart's whisper, dreams take their stand,
Bold in their silence, like shadows in sand.
Courage unfurls, like a dawn-lit stream—
Dare to do, what you dare to dream.

Stars in the night, a guide, a gleam,
Darkened pathways, more real than they seem.
Chasing the comet's fleeting beam—
Dare to do, what you dare to dream.

Mountains high, where eagles scream,
Valleys deep, where rivers teem.
Nature's call, a constant theme—
Dare to do, what you dare to dream.

With each new step, horizons gleam,
The world expands in light supreme.
Beyond the known, we push extreme—
Dare to do, what you dare to dream.

In every struggle, against the stream,
Against all odds, or so it may seem.
In every effort, where passions gleam—
Dare to do, what you dare to dream.

At journey's end, when the last light demeans,
And the night enfolds our final scene.
In the heart's echo, a persistent theme—
Dare to do, what you dare to dream.

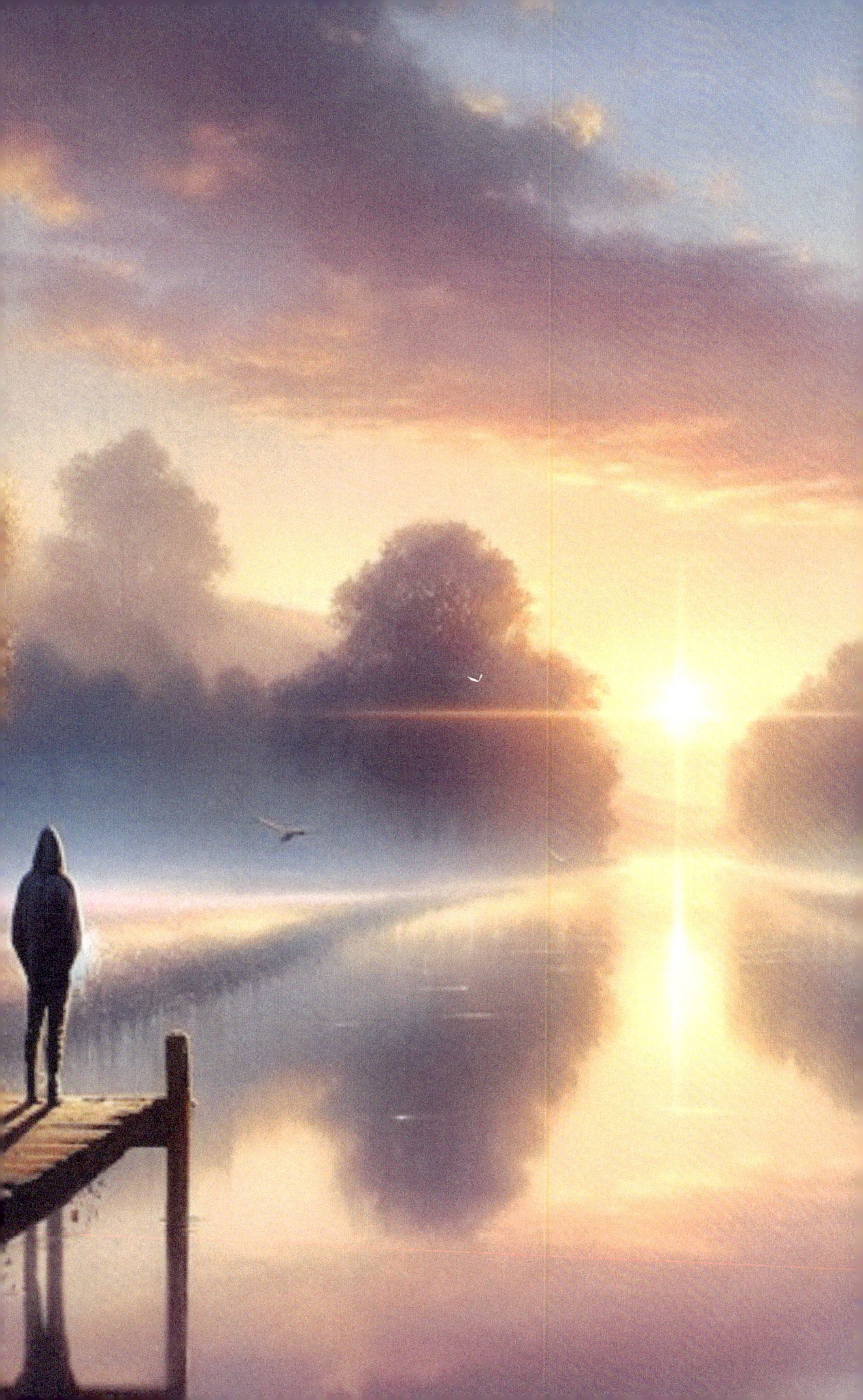

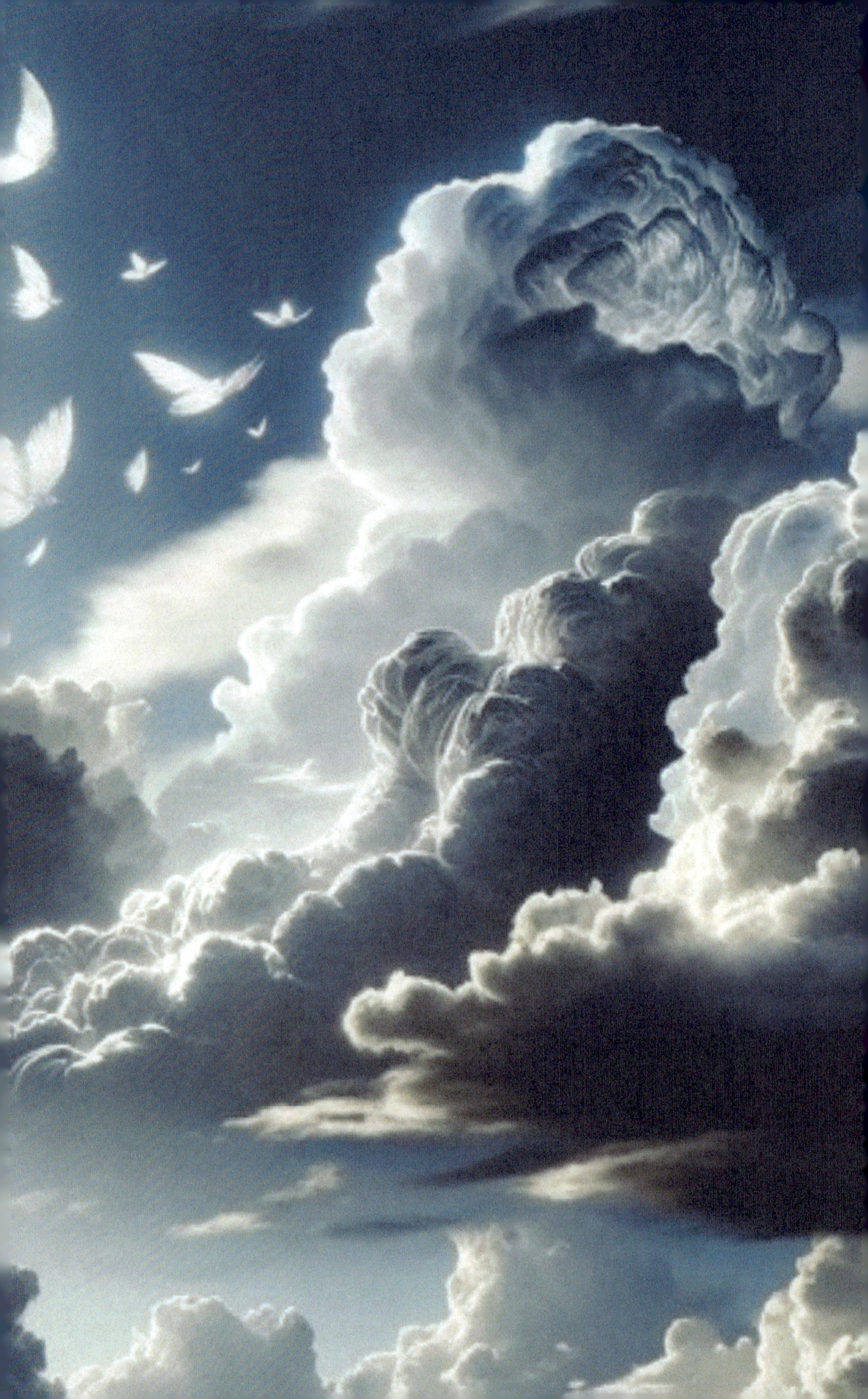

Echoes from the Heart

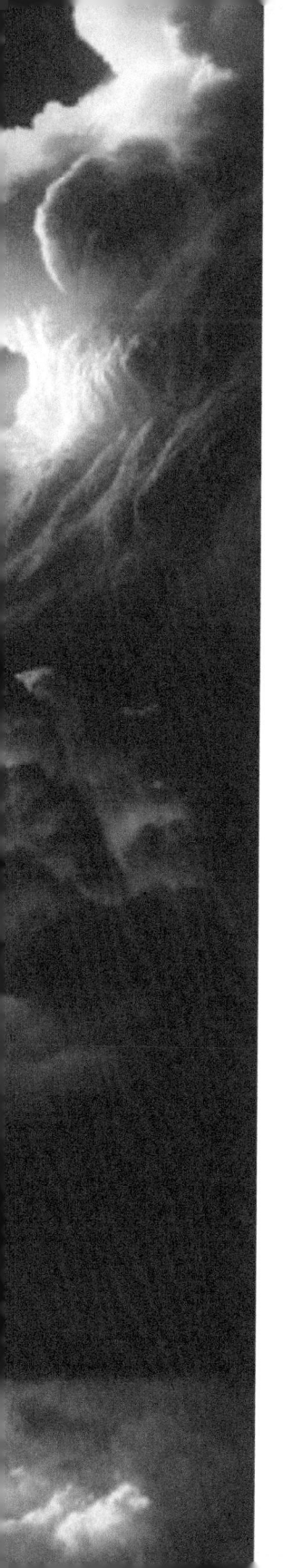

Silver Threads in Shadowed Skies

In the vast expanse where darkness sprawls,
Threads weave through night's shrouded veils.
Each glimmer, a story of resilience calls,
In the heart of storms, hope prevails.

Beneath the cloak of night's deep sorrow,
Lies a promise of a brighter morrow.
For in every tear that the heavens shed,
Gleams a silver lining, delicately spread.

Through the tumult, we come to see,
Strength revealed in winds set free.
In every cloud that dims the sun,
Lies a silver thread, quietly spun.

In the stillness after the thunder's wail,
Whispers rise upon the gale.
Soft voices hum of battles won,
Of light reborn when shadows run.

In the whispers of the rain's soft sigh,
Resides a truth that never dies.
Every drop holds light, refined,
In darkened skies, silver lines entwined.

At the end of each tempest's furious roar,
Rests a peace, not felt before.
In the darkest clouds, high above,
Dwells the silver lining, a symbol of love.

Embrace with Love

In moments dim, when shadows loom,
And pain whispers an eerie tune,
Ask with heart, in silent room,
What would love, in kindness, bloom?

In valleys deep where sorrows dwell,
And tears like rivers, stories tell,
There, love's warmth can softly quell,
The icy fears and break their spell.

For love, a lantern in the night,
Sheds gentle rays, a guiding light,
In pain's embrace, it holds us tight,
And lifts us high, beyond our plight.

In tender hands, love cradles fear,
Transforms the dark, makes all things clear.
Its whispered words we hold so dear,
In love, we heal, year after year.

In love's response, find strength anew,
A path of hope, a brighter view,
For every ache, love has a clue,
In kindness, finds a way through.

So, when you're lost, in depths of woe,
Remember love's eternal glow,
Its tender touch, a healing flow.
In love's response, our spirits grow.

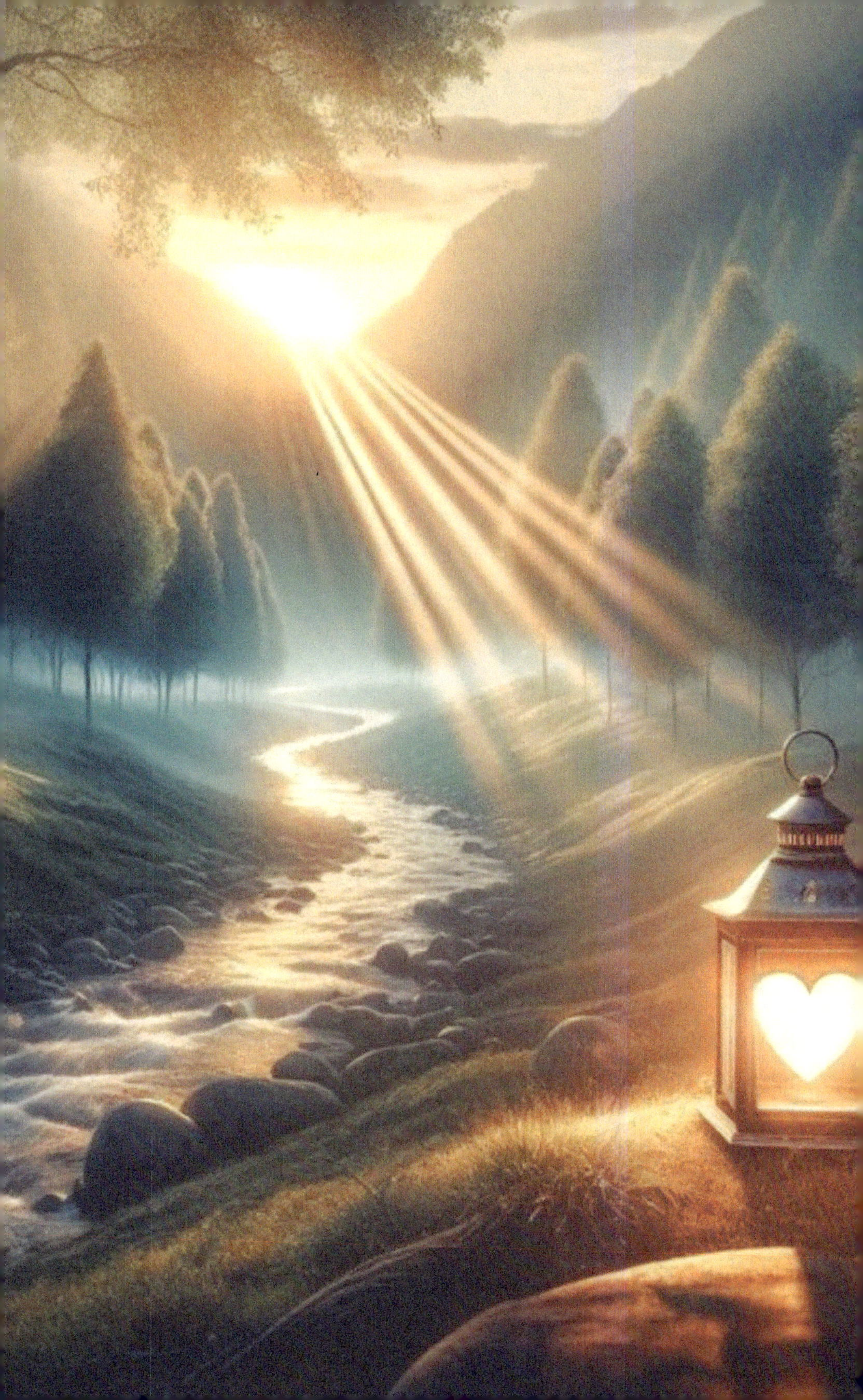

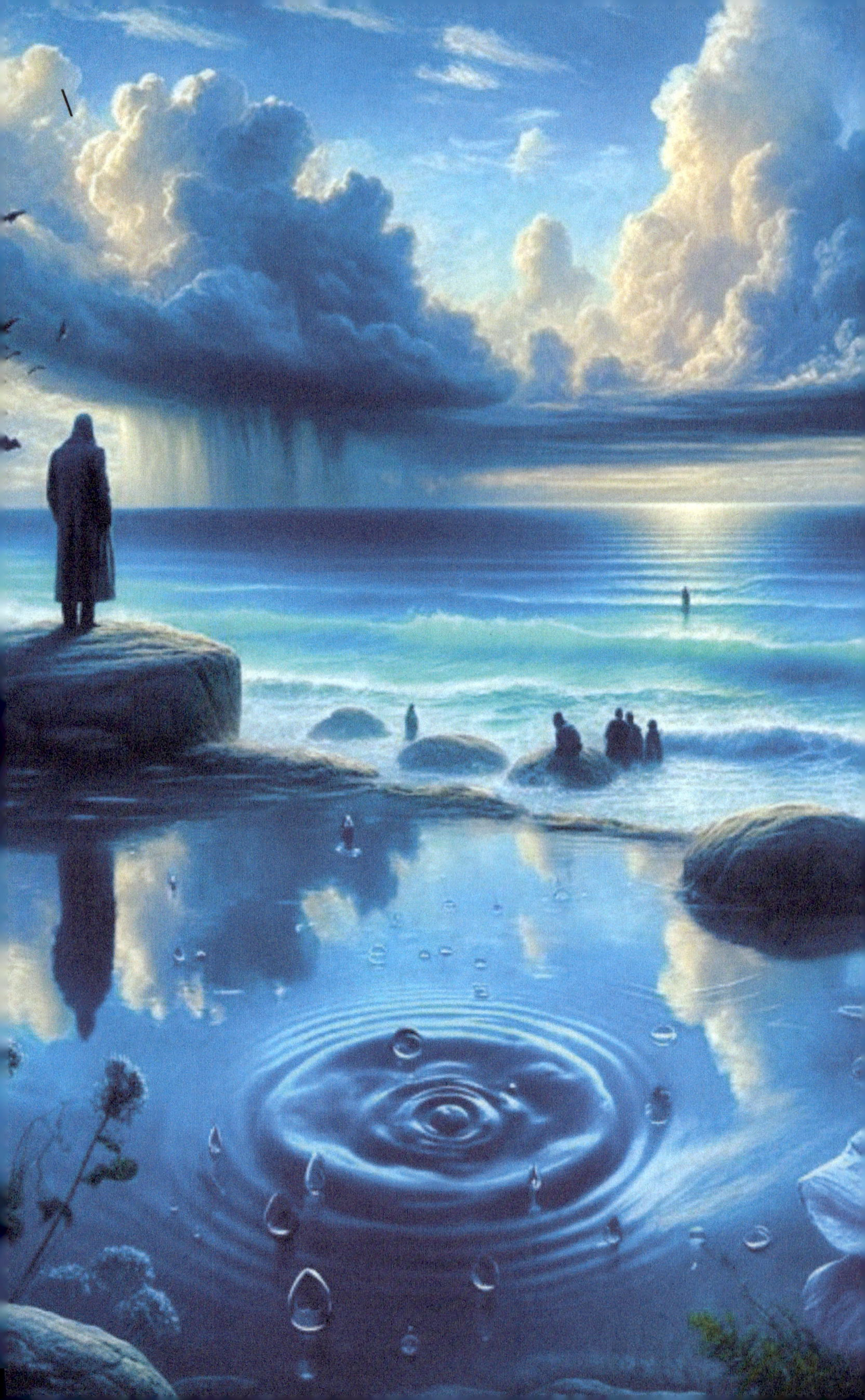

Echoes from the Heart

Azure Hues

Blue, a color's simple name,
Conceals a world, beyond the same.
Azure skies, a boundless view,
Turquoise oceans, vast and true.

In its depths, emotions hide,
Feelings that we often bide.
When hearts are heavy, eyes are wet,
Blue's the shade that sorrow met.

It paints the world when tears are near,
A universal sign, so sincere.
Yet in its melancholy state,
It binds us all, entwines our fate.

But blue is more than grief's embrace,
It dances in the open space.
In bright horizons, oceans wide,
Blue holds the joy we cannot hide.

A peaceful hue, both calm and strong,
In blue, we find where we belong.
It lifts us up, it pulls us through,
In every shade, a life anew.

From sky to sea, from dusk till dawn,
Blue's steady rhythm lingers on.
In every tone, we hear its song,
A color vast, where hearts belong.

Dreams Unleashed

Whispers of courage, in the silent night,
Stars above, shining oh so bright.
In each heart, a dream's flight,
Dare to do, what you dare to dream, a sight.

Through the forests, dark and deep,
Where secrets and ancient whispers creep.
In every step, a promise to keep,
Dare to do, what you dare to dream, a leap.

Mountains high, where eagles glide,
Scaling peaks with strength inside.
Through every climb, fears subside,
Dare to do, what you dare to dream, with pride.

Oceans vast, with mysteries untold,
Waves that dance, bold and cold.
In every tide, stories unfold,
Dare to do, what you dare to dream, be bold.

In the sky, where dreams soar free,
Beyond the reach of you and me.
In every cloud, a destiny,
Dare to do, what you dare to dream, a key.

At the end of the path, when journeys cease,
And hearts find courage, their quiet peace.
In every soul, dreams find release,
Dare to do, what you dare to dream, increase.

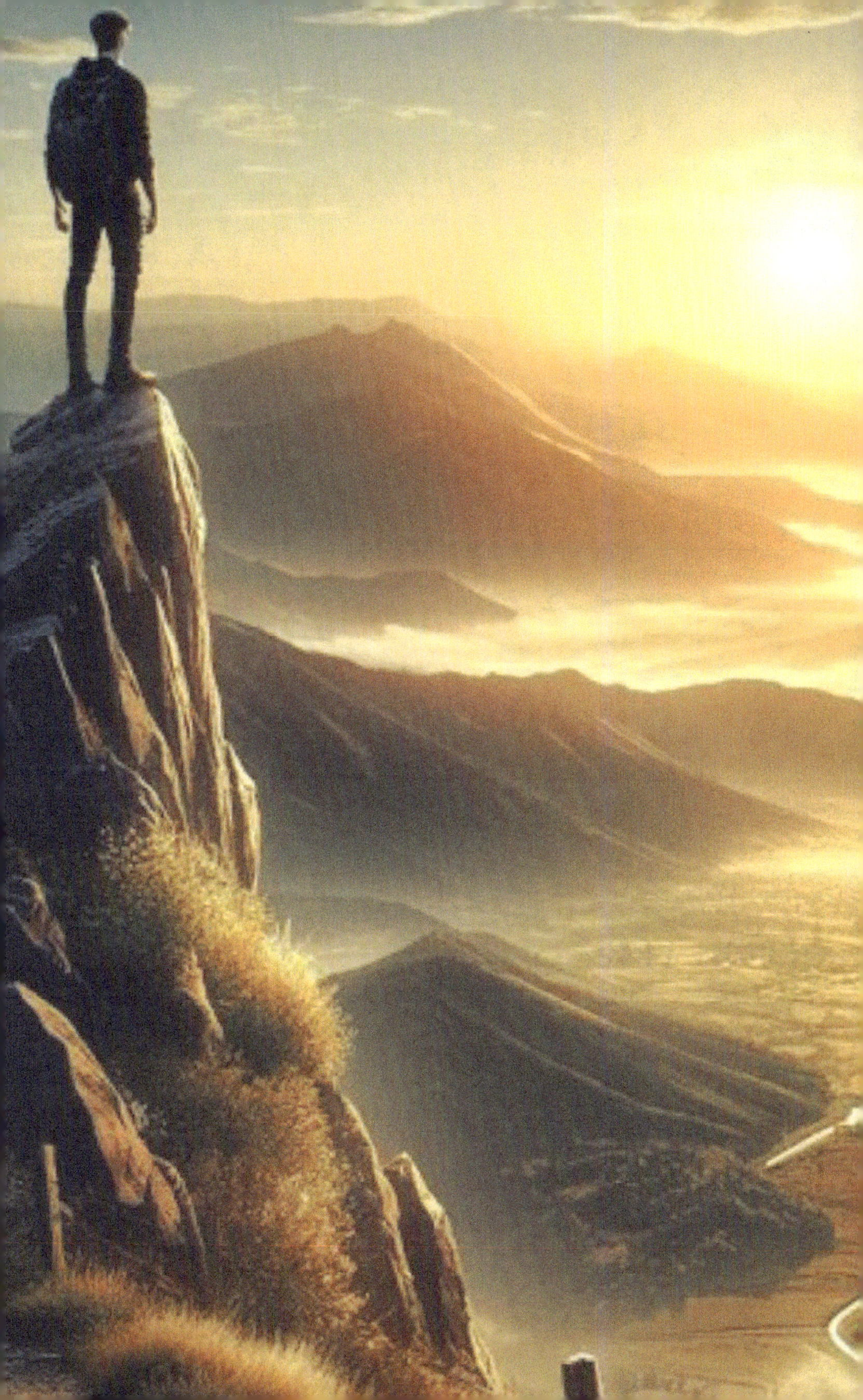

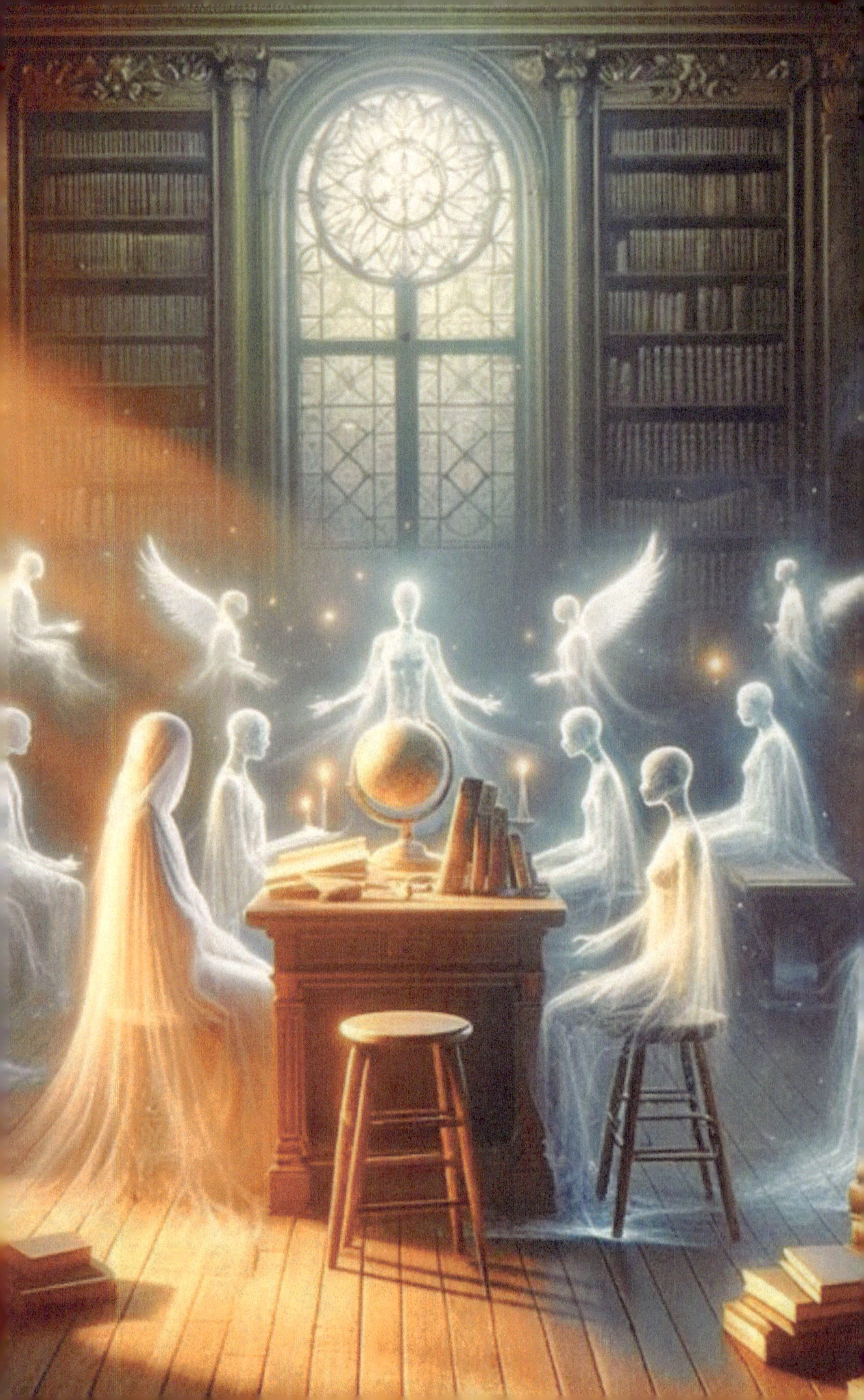

Echoes from the Heart

Guardians of the Mind's Realm

In the mind's halls, tread with care,
For thoughts are tenants, with stories to share.
Welcome the ones with light and song,
Turn away shadows where they don't belong.

Within these walls, let kindness reside,
Banish doubt, and humble pride.
Invite the laughter, hope, and dreams,
Let them flow like gentle streams.

Guard perception, hold the key,
The mind's a place where spirits fly free.
Cherish wisdom, let it speak,
Lighting the path to peace we seek.

In this realm, let harmony dwell,
A sanctuary where good can swell.
In heart's chambers, let truth stay,
Guiding the soul on its way.

From fleeting thoughts, a world takes form,
Shaped by love, or silent storm.
Choose the bright, dispel the gloom,
Foster light in every room.

Be wise in thoughts you allow to rise,
For they shape your world, touching the skies.
Let good alone in your headspace rent,
Creating peace, where minds are meant.

Journey of Belonging

With blisters on my feet, I tread,
On paths unknown, where dreams are led.
Through fields and hills, under the moon's soft song,
I search for the place where my heart belongs.

The wind whispers tales, old and new,
Of distant lands, under skies so blue.
Each step, a story, a memory prolongs,
In my quest to find where I truly belong.

Across valleys low, and peaks so high,
Beneath the sun, beneath the sky.
Each trial faced, each battle strong,
Brings me closer to where I belong.

Through forests deep, and rivers wide,
I journey forth, with hope as my guide.
The stars above, like a guiding throng,
Light my way to where I belong.

Amidst the shadows, in the night's embrace,
I find strength in this endless chase.
With every dawn, my spirit grows strong,
Closer to where my soul belongs.

At journey's end, I shall see,
The place that calls, whispers to me.
In that haven, my heart will sing a song,
At last, I'll be where I belong.

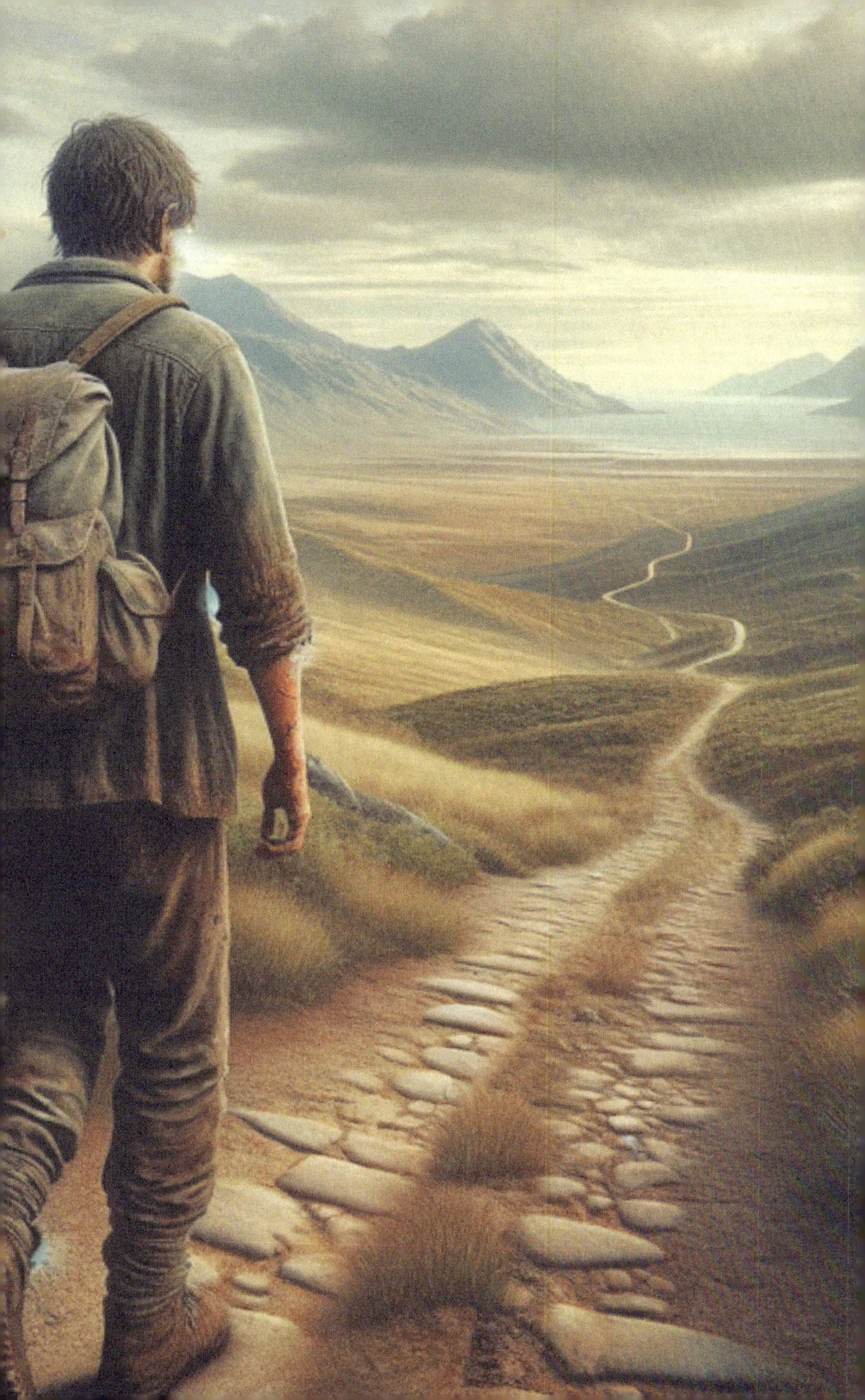

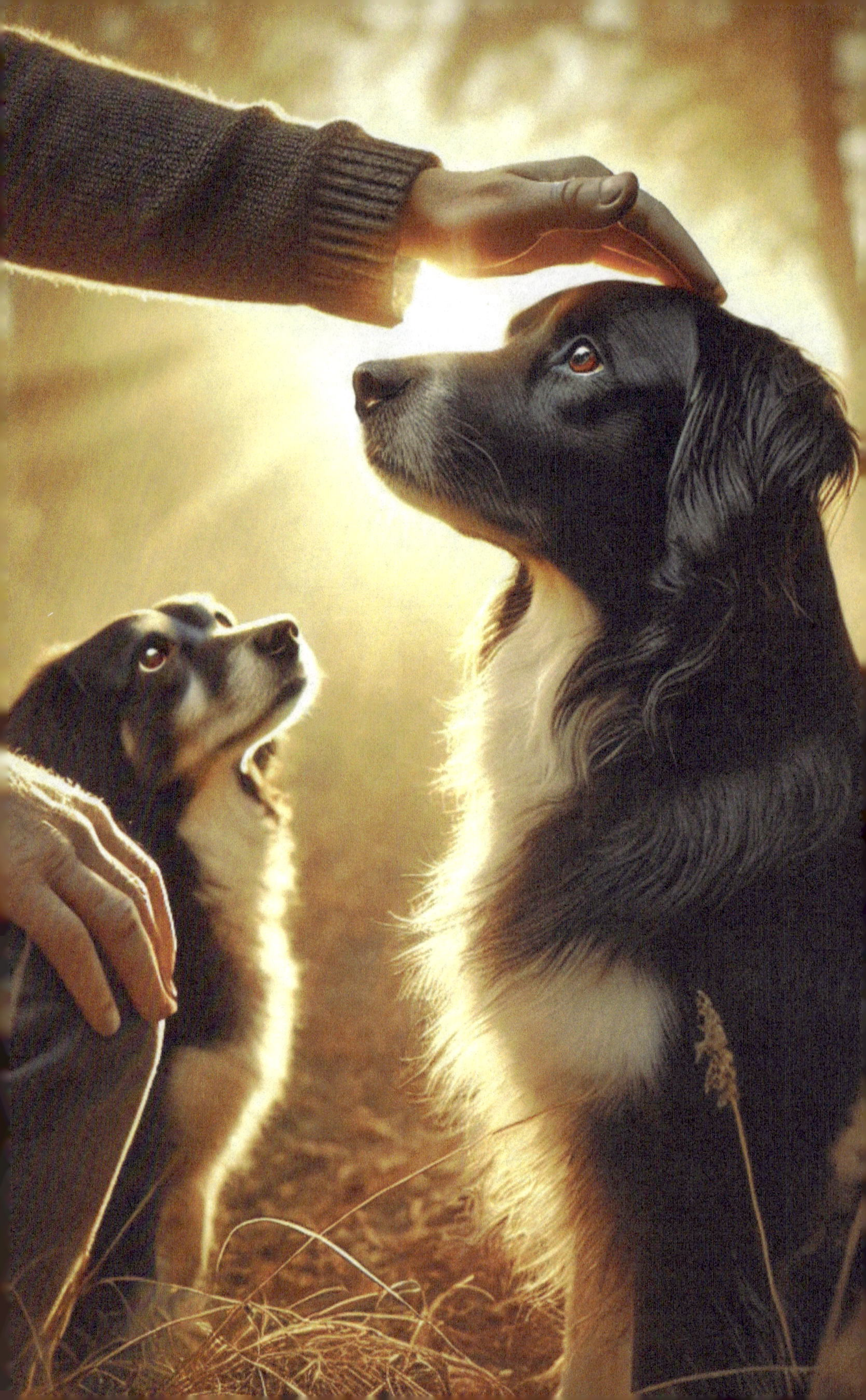

To Be a Dog

I want to be a dog, so free,
With love that's endless, always true,
No burdened mind, no need to flee,
Just loyalty in all I do.

A wagging tail, a simple touch,
My heart would beat with boundless care,
Not asking much, but giving much,
Content to always just be there.

I'd greet each day with gentle eyes,
No worry weighing on my brow,
Each sunrise new, no need for lies,
Just living purely in the now.

I'd chase the wind, the grass, the sky,
And find joy in the smallest things,
A bark, a howl, a carefree cry,
In every moment, freedom sings.

For love I'd give, not ask to earn,
A faithful friend through thick and thin,
In every corner, love would burn,
No end to where it could begin.

To be a dog, without the pain
Of human hearts that break and bend,
Just love, pure love, without a stain,
Until my days come to an end.

Unveiled

Do you glimpse me through the gaps,
In the barriers I've wrapped.
Guarding self from hurt and woe,
Pushing you yet can't let go.

In the labyrinth, I stride,
Hiding tears, I've tried to hide.
Will you venture, seek the start,
Find the rhythm of my heart?

With a whisper, can you call,
Break the fortress, watch it fall?
Reach out, melt the icy guard,
Ignite feelings, once too hard.

See me, beyond the guise I wear,
Not the shield, but soul laid bare.
In the night, can you trace,
The silenced fears, I embrace.

Will your affection ever stand,
Against the walls, I've planned.
Embrace the spirit, once remote,
And find the song, in notes I wrote.

For in your eyes, a light does gleam,
A warmth that wakes me from the dream.
If you can stay, through storm and fire,
You'll unveil the love I desire.

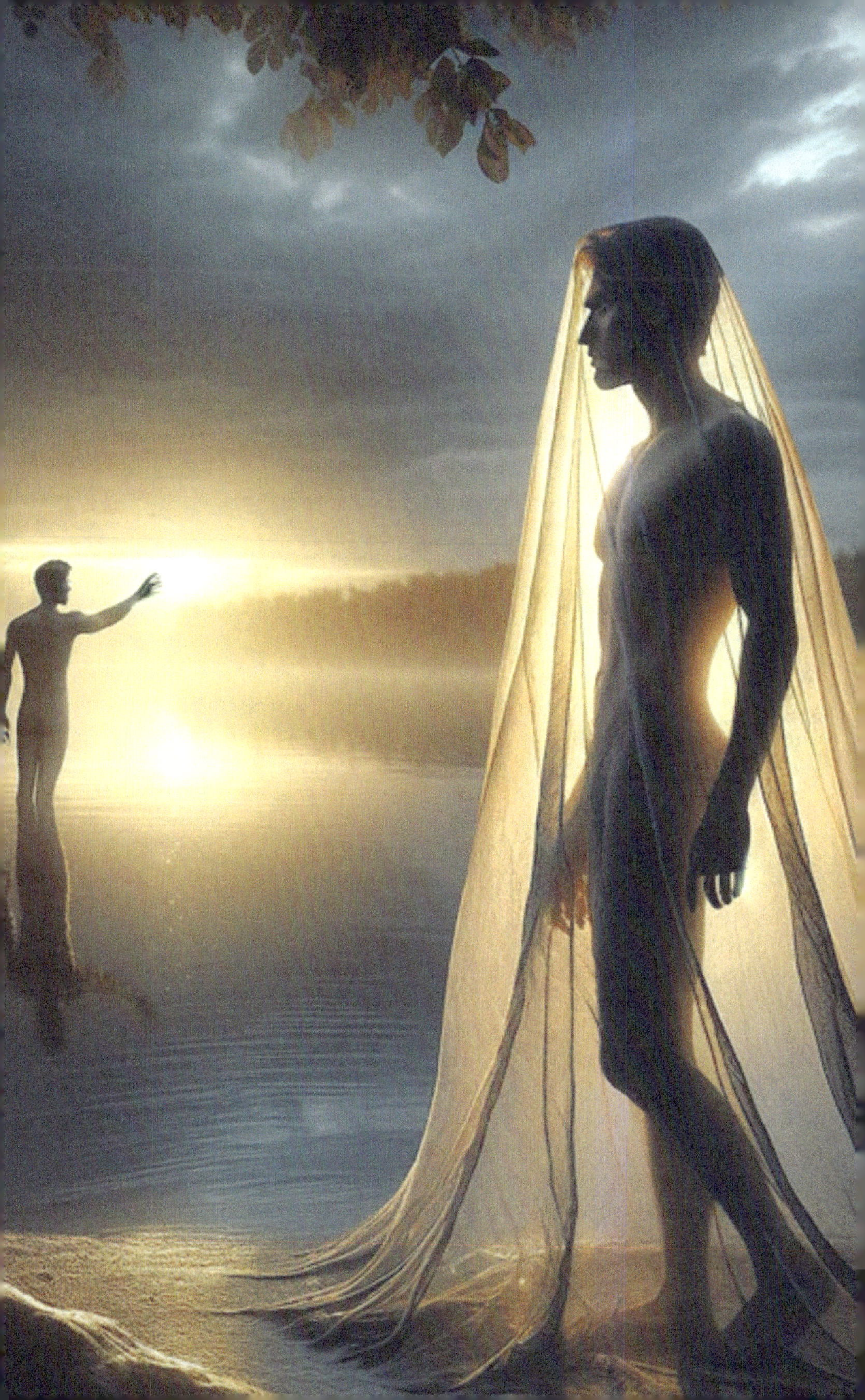

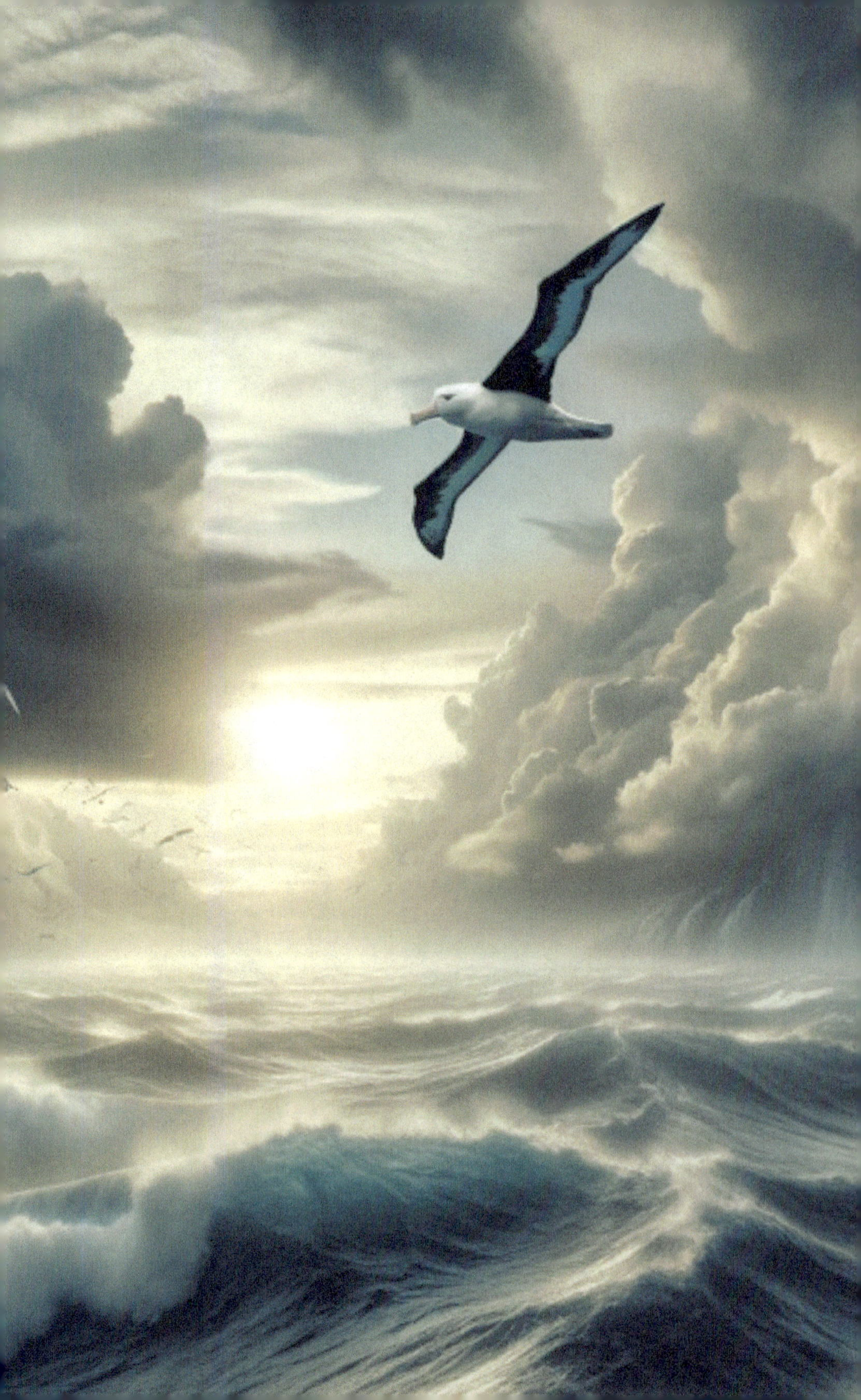

Echoes from the Heart

Albatross

I know why the albatross soars,
Eluding mankind's deceptive cores.
It glides on heaven's gentle breeze,
Observing humanity's ceaseless decrees.

In search of lands unmarred by hand,
Paradises where no humans stand.
Yet, no haven for its wings to rest,
To the winds, it remains a guest.

Amid uproars, formless, wild,
It seeks a sanctuary, nature's child.
Awaiting Earth's rebirth, anew,
A renewal not destined to ensue.

Bound to the skies until life's end,
In pursuit of peace, its eternal friend.
The albatross discerns below,
Earth, a land where turmoil flows.

On Satan's soil, it sees the strife,
A world embroiled in endless life.
Yet, in its flight, there lies a tale,
Of resilience, beyond the gale.

Through storm and calm, it finds its way,
A silent guardian, day by day.
In its journey, there's truth to find,
About our world, and humankind.

Echoes from the Heart

Something Will Bloom Tomorrow

Amidst the tempest's furious roar,
Raindrops dance on the trembling floor.
Lightning splits the ink-black sky,
As thunder's voice echoes, oh so high.

But within this chaotic display,
A tranquil beauty finds its way.
The storm's wild rage begins to wane,
As gentle whispers soothe the pain.

Cloud's part to reveal a silver moon,
Casting a tranquil, silvery tune.
The thunder's growl turns to a sigh,
As the storm bids the night goodbye.

In nature's dance, both fierce and grand,
Destruction weaves with a careful hand.
From every tear the heavens cry,
Sprouts the seed of earth and sky.

In the stillness of the aftermath,
Nature's fury takes a quiet bath.
A moment's respite, a hush profound,
In the calming of a thunderstorm found.

As the night gives way to light's soft glow,
In the earth's embrace, new life will show.
And in this peaceful, tranquil morrow,
Indefinity, something will bloom tomorrow.

Inspired by Leslie Crosby

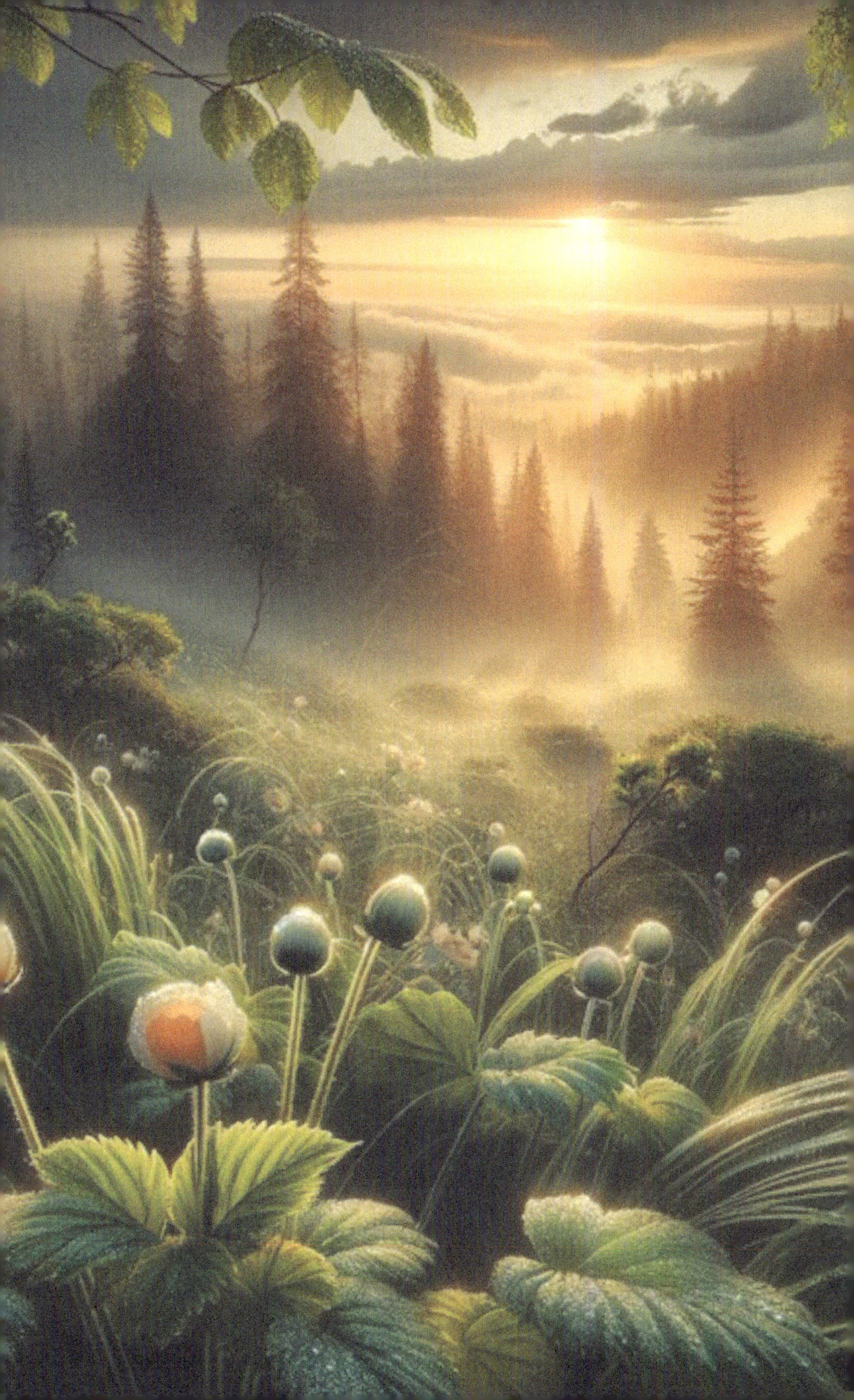

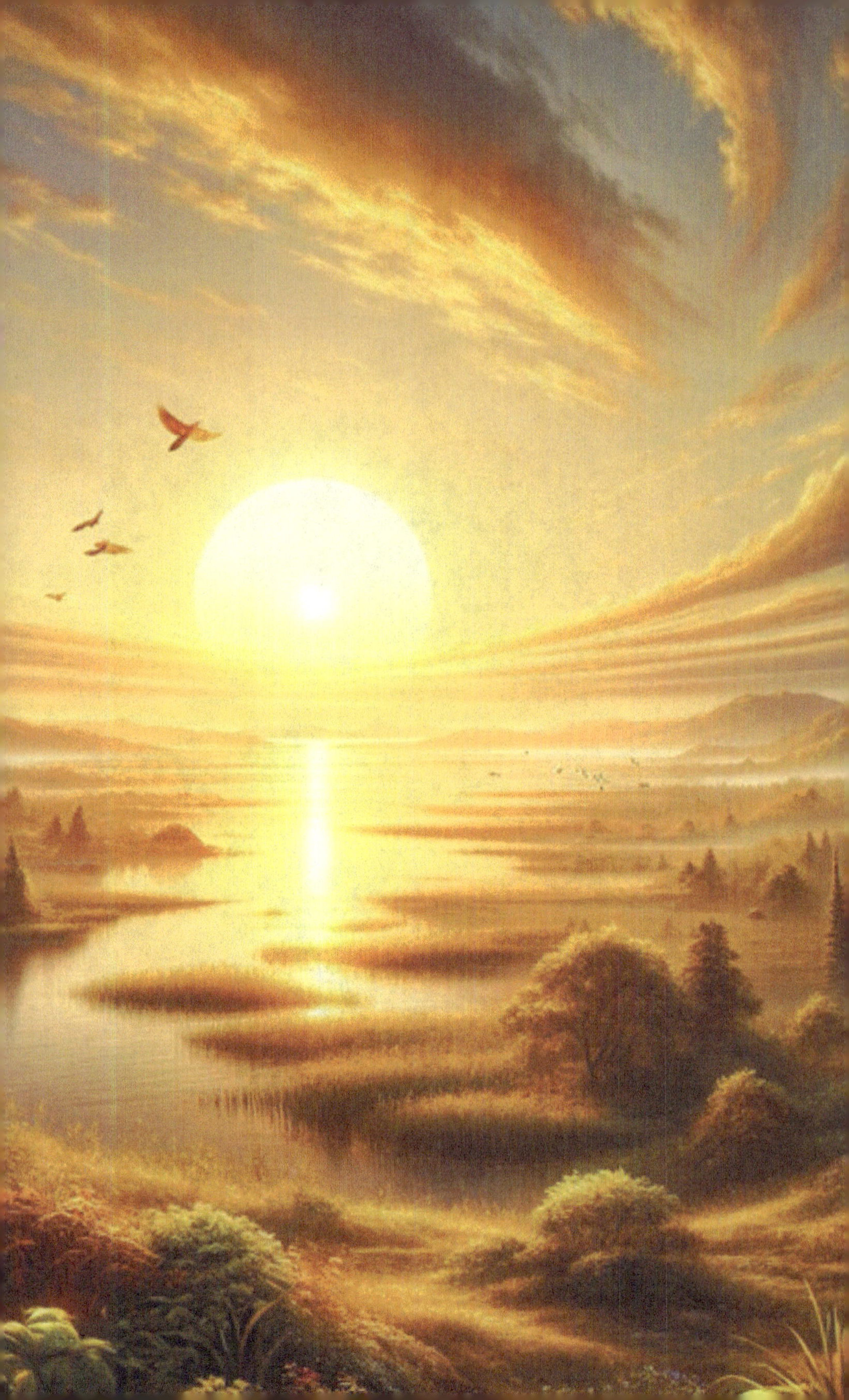

Echoes from the Heart

Sunrise Serenade

The sun peaking in, God's flashlight gleams,
A dawn's soft kiss, in morning's streams.
Golden hues dance, as day redeems,
Nature awakens, in joyful beams.

With gentle touch, the world's adorned,
God's flashlight paints, a canvas transformed.
Life stirs awake, from slumber's yawn,
A symphony of colors, a new day's spawn.

Casting away shadows, it takes its stand,
God's flashlight's touch, on sea and land.
A masterpiece born, so vast and grand,
Morning's embrace, across the land.

So, rise with the sun, let your spirit ignite,
In God's flashlight's glow, take flight.
Embrace the day with all you're might,
A symphony of hope, in morning's light.

In whispers of light, the birds take wing,
Harmonies of dawn, they gracefully sing.
Every hue, a promise does bring,
In this serene hour, hearts cling.

Beneath the sky, so brilliantly lit,
In this tranquil moment, we quietly sit.
The world anew, in splendor fit,
With every sunrise, we recommit.

In the soft glow, life finds its pace,
Each creature awakes, with unique grace.
In God's grand design, all find their place,
In the morning's glory, we embrace.

Whisper of Cascading Waters

Hush, murmurs the rushing stream,
Share your sorrows, let them gleam.
In the gentle flow, they sway,
Washed to peace, they find their way.

Amidst the rocks, they softly weep,
Secrets in the water's keep,
With liquid grace, they twist and play,
Released, they dance, in the light of day.

As moonlight paints a silver scene,
Your worries, here, need not convene,
For nature's choir, a soothing display,
Sings solace, where your heart can sway.

The stars above, a calming sight,
Reflecting in the waters' light,
Embrace the night, in dreams array,
Your troubles, like ripples, fade away.

Beneath the surface, shadows slide,
Tangled thoughts, no need to hide.
The stream will take them all away,
In whispered currents, calm will stay.

So, by this stream, in tranquil peace,
Let your cares and fears release,
In nature's arms, you'll find your way,
In the whisper of waters, come what may.

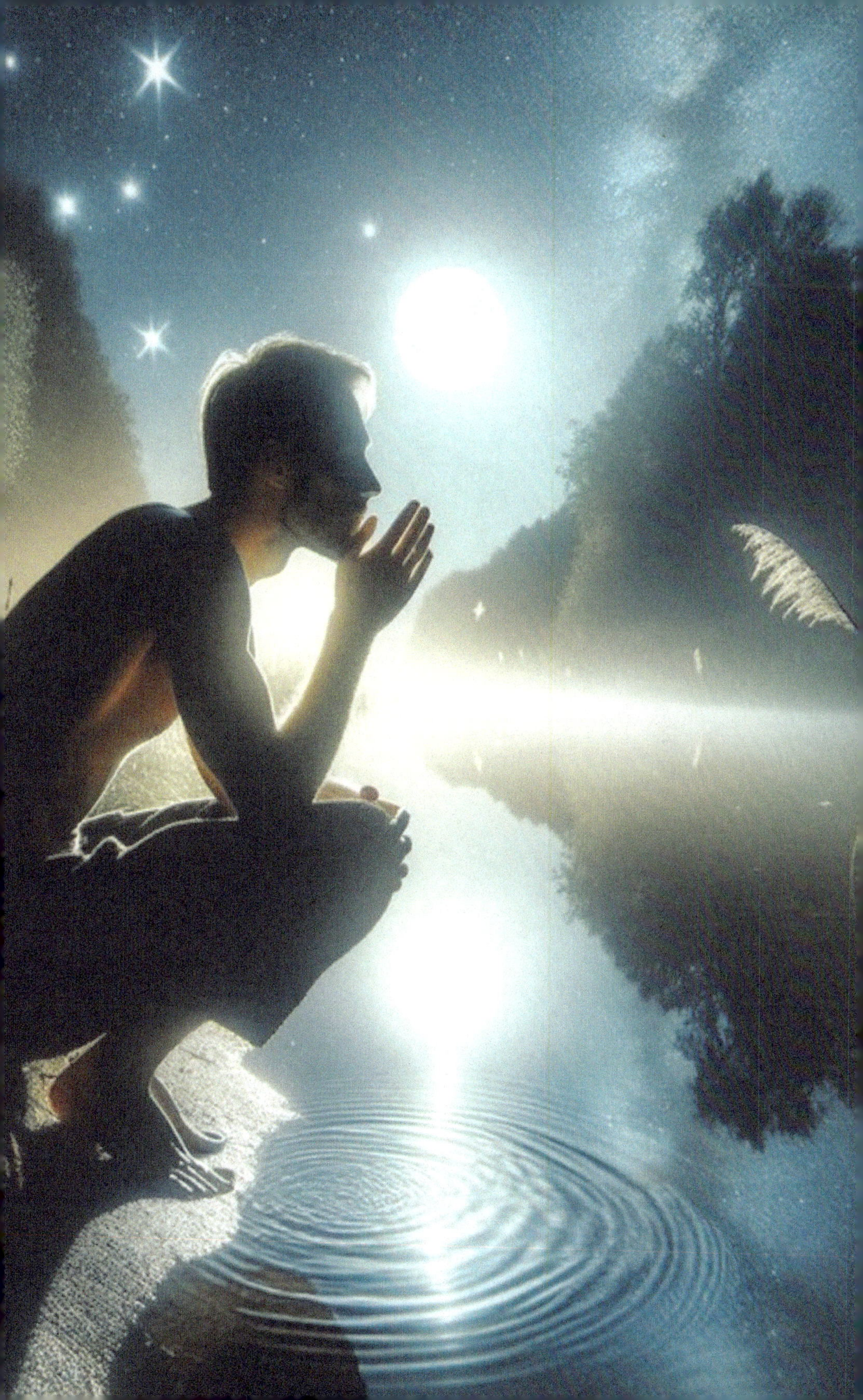

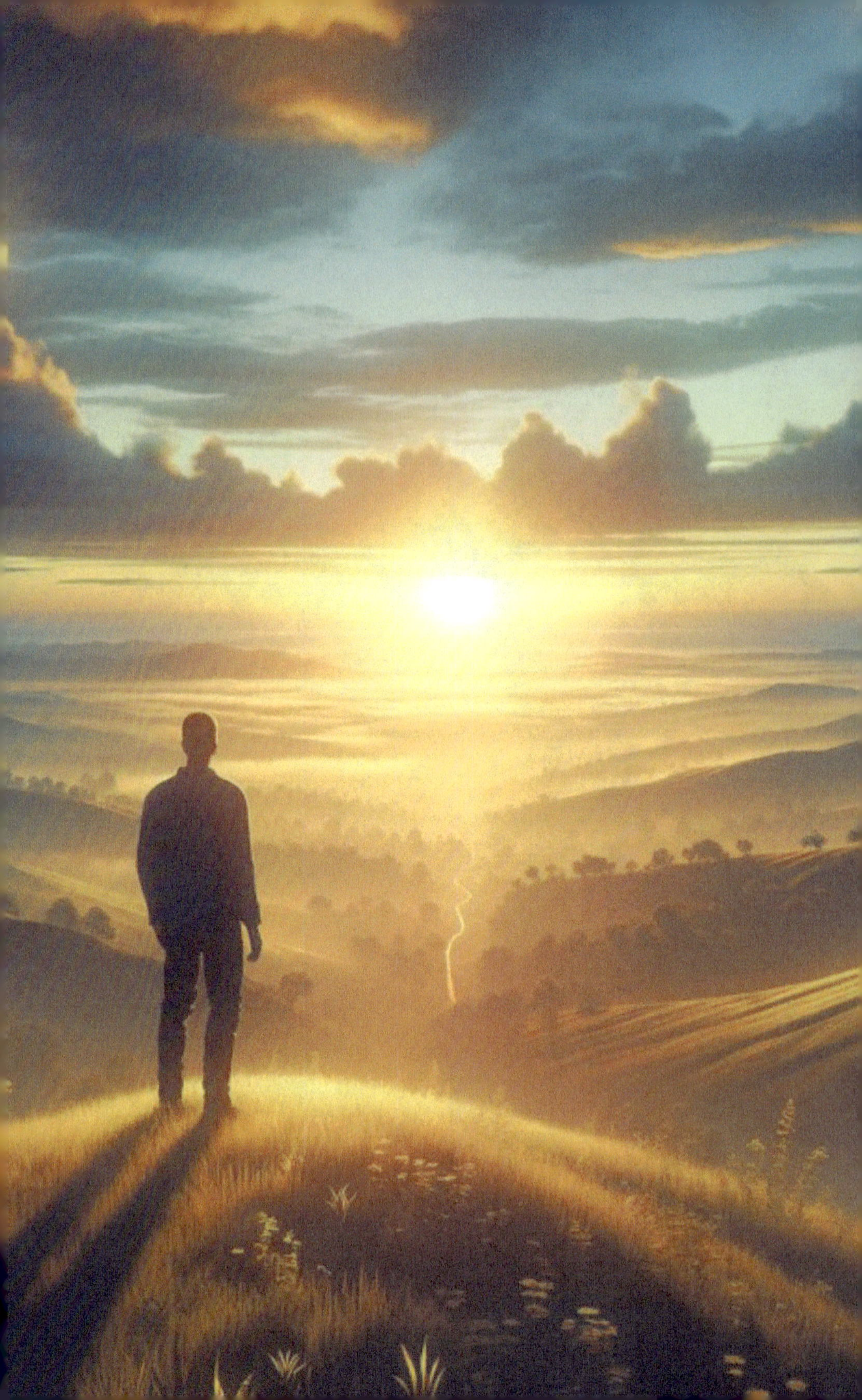

Echoes from the Heart

Journey of Life

In the realm of existence, fees unpaid,
Life's membership bestowed, a debt displayed,
Through trials and tribulations, we must sway,
But the cost, oh, the cost, it seeks to prey.

In the dance of days and nights, we find our role,
Navigating obstacles, each heart and soul,
With every challenge faced, we find our goal,
To cherish the moments that make us whole.

So, embrace this journey, both bold and true,
The membership to life, it's meant for you,
Though the dues may test your strength and virtue,
In the end, you'll find a world anew.

For every dawn brings hope, a fresh new start,
Life's canvas awaits your artful heart,
With colors of experiences, play your part,
In weaving the tapestry of your life's chart.

In the whispers of the wind, hear life's song,
A melody of where you truly belong,
In its harmonies, you'll grow strong,
Guided by the rhythm, you'll stride along.

And as the sunset hues kiss the day goodbye,
Reflect on the beauty, don't just pass by,
Each moment a lesson, a reason to try,
Under the vast, ever-changing sky.

Everything Has Beauty

In life's vast puzzle, every piece unique,
Bestowed with gifts, both strong and meek,
A world abounds in splendor, a variegated streak,
Yet its beauty's secret, we must seek.

Amidst life's whirl, a symphony plays,
A spectrum of life in sun's golden rays,
Nature's masterpiece, in countless ways,
Hidden in plain sight, through time's haze.

Beauty lives in simple, everyday sights,
In laughter and love, in soaring heights,
In shared moments, in day's delights,
A dance of experiences, in days and nights.

See the beauty in each dawn's early light,
In the stars twinkling, oh so bright,
In every kind gesture, in love's might,
Beauty unfolds, in our daily flight.

Hear it in the wind, in the ocean's deep call,
In mountains standing, proud and tall,
In every dream, big or small,
Beauty's there, encompassing all.

With hearts open wide, and eyes that truly see,
In every face, every moment, in you and me,
Everything holds beauty, vast as the sea,
A world of wonder, for all to see.

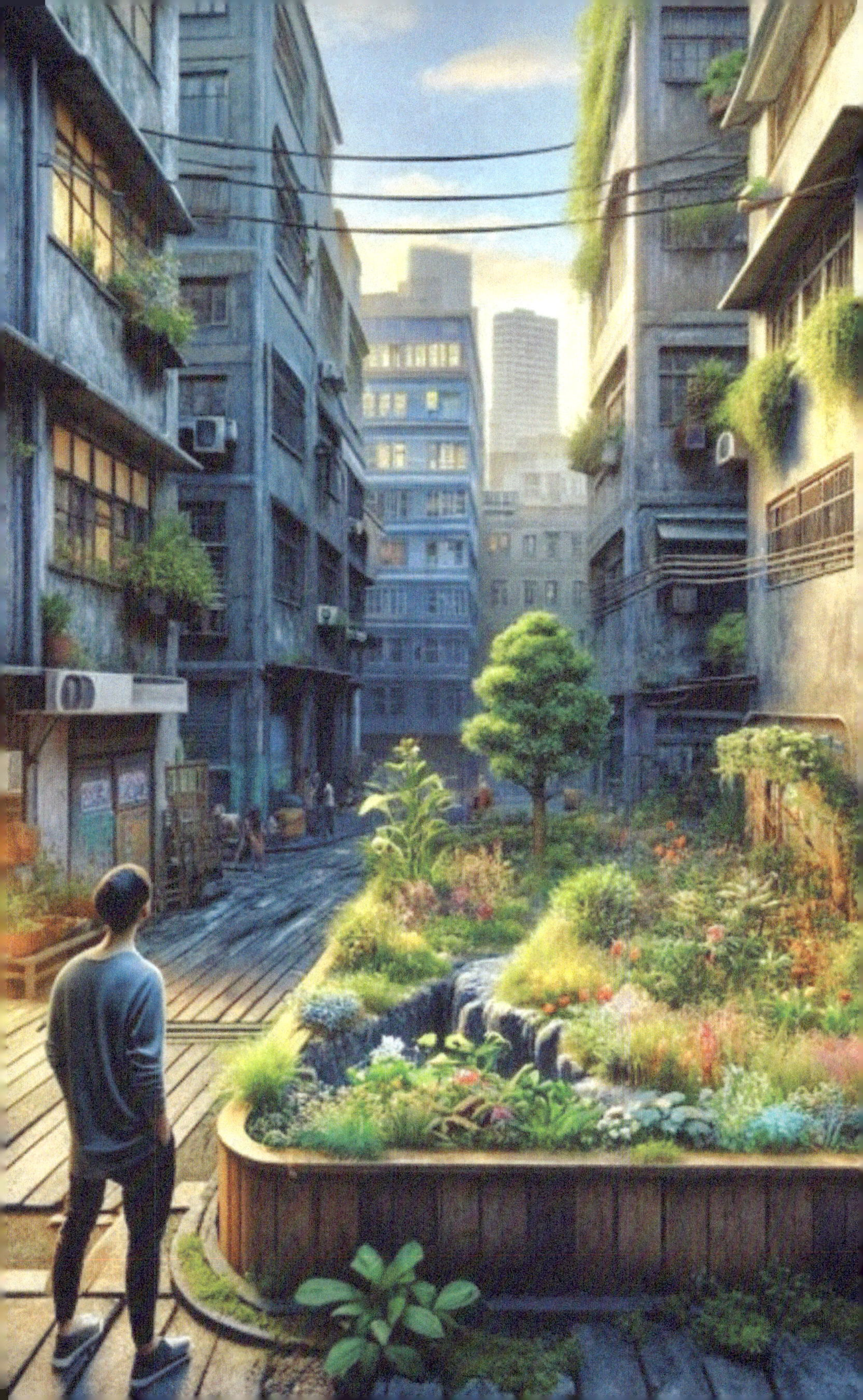

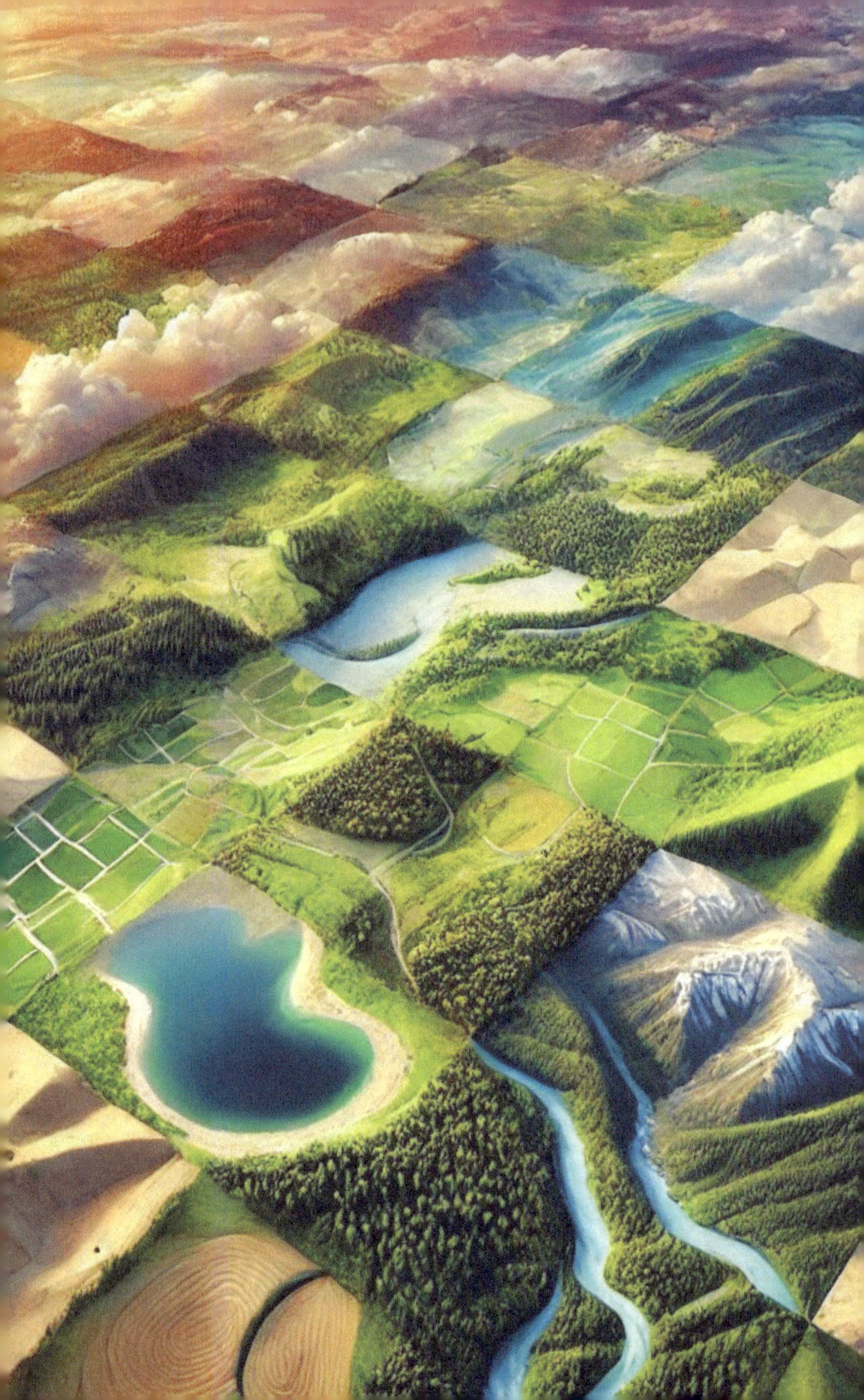

Echoes from the Heart

Quilt of Life
A Tapestry of Time and Tales

In a realm where colors blend and sway,
A patchwork of dreams at play,
In each square, a world unseen,
Stories told in hues of green.

A quilt of memories, stitched with care,
A canvas of moments, rare and fair,
Each fragment a whisper of time,
In this woven rhyme, sublime.

In every thread, a tale untold,
A narrative, both bright and bold,
A spectrum of life, in fragments caught,
A myriad of lessons subtly taught.

Gentle hands, with love, compose,
This masterpiece, where tranquility flows,
A symphony of shades, in harmony,
A visual ode, to memory.

In this picture, life's echoes dance,
Each piece, a chance for glance,
A journey through a kaleidoscope of light,
In this artwork, day meets night.

A tribute to the art of life,
Through joy and strife, in balance rife,
In this creation, stories interlace,
A vivid, living, breathing space.

Echoes from the Heart

Dusk's Embrace

In the realm where day bids night hello,
Horizon flames in fervent throw,
Evening whispers through the sky,
In colors bold, the clouds reply.

Mountains cut the sunset's flow,
Silhouettes against the glow,
Nature's brush in strokes so wide,
Paints the dusk in vibrant pride.

Crimson, gold, a visual feast,
In the quiet, the light decreased,
Stars prepare their nightly shine,
Above the earth, they'll soon align.

With every shade, the heart does leap,
In the canvas vast, emotions seep,
The world below in tranquil state,
Under heaven's fiery gate.

The final chorus of light retreats,
Leaving behind its fiery treats,
Darkness comes with a gentle hush,
The world awaits the night's soft brush.

As twilight yields to gentle moon,
The day's loud colors now immune,
Peace descends with velvet touch,
In the night's embrace, we trust so much.

©Photograph by Laura Tarnoff

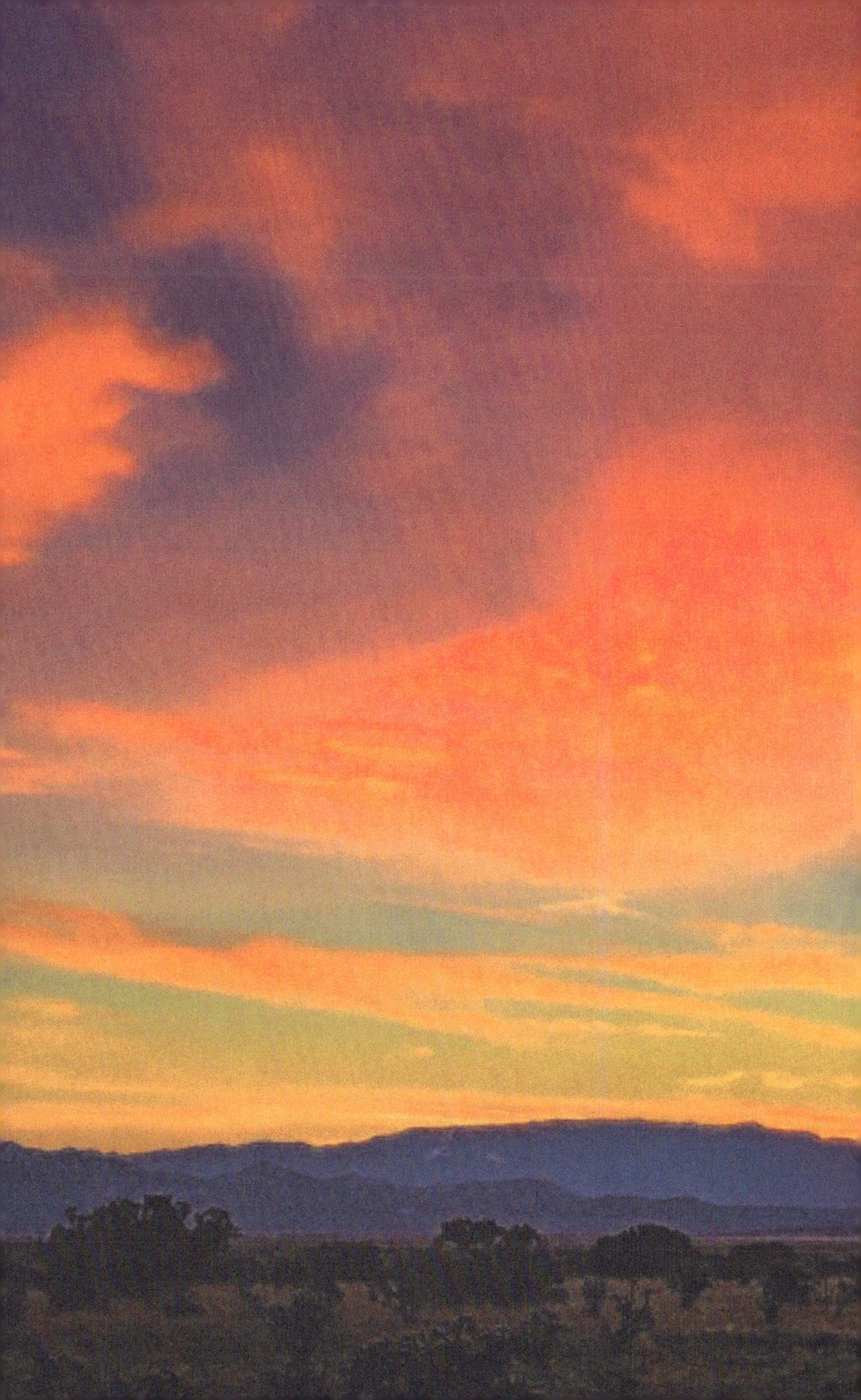

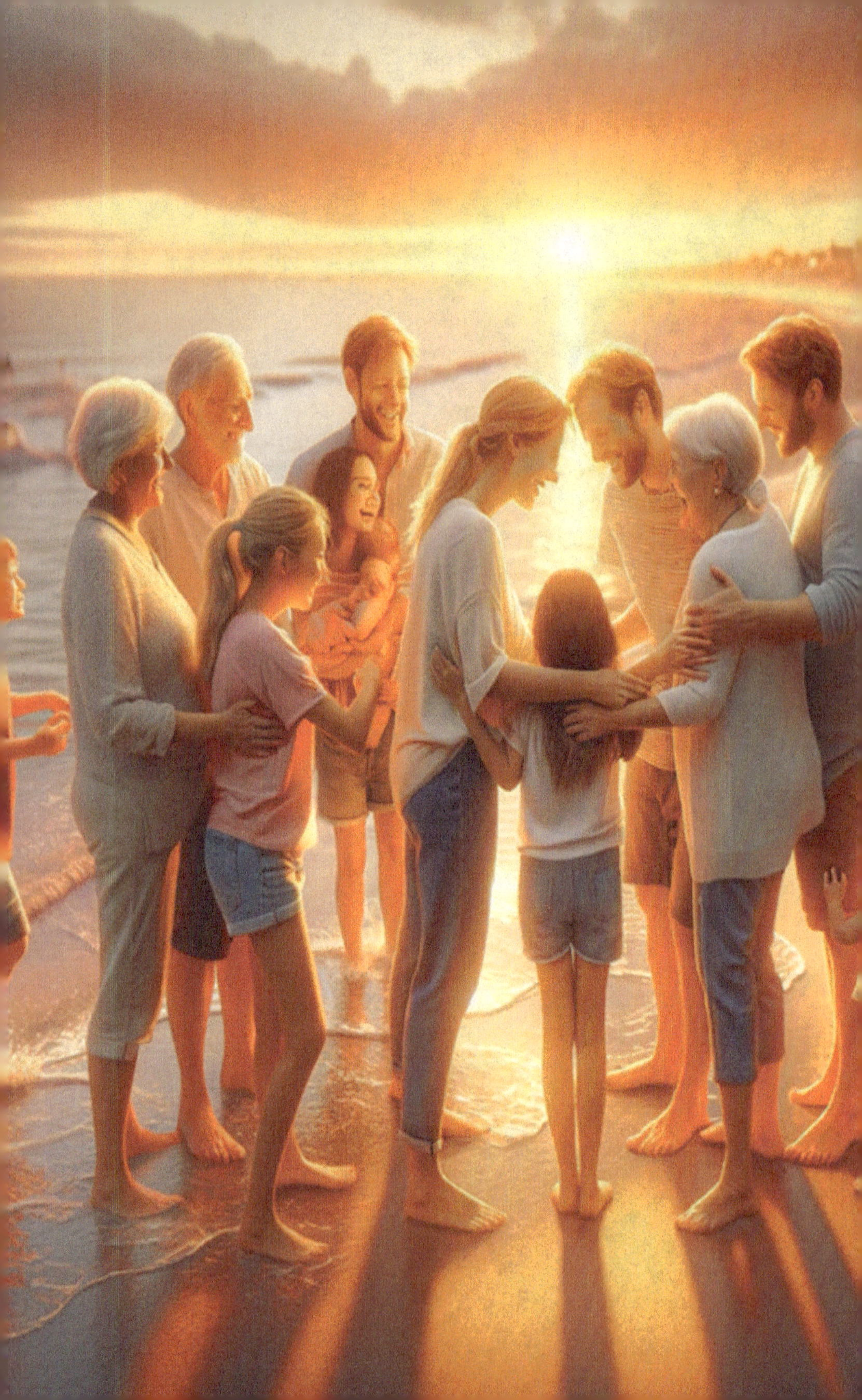

Echoes from the Heart

Finding Gold

In a world awash with dirt, anyone can see,
The flaws and blemishes, as plain as can be.
But be the one, with eyes so keen and bold,
To seek out the treasures, worth more than gold.

In every soul, a glimmer may reside,
Hidden beneath the scars, deep inside.
Dig through the layers, unearthing stories untold,
And you'll be the one who finds the gold.

Don't judge too quickly, the surface may deceive,
For beauty's not just what the eyes perceive.
In each heart, a story, waiting to be told,
So be the one who finds the gold.

In kindness and compassion, the true wealth lies,
Not in the judgments that too often arise.
Embrace the chance to cherish and uphold,
In precious hearts love's worth more than gold.

In the darkest nights, in the harshest climes,
Lies a chance to turn around the times.
See beyond the ordinary, break the mold,
For in the overlooked, you find the gold.

With every act of understanding and grace,
You illuminate the world, a better place.
In every moment, a new chapter unfolds,
In the book of life, where you find the gold.

Echoes from the Heart

The Karma Equation

In this modern world, we often find,
Karma's law, a truth of humankind,
What you put out, it comes around,
In this dance of life, a profound sound.

You reap just what you sow, no disguise,
Karma's rule, it's truly wise,
The energy we emit, it returns without fail,
In life's intricate web, like a cosmic trail.

So, be conscious of your actions and speech,
Karma's echo, it's not out of reach,
For the future unfolds, a reflection so clear,
Of choices you make, whether far or near.

In this digital era, where clicks resonate,
Karma's power, it's not up for debate.
Every choice you embrace, every path you take,
In the universal ledger, it leaves a stake.

Let kindness and love be your guiding light,
In this intricate journey, day and night,
For when you give your best, it shall unfold,
In karma's grand scheme, your story told.

In this modern narrative of cause and return,
Karma's wisdom, let us discern,
Blame it on karma, if you so wish,
It's the essence of life, in every twist and swish.

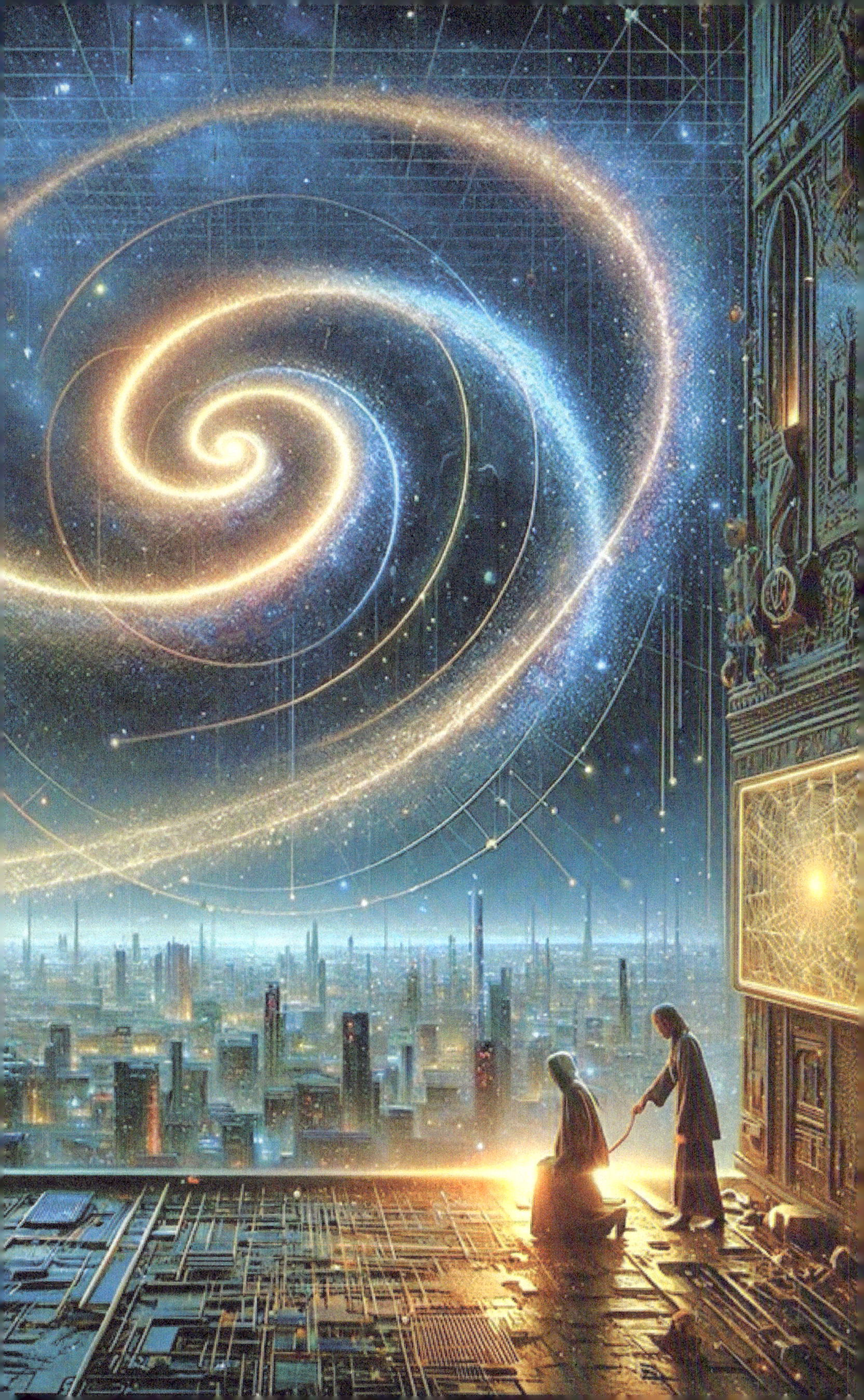

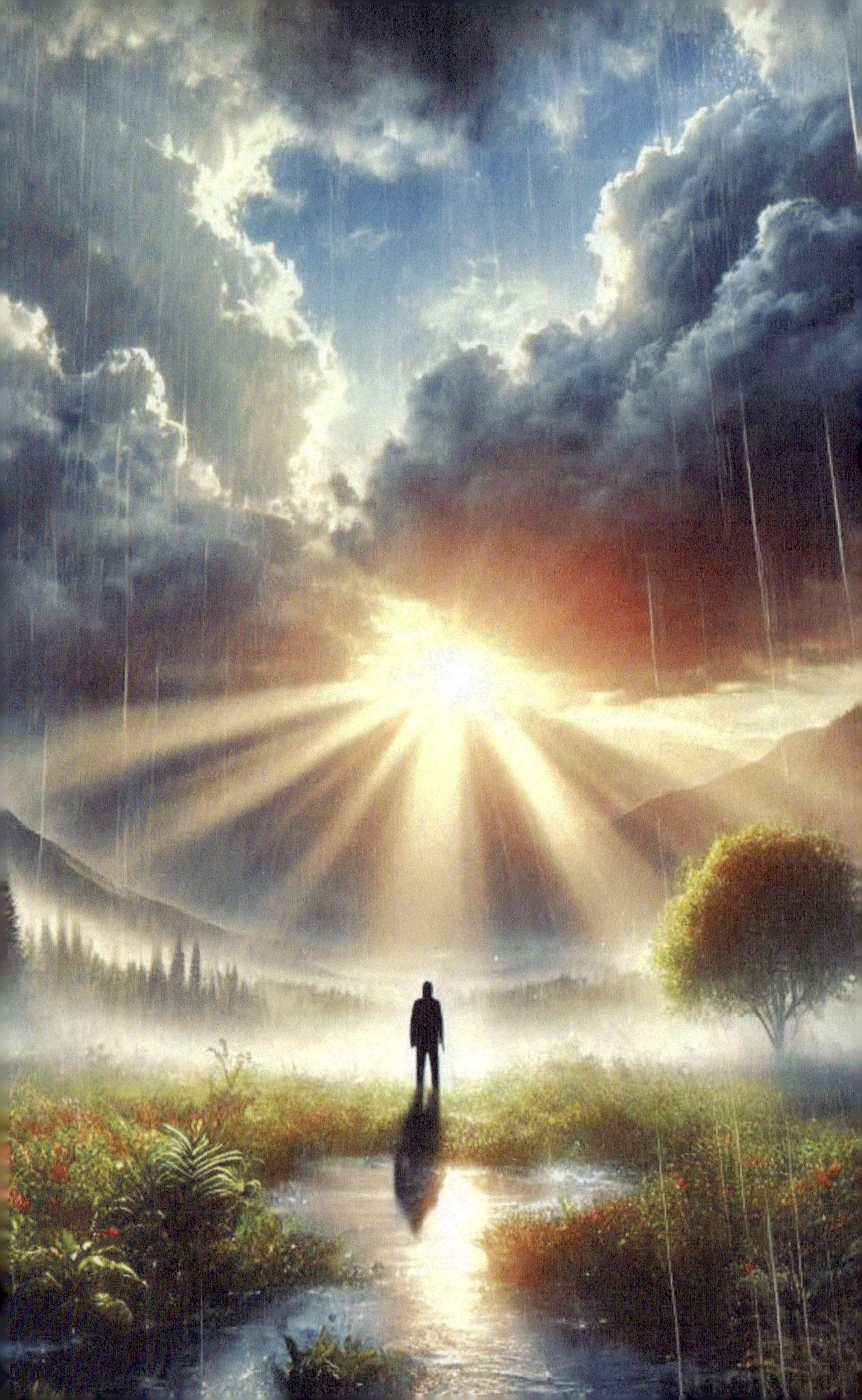

Echoes from the Heart

The Joy to Live

Though pain may press upon my chest,
And sorrow weigh on every breath,
I find a song within my soul,
A quiet joy, a life to bless.

The sun still shines beyond the clouds,
Its warmth can pierce the darkest days.
And even when the rain pours down,
The earth beneath still dances, sways.

Each morning brings a brand-new light,
A chance to rise, a choice to be.
Though aches may linger through the night,
The dawn is filled with possibility.

In every tear, there's something pure,
A lesson etched in gentle streams.
And in the cracks, I still endure,
I stitch my pain with thread of dreams.

For life, though woven with its thorns,
Still blooms in colors rich and rare.
In every moment, new reborn,
I find the strength to rise, to care.

So let the hardships come and go,
I hold my joy through all the strife.
For even in the pain, I know,
There's beauty in the gift of life.

NATURE

Stellar Symphony

Whispers of the cosmic dance,
Stars in twilight's deep expanse,
Each one a tale, a fiery glance,
In the universe's vast romance.

Galaxies twirl in a timeless waltz,
Nebulas paint with their ethereal faults,
Comets blaze with tails that exalt,
The mysteries the sky vaults.

In the silence of the astral sea,
Constellations tell tales of glee,
Legends of old, myths set free,
Woven in the fabric of the galaxy.

Under this canopy so profound,
I stand, my thoughts unbound,
In awe of the beauty all around,
In the skies where stars are found.

Planets orbit in harmonious grace,
Each in its own celestial space,
A cosmic ballet in endless chase,
In the boundless universe's embrace.

Moonlit nights and sun's warm face,
Both play their part in this cosmic race,
Illuminating time and space,
In this magnificent, starry place.

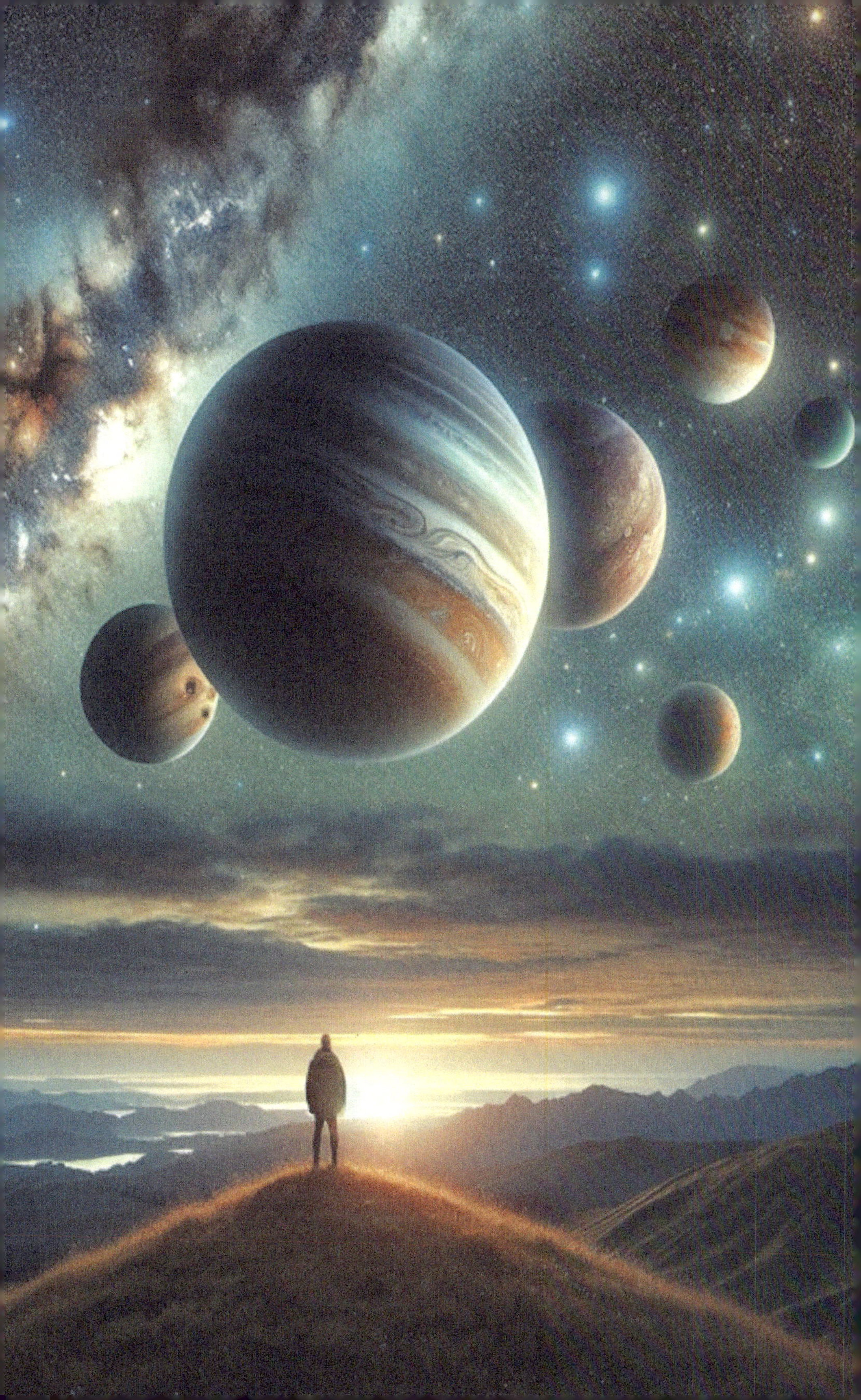

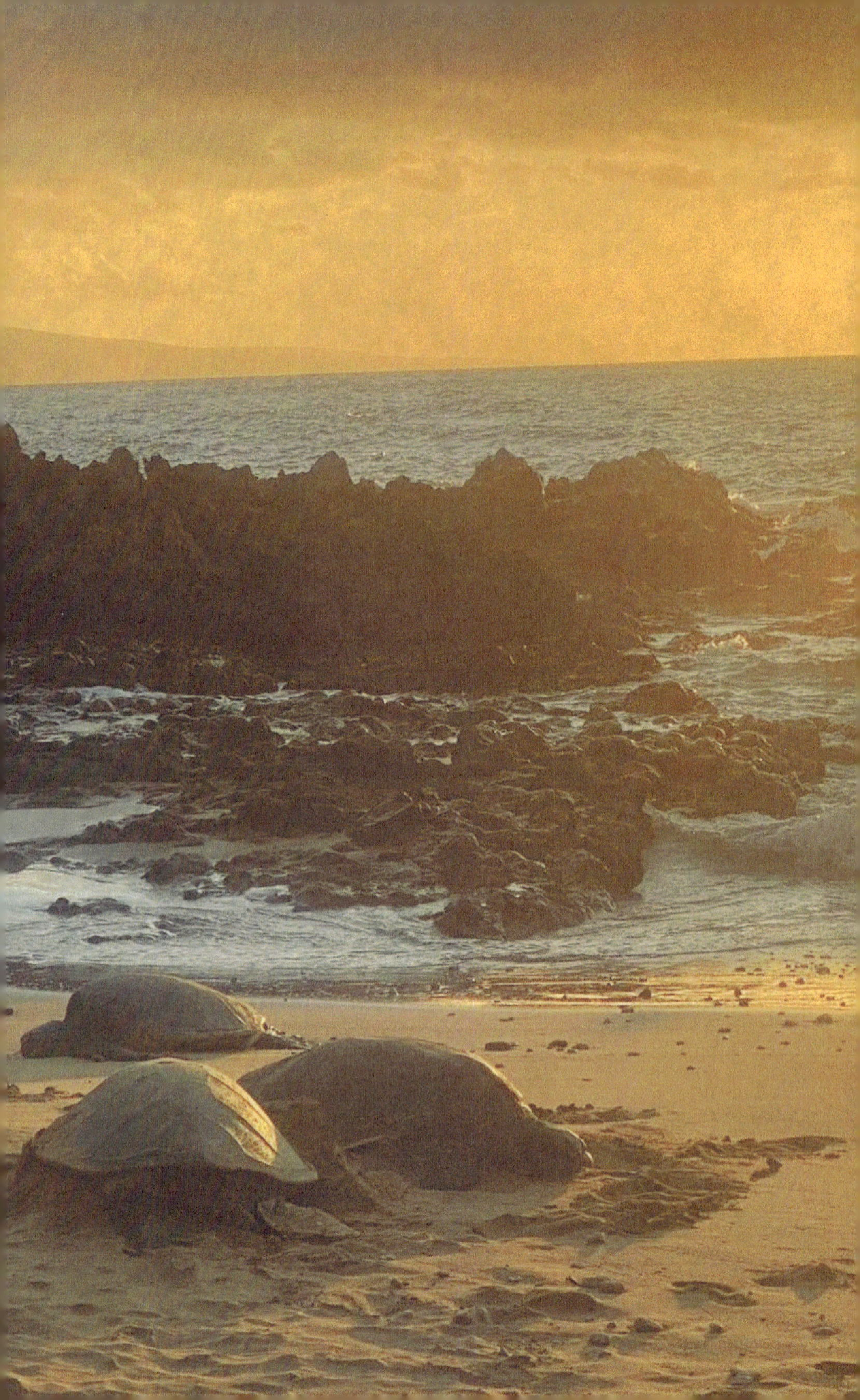

Echoes from the Heart

Sunset Serenity

Amidst the ebbing tide's gentle roar,
Sea turtles rest on sandy shore.
Golden sun bids the day goodbye,
In a tranquil surrender 'neath the sky.

Waves whisper secrets to the dusk,
Nature's embrace, soft and brusque.
Footprints etched in time's brief lease,
Speak of silence, and of peace.

The horizon, aflame with evening's glow,
Reflects life's constant ebb and flow.
In this fleeting, serene scene so lush,
Day's last light in a quiet hush.

In moonlit nights, on sands so fair,
Turtles glide with grace, through salty air.
Their ancient eyes, like stars aglow,
Whisper tales of depths below.

Beneath the waves, they dance and twirl,
In a world where coral castles unfurl.
With every stroke, they claim their reign,
Masters of the surf, in their domain.

As dawn paints skies in hues of light,
They vanish like phantoms into the night.
Leaving only tracks on sandy shores,
Echoes of a dance, in ocean's lore.

©Photograph by Kristen Wing[ii]

The Seasons of My Resolve

In spring's embrace, I found my loss,
Through blooming fields, I bore my cross.
Showers wept with me, skies so wide,
Yet in my heart, no dreams had died.

The summer's heat brought victory's taste,
On golden sands, time did not waste.
Triumph's sweet sweat, under the sun's gold,
I stood tall, in defeat not sold.

Autumn leaves fell, failures in tow,
Auburn sorrows in the wind did blow.
But with each leaf that touched the ground,
A stronger will in me was found.

Winter's chill provoked the tears,
Frosted echoes of my fears.
Yet amidst the silent night's hush,
A laughter's warmth turned sorrow to blush.

As spring returned, with blossoms bright,
I felt resolve take fullest flight.
Each petal soft, though storms had tried,
In every fall, my strength relied.

Through seasons turn, love was my guide,
In every moment, life did not hide.
This year I lived, every ebb and ahold,
I lost, won, failed, but did not fold.

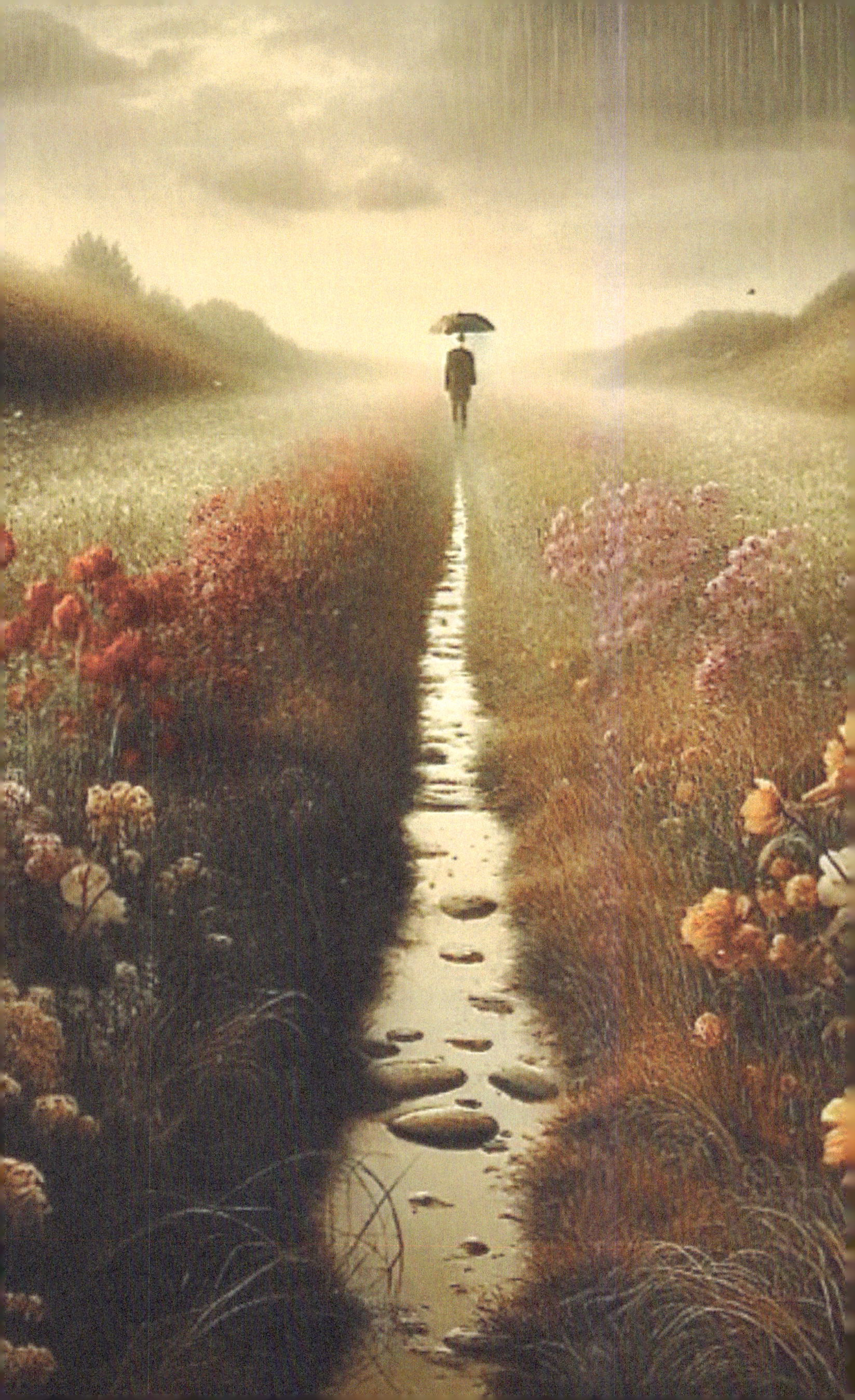

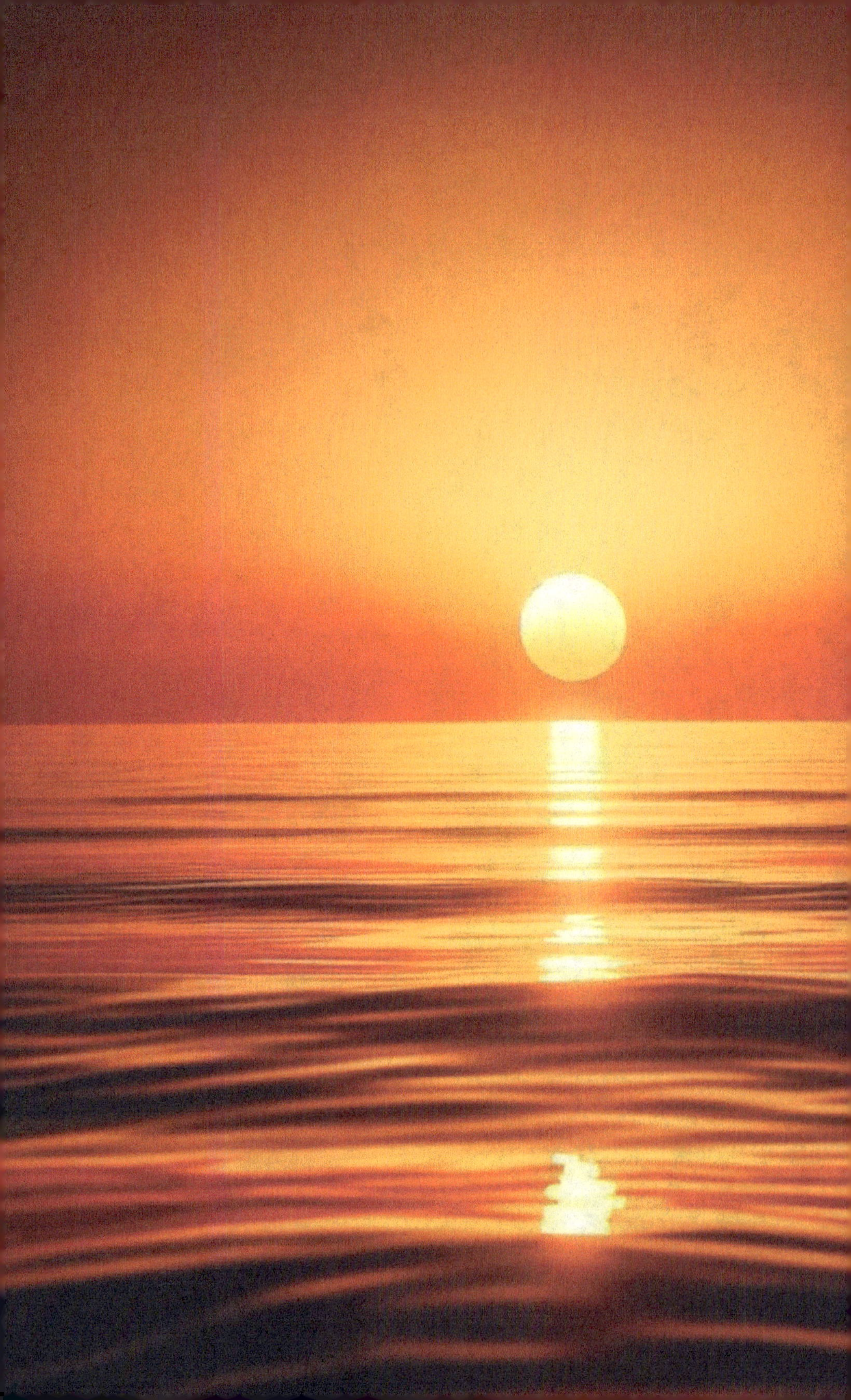

Echoes from the Heart

Sunset's Tender Farewell

The day fades with a quiet sigh,
As sun and sea meet, low and shy.
Night approaches, shadows rise,
Twilight settles in the sky.

Gold and crimson paint the west,
As time and light take their rest.
The cycle turns, forever blessed,
Sun and night, an endless quest.

Waves reflect the sun's last glow,
Night descends, soft and slow.
A promise waits in dawn's soft flow,
Light returning, sure to show.

Nature balances sky and sea,
In quiet, peaceful harmony.
Dusk brings night's tranquility,
Awaiting dawn's bright decree.

Each sunset holds a hidden vow,
Renewal waits beyond the now.
Darkness yields as light allows,
Morning comes, a sacred plow.

The sun departs with gentle grace,
Leaving stars to fill the space.
In the calm of dusk, we trace,
The endless sun's eternal chase.

Whispers of the Night

In the world of the night, where dead cells play,
Silhouettes dance in the moon's soft fray.
Stars twinkle secrets, old and grey,
As the dark cloaks the remains of day.

Shadows whisper of things not right,
Underneath the celestial light.
Lost dreams flutter in the flight,
In the quiet, my thoughts ignite.

Mysteries unfold in the starlit sky,
With hopes and fears silently lie.
In the night, alone, I sigh,
Watching time's silent reply.

Amidst the darkness, my soul does sway,
To the rhythm of night, in dismay.
In the silence, I find my way,
Embracing the night, till the break of day.

As the dawn approaches, soft and shy,
The night's embrace begins to die.
In its wake, a new day's cry,
In the world of the night, we're alive, not shy.

But even as daylight reclaims its hold,
The night's sweet secrets remain untold.
In every shadow, stories unfold,
Whispering truths that the dark has sold.

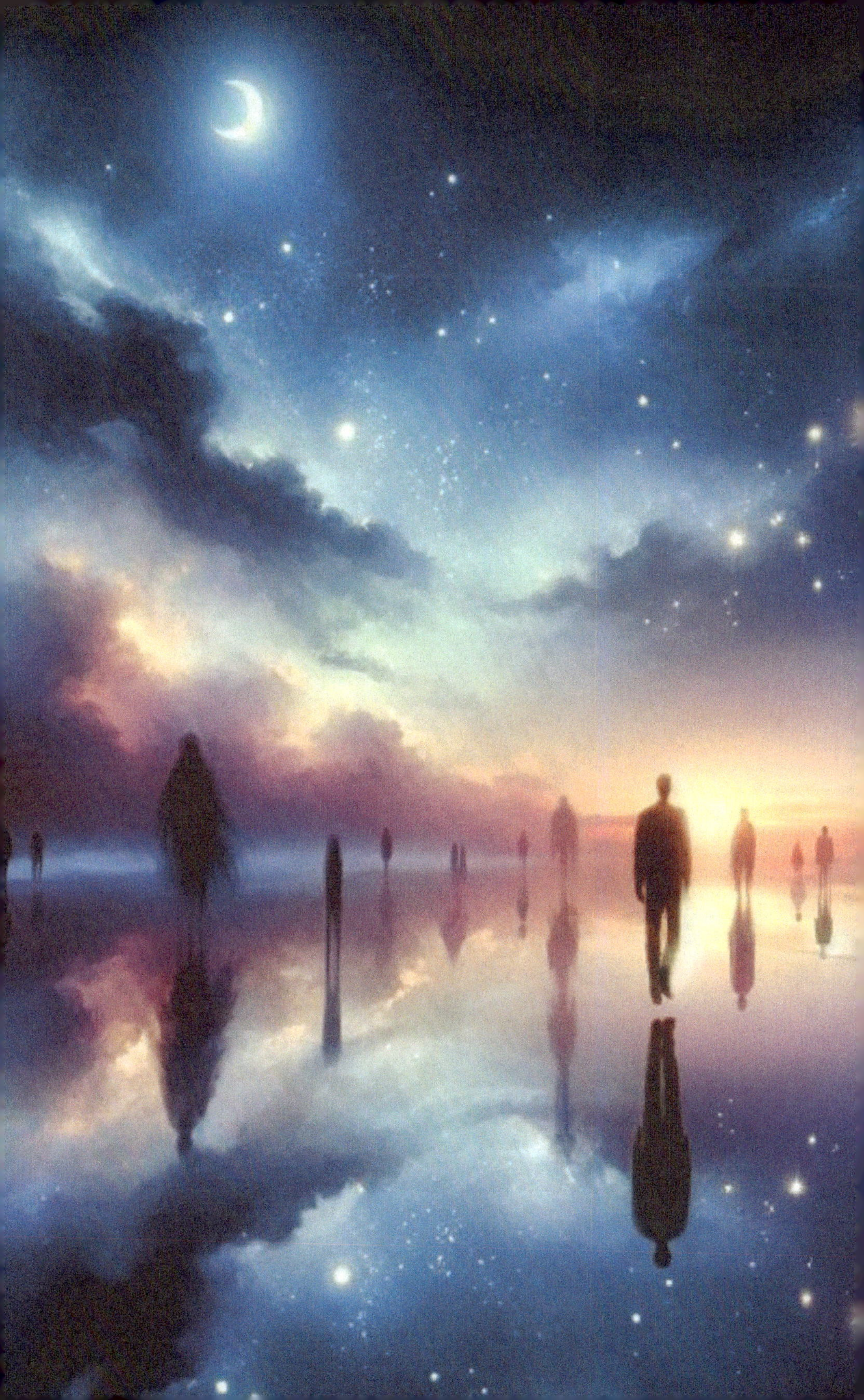

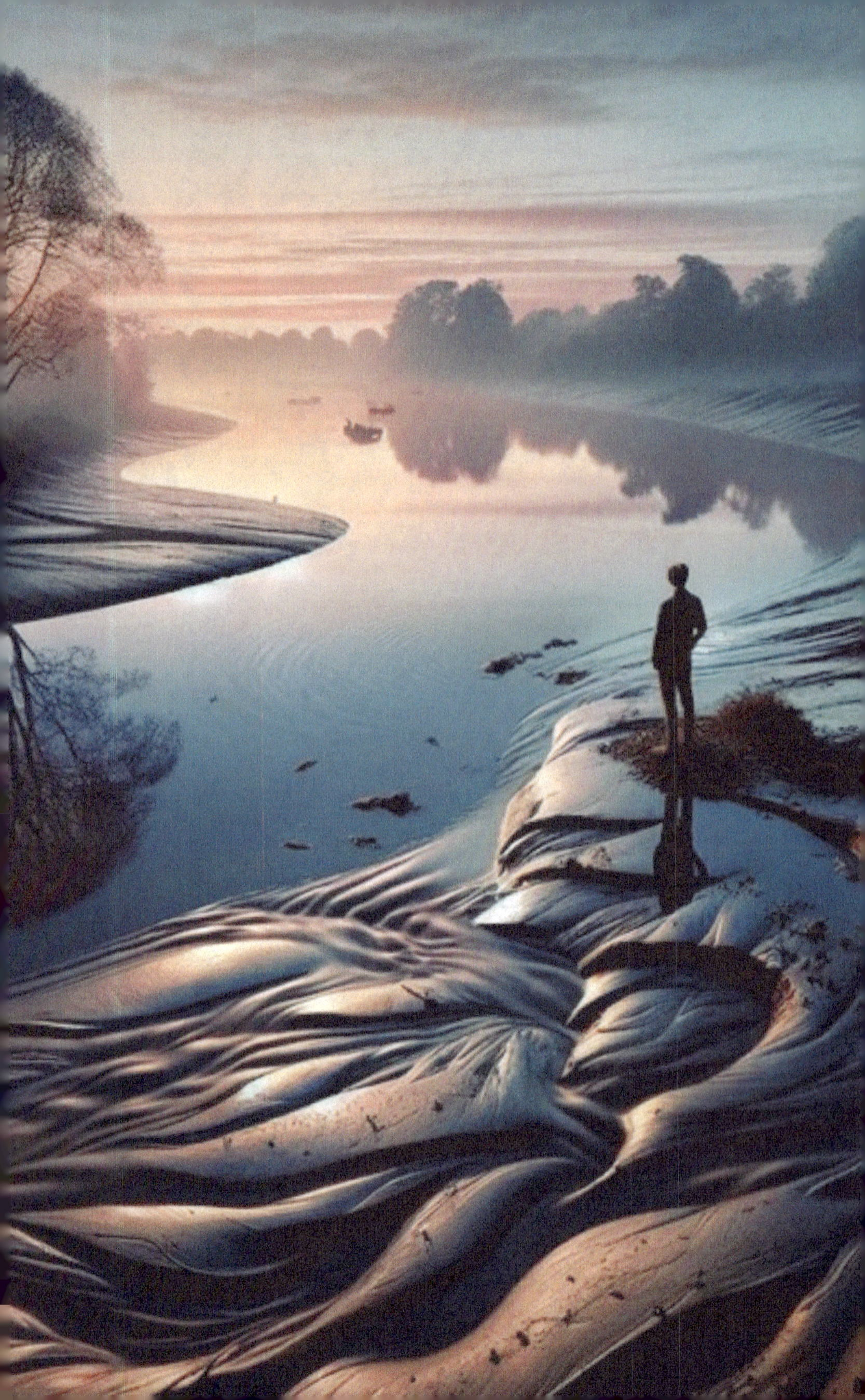

Echoes from the Heart

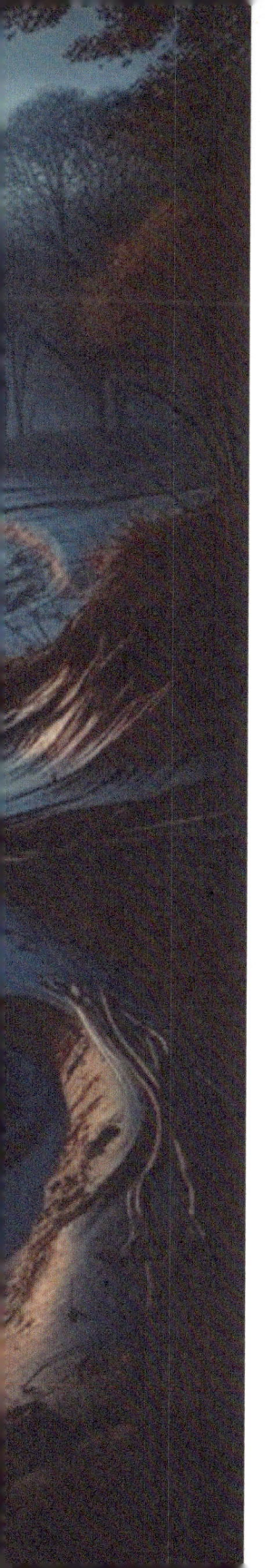

Muddy Water's Edge

In the hush where waters meet the land,
A symphony soft and grand.
Muddy waves, in gentle play,
Wash my worldly cares away.

Where liquid mirrors meet the skies,
My heavy heart finds its reprise.
Each ripple a tender embrace,
In nature's serene, tranquil space.

At water's edge, I stand in awe,
The muddy depths hold secrets raw.
In their whispers, soft and low,
My sorrows find the space to go.

The reeds bow low to kiss the tide,
Where fleeting dreams in shadows hide.
Beneath the sky's vast, silent dome,
I find a place that feels like home.

Here, where earth and water blend,
Broken spirits start to mend.
The water's touch, so soft, so kind,
Brings peace to my restless mind.

In this haven, so pure, so free,
I find a quiet symphony.
At the water's edge, I see,
A place where my soul can simply be.

Echoes in the Gale

Beneath the broil of a storm's might,
A man's face emerges from the night.
Lightning sketches the stern lines,
A map of life where darkness shines.

Each bolt, a chapter of hidden pain,
Of silent strength gained and retained.
Against the howl, his quiet fight,
An anchor in the tumultuous flight.

Chaos rages, a relentless spin,
Yet his resolve stirs from within.
In the storm's eye, his peace resides,
Where he confronts what the heart hides.

As transient as a lightning's course,
His spirit withstands the gale's force.
In the tempest's rage, he finds his part,
A quiet mind, a warrior's heart.

The winds may tear, the rain may blind,
But in the storm, his truth he'll find.
With every gust, he stands upright,
Unyielding in the endless fight.

And when the storm begins to fade,
He walks the path that fate has laid.
Through the echoes of the gale's refrain,
A man reborn from storm and pain.

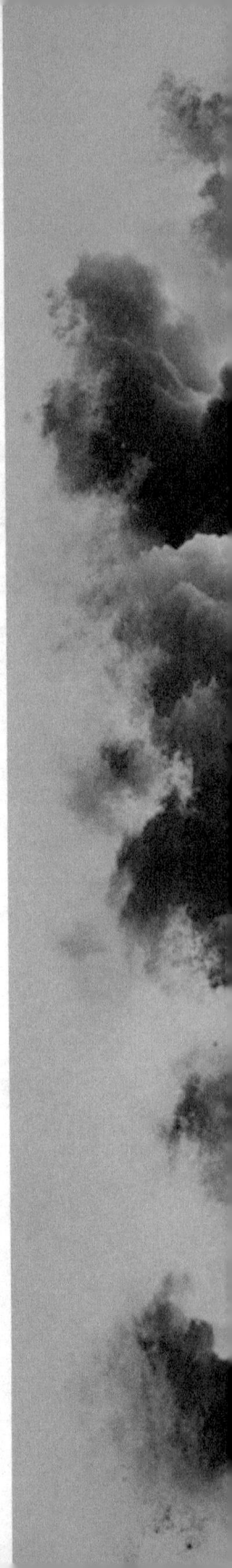

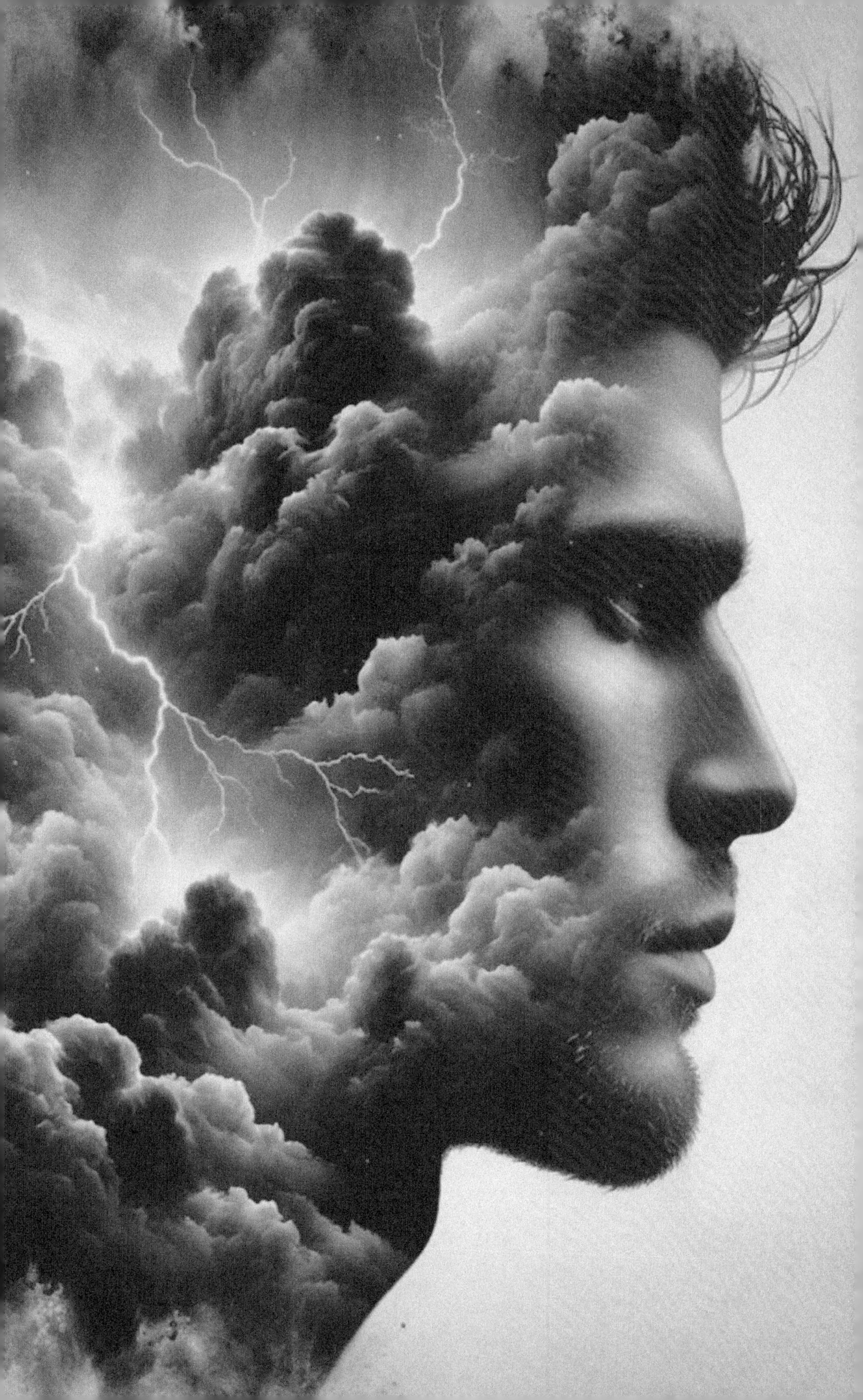

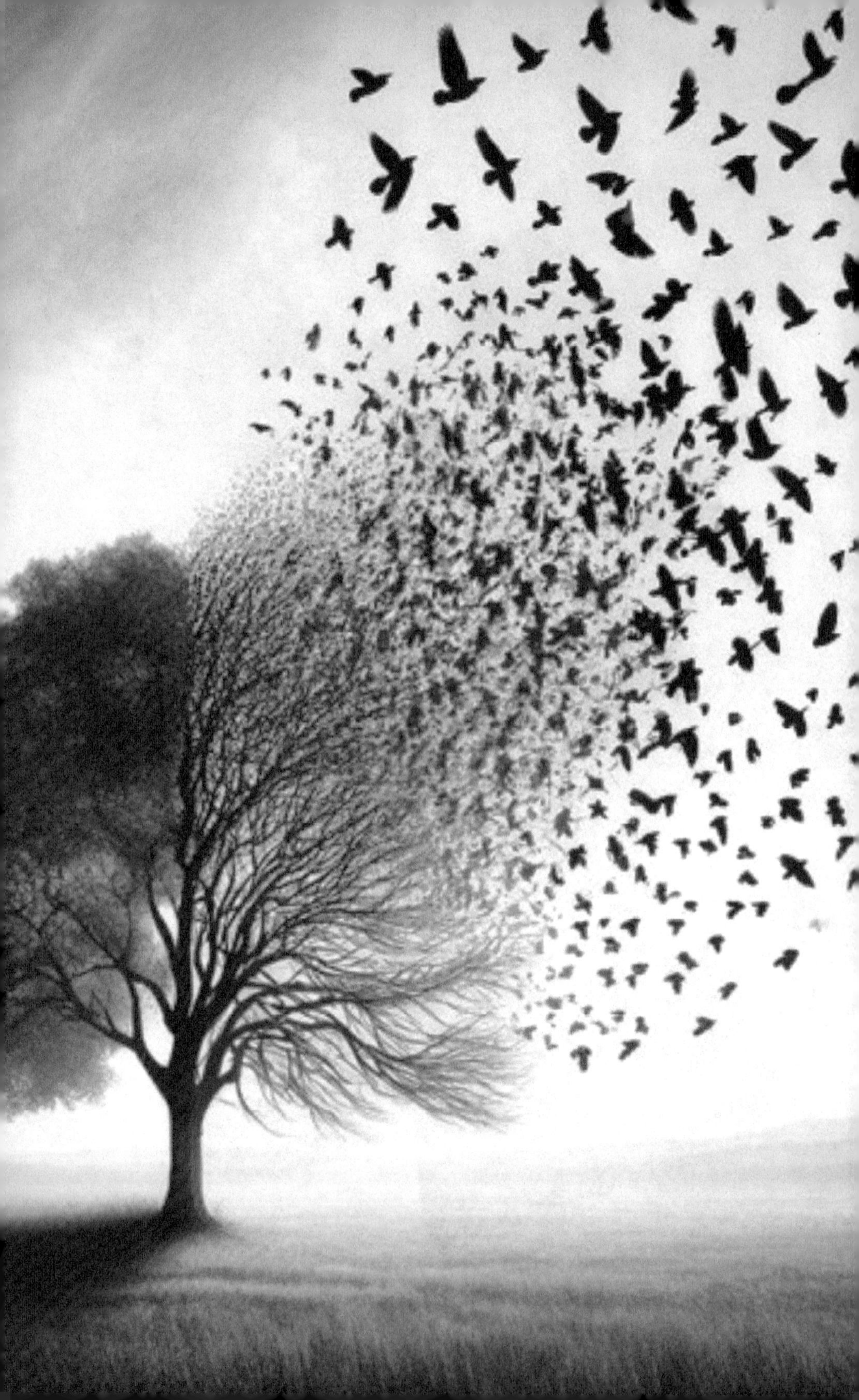

Echoes from the Heart

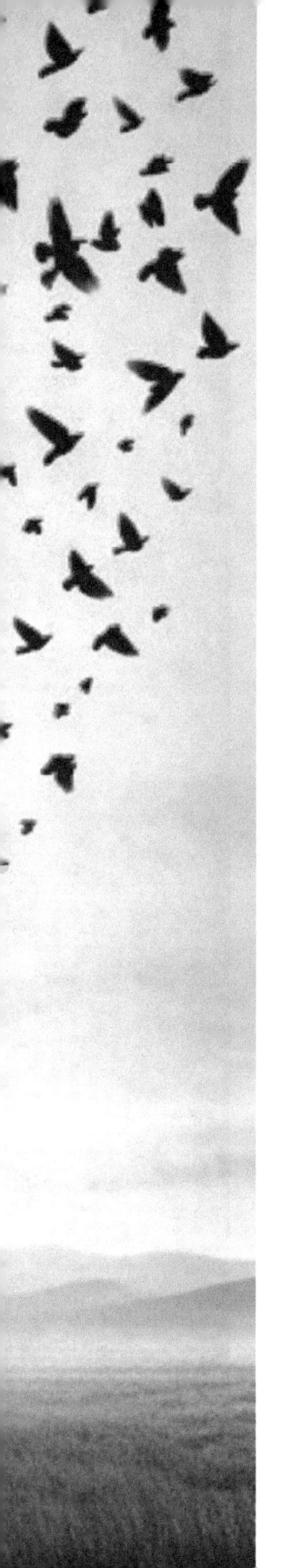

Whispers to the Wind

Beneath the brooding sky's embrace,
A tree stands alone in silent grace.
Its leaves to winged whispers yield,
In the vastness of the open field.

Birds like thoughts take flight in throngs,
A scattered dance to the wind's sweet songs.
Their silhouettes, a fleeting script,
On the canvas of the sky, they're cryptically writ.

The tree, a sentinel to time's soft treads,
Rooted deep where the earth's heart weds.
Its branches bare, yet full in might,
Cradling daydreams until the night.

A tale of freedom, in monochrome hues,
Where every flight, destiny pursues.
In this quiet spectacle of life's soft kiss,
Lies a world of meaning, of quiet bliss.

Yet seasons turn, as they always do,
The tree endures, its strength renews.
In winter's chill, or summer's glow,
Its steadfast form, through all, will grow.

And so, it stands, both still and free,
A witness to all that comes to be.
In whispered winds or storm's refrain,
The tree endures, through joy and pain.

Echoes from the Heart

Rhapsody of the Storm

In the heart of the heavens, a tumultuous scene,
The sun's golden tendrils and tempest convene,
A dance of the elements, fierce and untamed,
As the sky paints its fury, unnamed.

Mighty peaks stand as sentinels, ancient and wise,
Gazing up at the theater of turbulent skies,
Electric veins course through land's open palm,
A display of raw power, a natural psalm.

Clouds heavy with sorrow, weep tears of light,
Flooding the world below with the plight,
Of a storm's soulful cry, in silver they thread,
Illuminating earth where their sorrow is shed.

The mountains whisper secrets of old,
In silhouettes against a sky so bold,
While lightning strikes in a rhythm, a beat,
An orchestra of nature, none can defeat.

Here lies the boundary, where day meets night,
A symphony of chaos, a breathtaking sight,
The horizon ablaze with the storm's fierce glow,
A masterpiece only the wild winds can sow.

And when the fury subsides, the calm restores,
The mountains and sky tell tales of the lore,
Of a world that dances on the edge of a knife,
The enduring beauty, the storm of life.

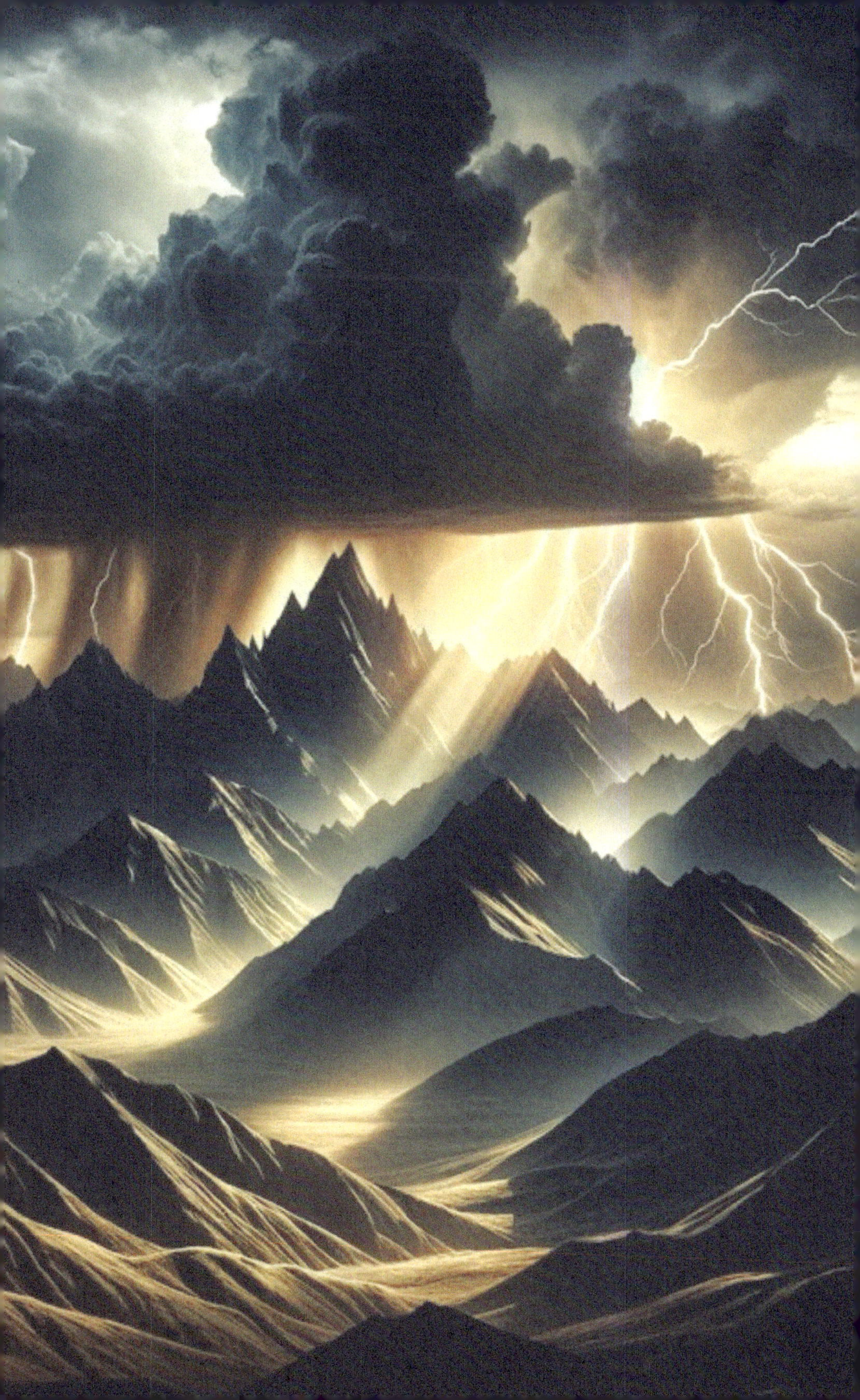

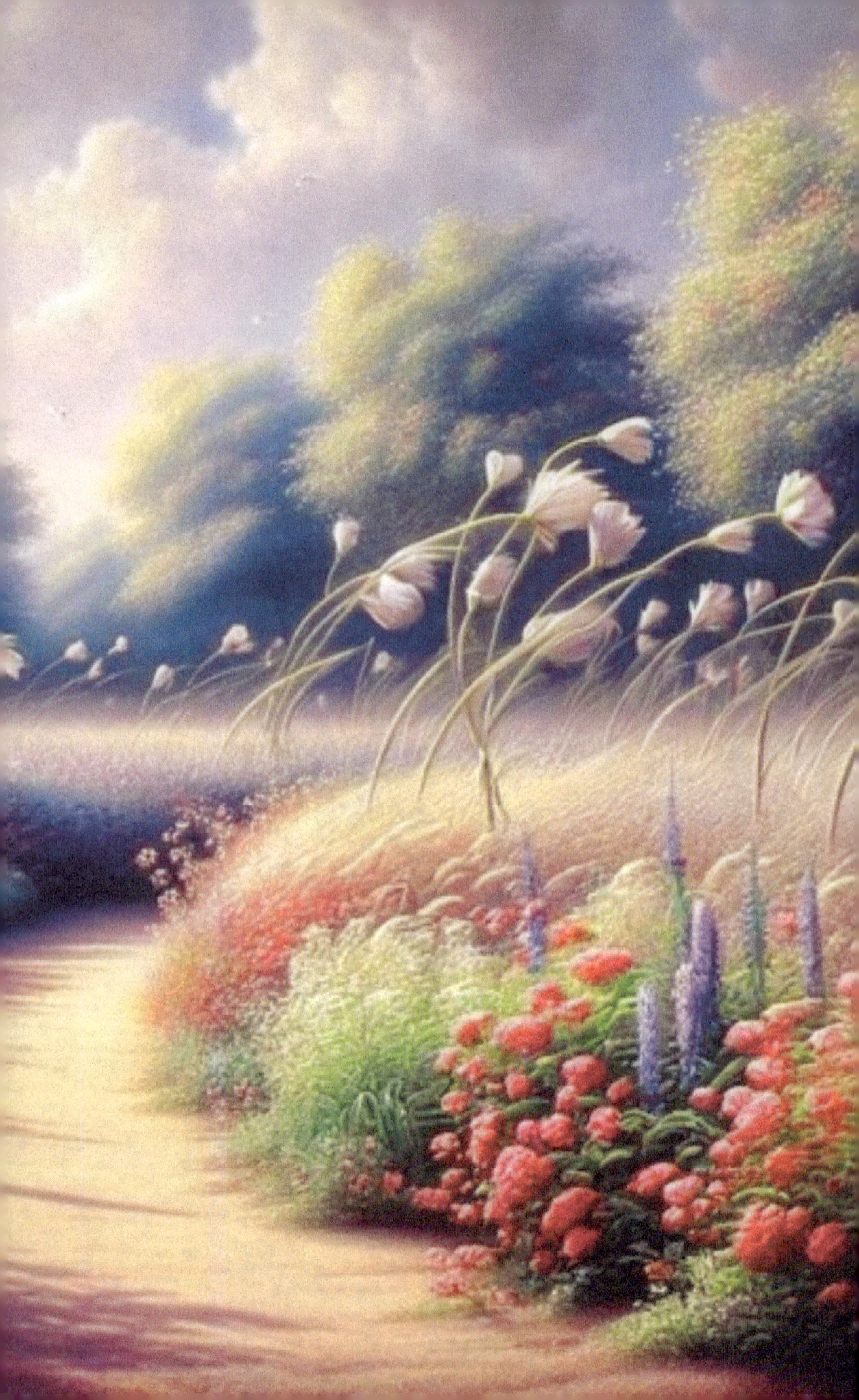

Echoes from the Heart

Garden of Thoughts

In fields of dreams, thoughts like flowers grow,
Each petal a memory, tenderly sown.
For every time you cross my mind, behold,
A bloom arises, in love's garden owned.

Amidst these rows of endless, vibrant hues,
Your essence lingers like morning's first dew.
If thoughts were flowers, forever I'd stroll,
In gardens vast, where love eternally grew.

In this lush landscape, where our hearts converse,
Each thought a seed, in the soil immersed.
Together they flourish, beyond measure,
In the haven of our silent verse.

Your whispers in the wind, a melody,
Turn empty fields into a symphony.
A floral testament of endless days,
Where thoughts of you are my sole company.

If I had a flower for each thought so true,
I'd wander forever, lost in thoughts of you.
In my garden of eternity's bloom,
Love's timeless dance, forever to pursue.

And as seasons shift, and petals may fall,
Our love, like nature, transcends them all.
With each new blossom, our bond renewed,
In fields of dreams, forever imbued.

Fire Tree

In winter's grasp, the tree stands bare,
Leaves long gone, branches stark and spare.
Above, the fiery clouds dance with flair,
Kindling life, in the cold, thin air.

Roots deep in earth, quiet, unseen,
Holding fast to dreams of spring's green.
Fire in the sky, a majestic scene,
Promises whispered, where light has been.

Beneath the fiery twilight's gaze,
The tree endures the frosty days.
In its silence, a hope ablaze,
For the bloom that comes after the phase.

As night descends, stars twinkle high,
The tree beneath the fire-streaked sky.
In stillness, it hears the night's soft sigh,
Dreaming of days when it will again stand spry.

With dawn, the fire clouds fade away,
But in the tree, a spark will stay.
Awaiting spring's warm, golden ray,
In hibernation's embrace, it sways.

Though winter's chill may grip the land,
The tree holds fast, its strength will stand.
In every branch, a quiet command,
To bloom anew when touched by spring's hand.

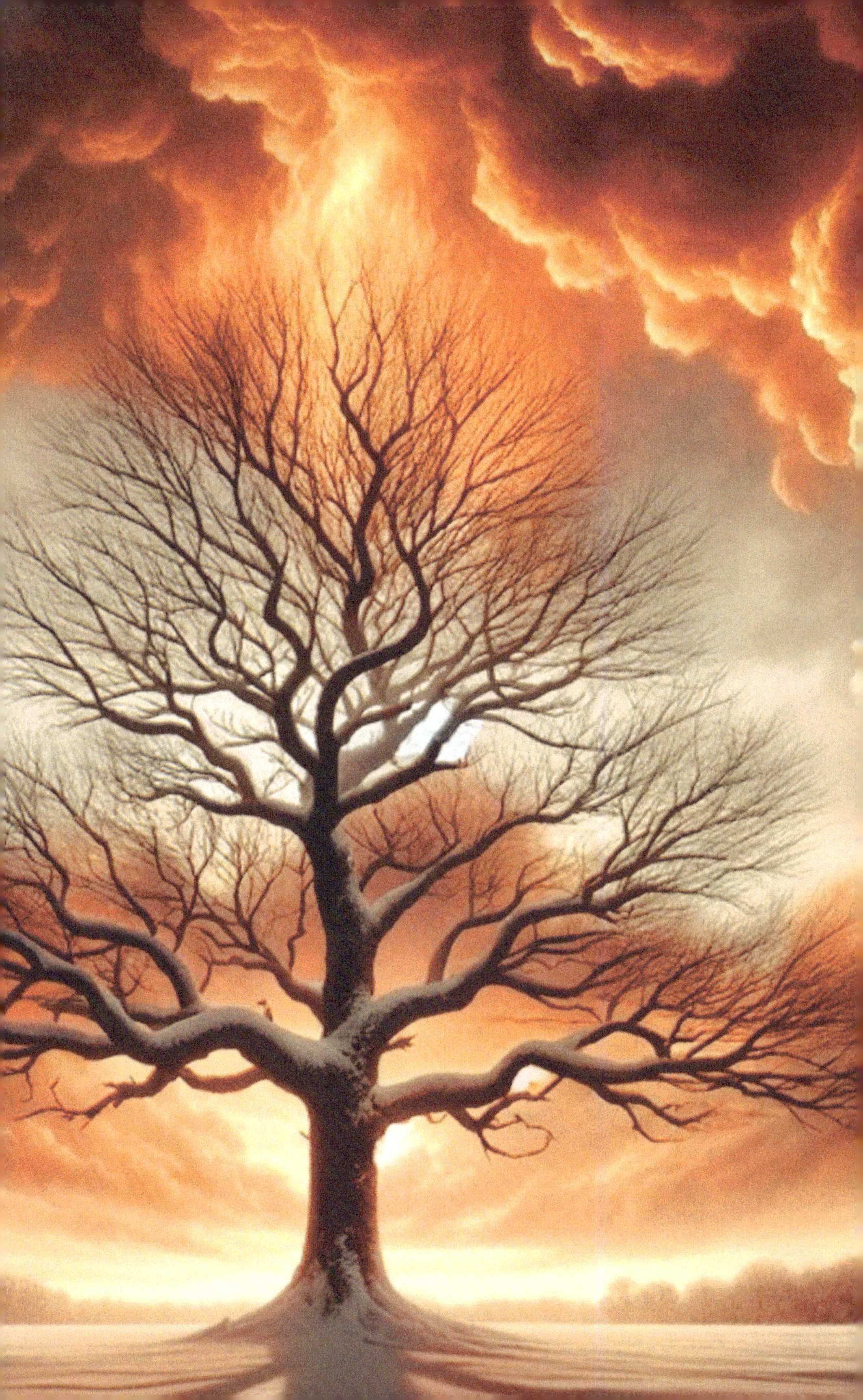

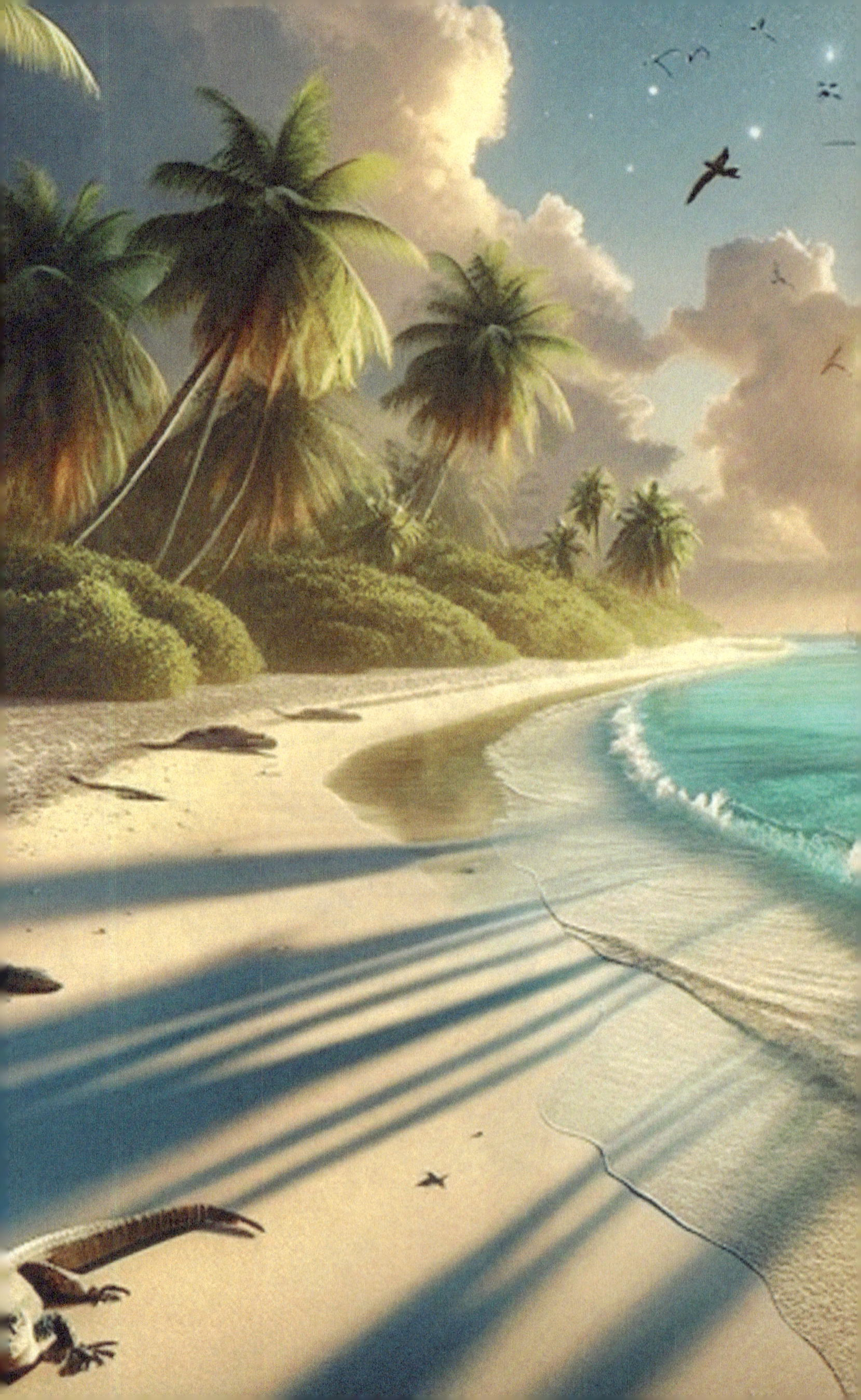

Echoes from the Heart

Whispers of Ambergris Caye

Sapphire whispers 'long the shore,
Sails dance to an unseen score,
Palm shadows stretch, evenings greet,
The horizon kisses the ocean's feet.

Barefoot trails in silver sand,
Nature's craft, the artist's hand,
Stars above in festoons drape,
Nighttime's shawl, a perfect shape.

Mangroves stand in silent choir,
Rooted deep, aspiring higher,
Iguanas bask in balmy grace,
Time slows down to nature's pace.

Salted breeze, the air so sweet,
Where the skies and waters meet,
Laughing gulls in arcs so free,
Scribe tales in the boundless sea.

Dreams alight on gentle waves,
Peace resides in hidden caves,
Ambergris, a jewel so rare,
Each moment's a solitaire.

Beneath the moon's soft silver gaze,
The island hums in twilight's haze.
In every breath, a story told,
Of timeless beauty, pure and bold.

Resilience's Gem

A piece of earth, shrouded in night,
Bears silent weight with hidden might.
Under pressure's endless fight,
A diamond forms, from coal to light.

In shadows deep, it finds its grace,
Strength grows in a carbon embrace.
Through time's long, unyielding race,
It shines with patience in its place.

From rough beginnings, light breaks free,
A spark of battles fought with glee.
Each facet tells a history,
Of strength born out of agony.

Within the earth's relentless hold,
The dust transforms, a story bold.
Coal to diamond, bright and cold,
Forged by trials long foretold.

Behold the gem, once mere fuel,
Now radiant under nature's rule.
Its rise through hardship, sharp and cruel,
A shining testament, calm yet cool.

A diamond's path is never brief,
Carved by time, and honed in grief.
A symbol of resilient belief,
Born of struggle, finding relief.

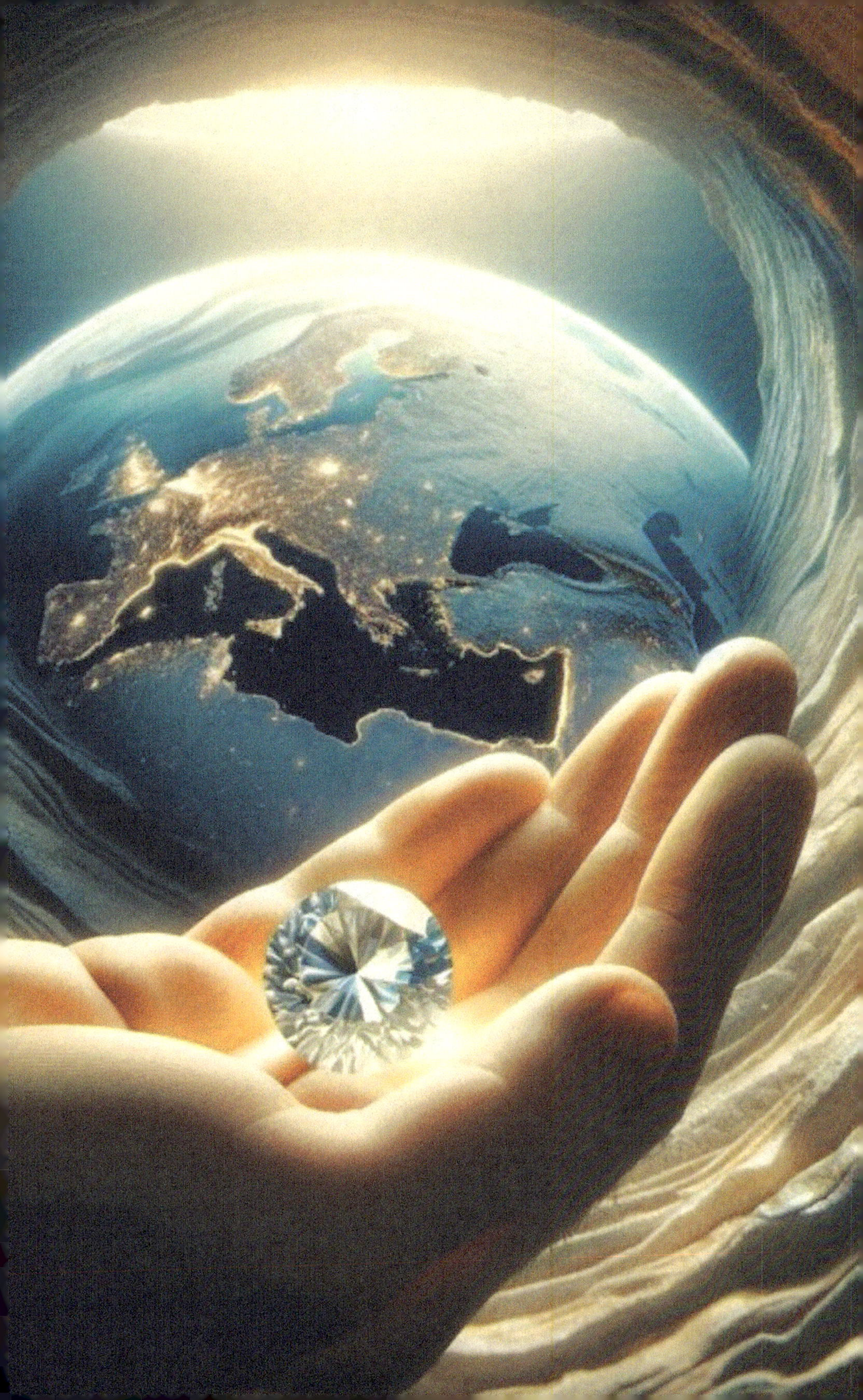

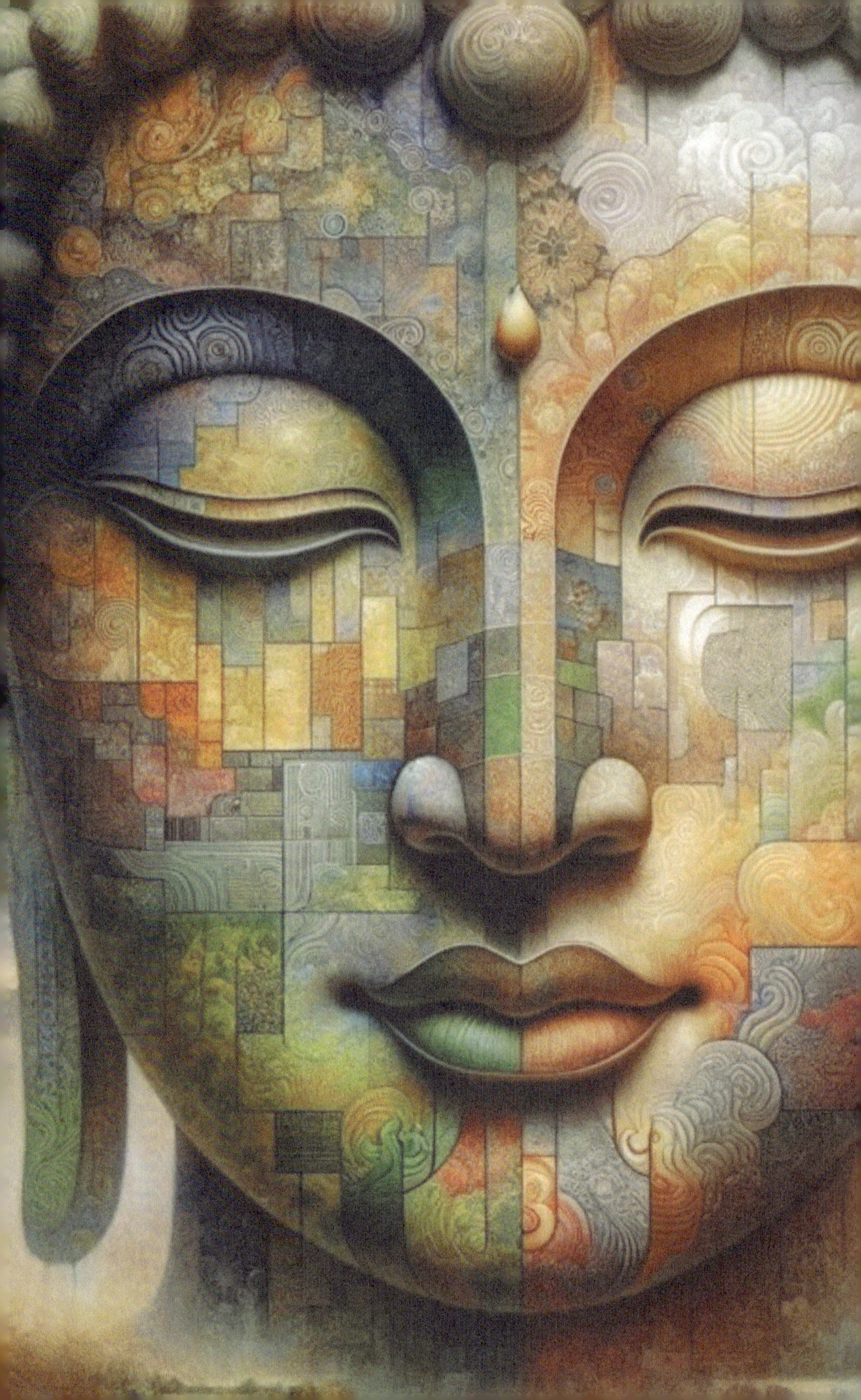

Echoes from the Heart

The Serenity of Reflection

In the stillness of a visage, stories unfold,
A garden of memories in each crease is told.
Eyes like silent lakes, mirrors to the soul,
Where time's soft ripples gently roll.

Cheeks bear the artistry of life's embrace,
Shades and hues of every heartfelt trace.
A map of journeys in golden lines,
Each a path where the spirit shines.

Lips, a horizon where silence blooms,
Red whispers of joy, and sometimes dooms.
The tranquil air of a meditative state,
Holds a universe where dreams conflate.

Brow, an arch that weathers storm and sun,
Marks the battles fought, the victories won.
Its furrows speak of wisdom's rise,
Etched by truth, beneath the skies.

In this quietude of contemplative grace,
A universe thrives in a sacred space.
A face, not merely surface but depth untold,
In its silence, a masterpiece bold.

For in the calm of this sculpted scene,
Lies a narrative, tranquil and serene.
A testament to history's song,
In the silence where secrets belong.

Echoes from the Heart

Whispers by the Watermill

At forest's edge, by pond's still grace,
The watermill stands in its place.
Logs weathered, ivy's slow embrace,
A wheel once turned, now lost in space.

Water whispers, old tales to tell,
Of work once done, now bid farewell.
The chimney stands, though fires are cold,
Once warm with stories, now left untold.

Autumn paints with a golden hand,
Leaves fall like sunbeams on the land.
Reflections shimmer in the pond,
Of silent wheels and skies beyond.

This quiet place, time's gentle grip,
Where nature's slow reclaim does slip.
The mill, a witness to days gone,
Where life persists, though work is done.

The air is still, the world serene,
A glimpse of what once might have been.
Beneath the trees, the mill remains,
A relic freed from time's harsh chains.

In the stillness, whispers revive,
A tale of life that once did thrive.
The mill endures, though work has ceased,
Its quiet soul forever at peace.

©Photograph by Tina Vos[iii]

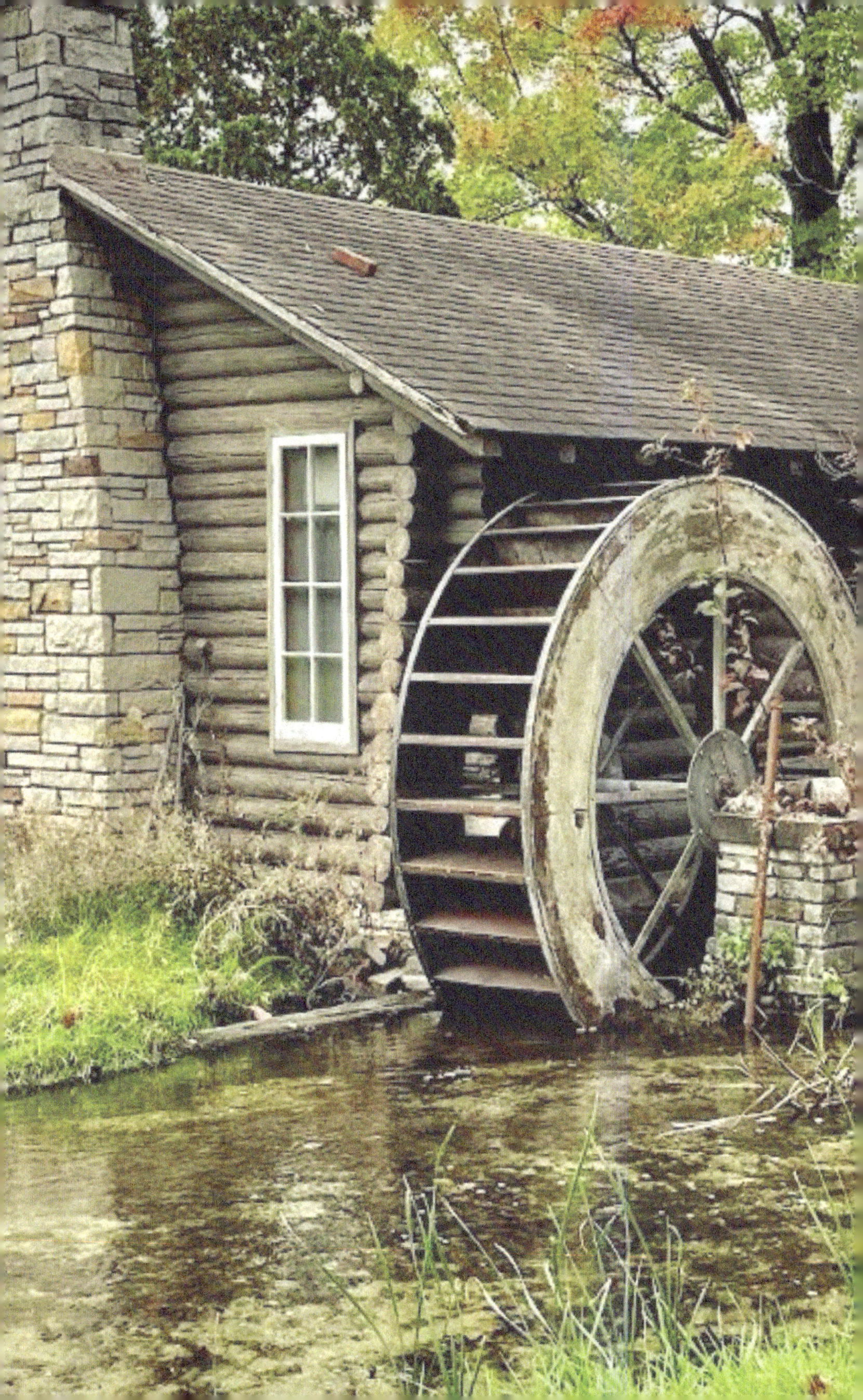

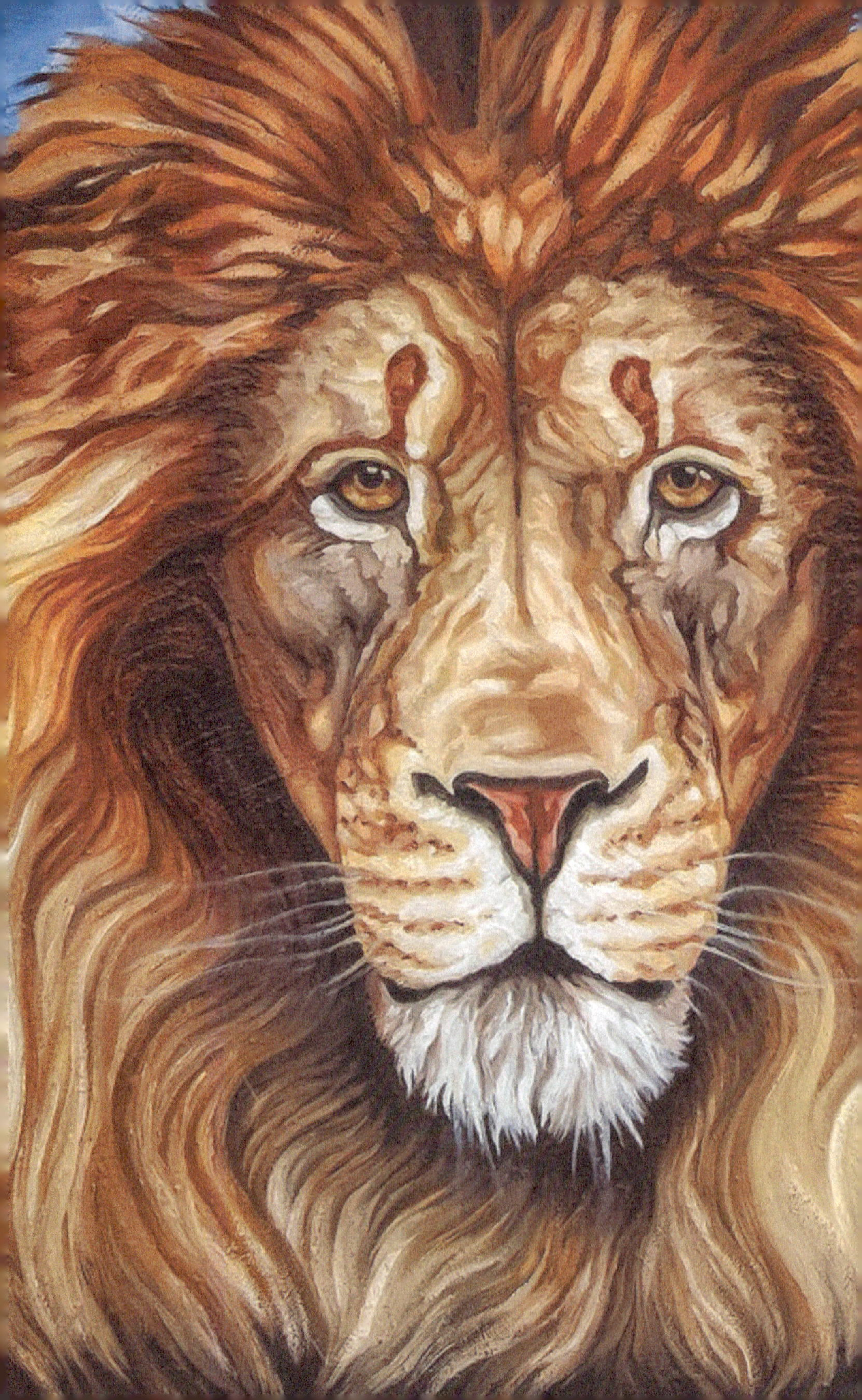

Echoes from the Heart

Sovereign of the Serengeti

Upon the endless plains he stands,
With mane like fire, and noble demands.
His eyes, a mirror of the skies above,
Reflect the world with wisdom and love.

In every tuft and whisker, life's art,
Under the celestial dome so wide,
He rests with pride by his side,
A sentinel framed by the day's last light.

Casting shadows, commanding the night.
As dusk descends with a hushed decree,
The king's silhouette is the last to flee,
His kingdom sleeps under starry sheen.

Yet in the grass, where silence creeps,
His heart hears what the quiet keeps.
A symphony of unseen life,
A balance held in primal strife.

And he, the silent, ever-watchful dream.
Nature's own design, a master's part.
With each brush stroke of the sun's embrace,
His presence is painted with dignified grace.

He surveys his realm with a steady gaze,
Unspoken laws, the wild obeys.
The zephyrs weave through his golden hair,
Whispering tales of the lands laid bare.

©Painting by Laura Tarnoff[iv]

Echoes from the Heart

Echoes in the Desert Homestead

Beneath the vast New Mexico skies,
Where clouds like cotton softly rise.
An olden cabin, walls weather-worn,
Stands solemnly in the desert, forlorn.

The mountain guards in stony might,
A silent sentinel in the light.
Its shadow stretches over the land,
Over the cabin, over the sand.

The porch is empty, the doors askew,
Echoing tales that the wind once blew.
Through broken windows and gaping doors,
Where silence now dances on dusty floors.

The snowflakes kiss the thirsty ground,
A fleeting beauty in the quiet found.
They rest in patches, cold and rare,
A contrast stark in the desert air.

The trees bear witness, boughs held high,
To time's relentless march, the open sky.
Their roots entwined with the earth's own heart,
In this tranquil scene, they play their part.

Here, the world seems to hold its breath,
In this corner of life, of time, of death.
The cabin whispers of days gone by,
Under the wide and watchful New Mexico sky.

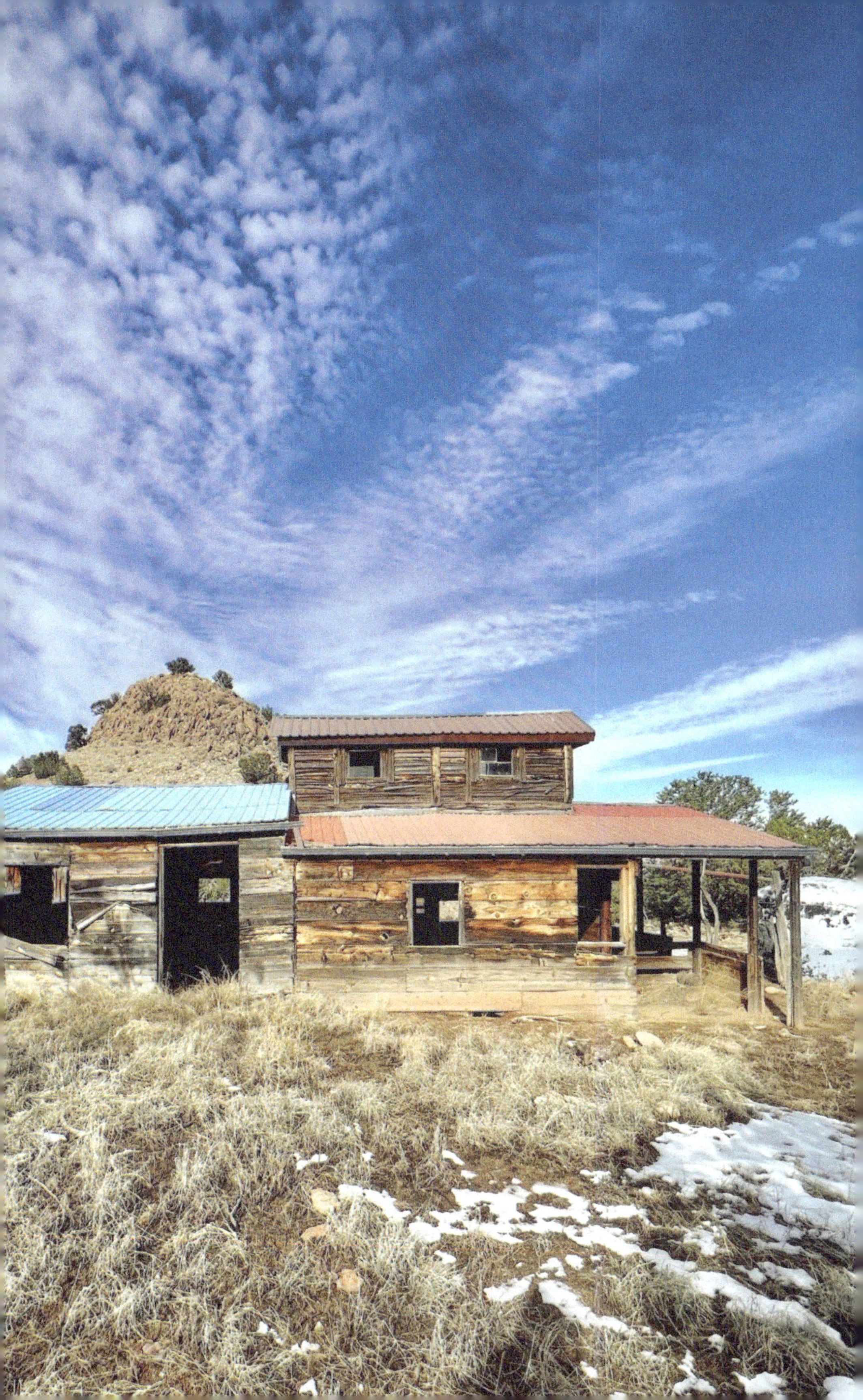

SORROW

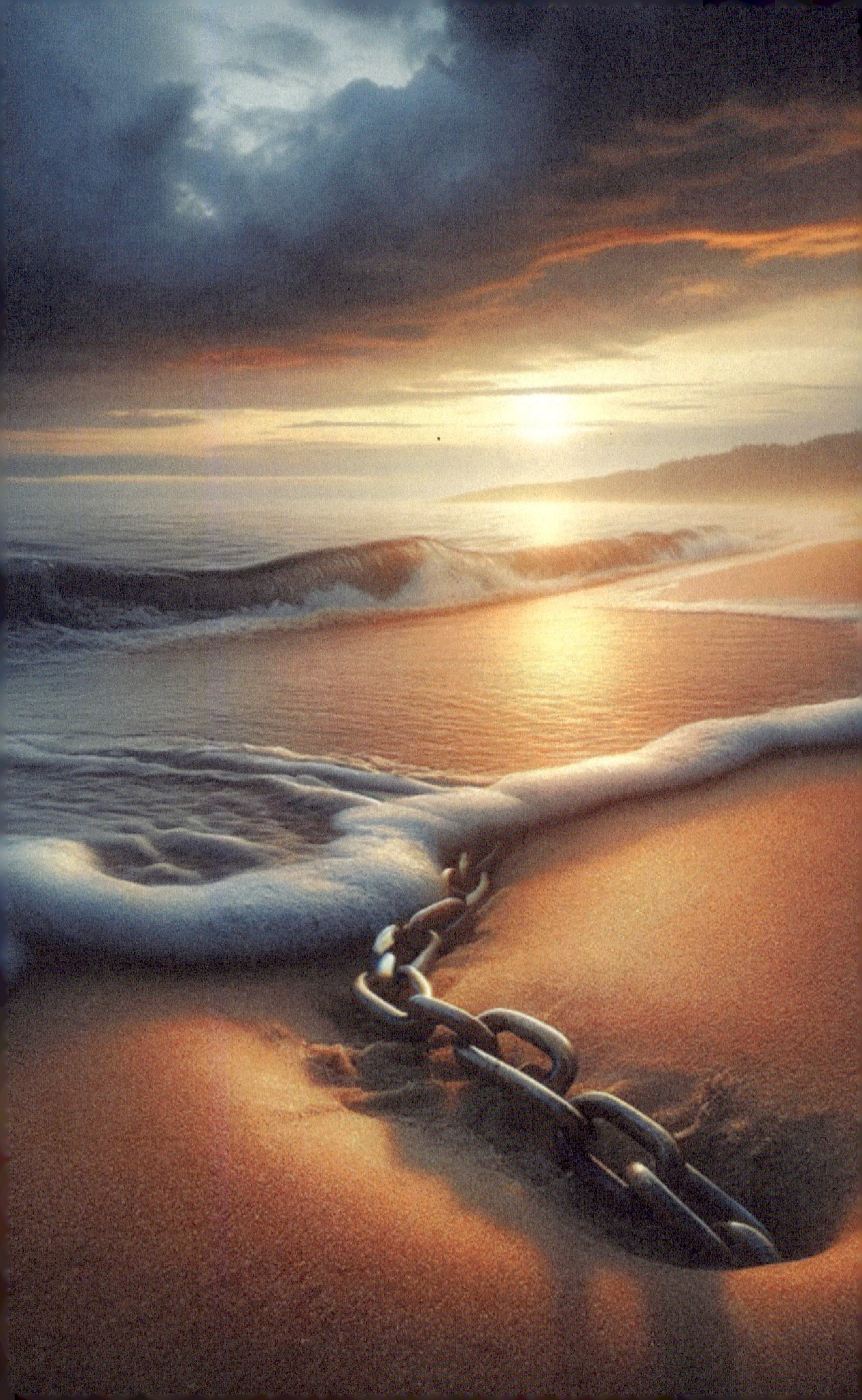

Echoes from the Heart

Why Love Feels Like a Penitence

Love, a heavy chain we bear,
Binding hearts in deep despair.
It feels like penance, harsh and grim,
Yet we chase it on a whim.

Each glance, each touch, fleeting grace,
Longing carved upon the face.
A punishment in sweet disguise,
Pulling us with tear-filled eyes.

Waves crash, retreat, then disappear,
Close one moment, distant, unclear.
A torment wrapped in passion's flame,
We suffer, yet we play the game.

A labyrinth of choices made,
Paths unclear, yet unafraid.
Love's weight, a burden hard to lift,
A punishment we still insist.

The wind whispers of what's been lost,
In love, we pay a heavy cost.
It binds, it breaks, then leaves behind,
A tortured heart, yet still we find.

In memories, love lingers still,
A punishment both sweet and cruel.
No end in sight, no final rest,
But in its grip, we feel our best.

Why Does Love Hurt

In shadows deep, emotions twine,
A question asked, a timeless sign.
Why does love, in its tender grace,
Bring tears that stain a fragile face?

In moonlit nights, hearts interlace.
Yet pain resides in this sacred place,
A paradox, where feelings birth,
The bane and boon of love's own worth.

A symphony of joy, love's sweetest song,
Can turn to sorrow, right and wrong.
It dances on a tightrope's edge,
Both ecstasy and silent pledge.

Like roses' thorns on petals fair,
Love's tender touch can bind or tear.
A conundrum that's as old as time,
Why does love hurt, a truth sublime?

For love, a force that none can shun,
It's both the moon and burning sun.
In its embrace, we find our worth,
But sometimes, love can hurt the Earth.

So let us cherish, despite the ache,
The love we give, the love we take.
For in its depths, we find our way,
Through joy and pain, come what may.

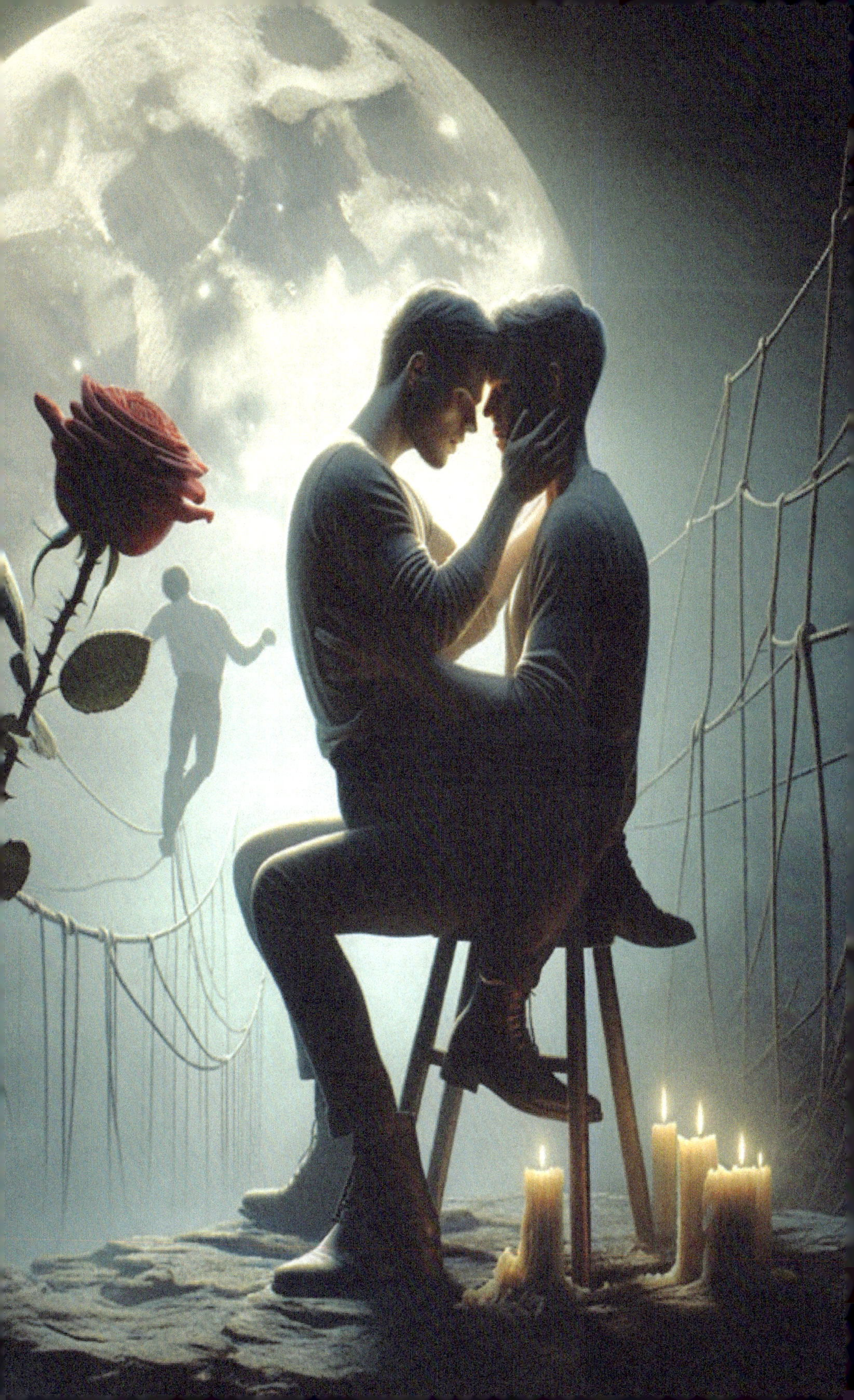

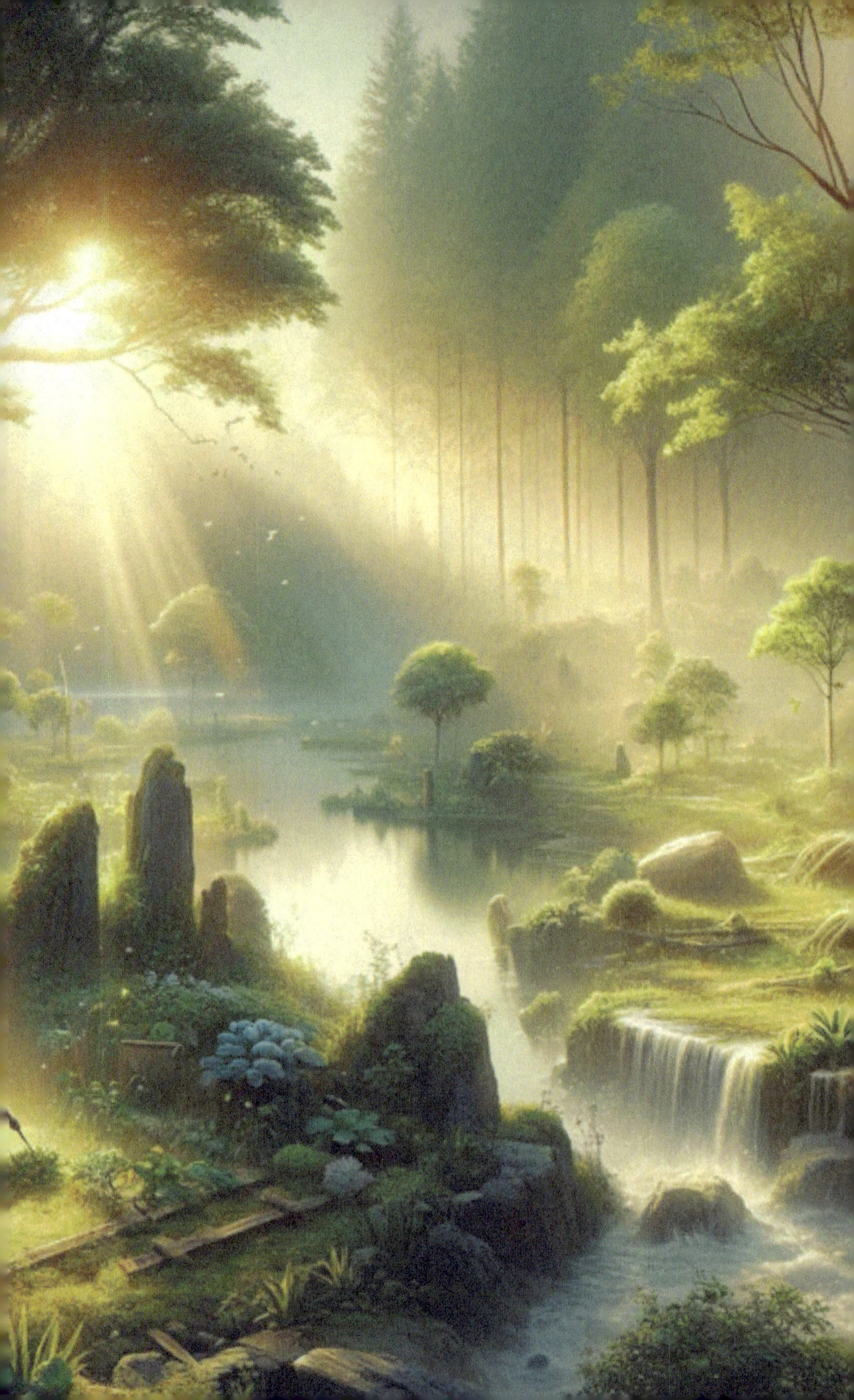

Echoes from the Heart

Fragments of Serenity

In the depths of time, the canvas torn,
I sought solace, a refuge reborn.
For in my universe, once shattered and bleak,
A tapestry of peace, anew I'd seek.

Through eons of trials, the struggle endured,
Each piece of happiness carefully secured.
For I knew the labor, the sweat, and the tears,
That mended my world, dispelled all my fears.

If you could fathom the arduous path,
The toil and the strife, the aftermath.
Then, perchance, you would comprehend,
Why my choices are few, my trust I defend.

Not one to surrender my fragile domain,
To those who bring chaos or cause me pain.
With discerning eyes, I carefully glean,
Who enters my haven, who forms my scene.

For the energy exchanged within these walls,
Determines the height where my spirit calls.
And though it may seem a picky decree,
It safeguards the peace that exists within me.

So, judge me not for the walls that I raise,
For in them, my universe finds its blaze.
A symphony of souls, harmonized true,
Building a haven where serenity grew.

Echoes from the Heart

Field of Valor

Amidst the green, flags stand proud in rows,
A tribute to the brave, where honor grows.
Stars and stripes catch light, a bright display,
Symbols of love and loss, the price they pay.

Grass whispers beneath, a hushed refrain,
A melody of cost, where memories remain.
Each banner tells a tale, a legacy,
A chapter of valor in history.

Not fabric by hand, but woven by the brave,
Who stood for duty, the soul to save.
In this field, where silence speaks the tale,
Of lives lived large, where courage didn't fail.

As night falls, their shadows blend and stretch,
A vow to truths we must protect.
Here, where stars and stripes still fly,
Every flag brings peace, raised high.

Beneath the moon, flags keep watch in the dark,
Each one a flame, a nation's spark.
In every gust, they speak of light,
Their memory held in cloth, through the night.

At dawn, the light brings pride once more,
For those who stood with strength before.
In rows they rest, in peace they lie,
Their legacy will never die.

©Photograph by Tina Vos[v]

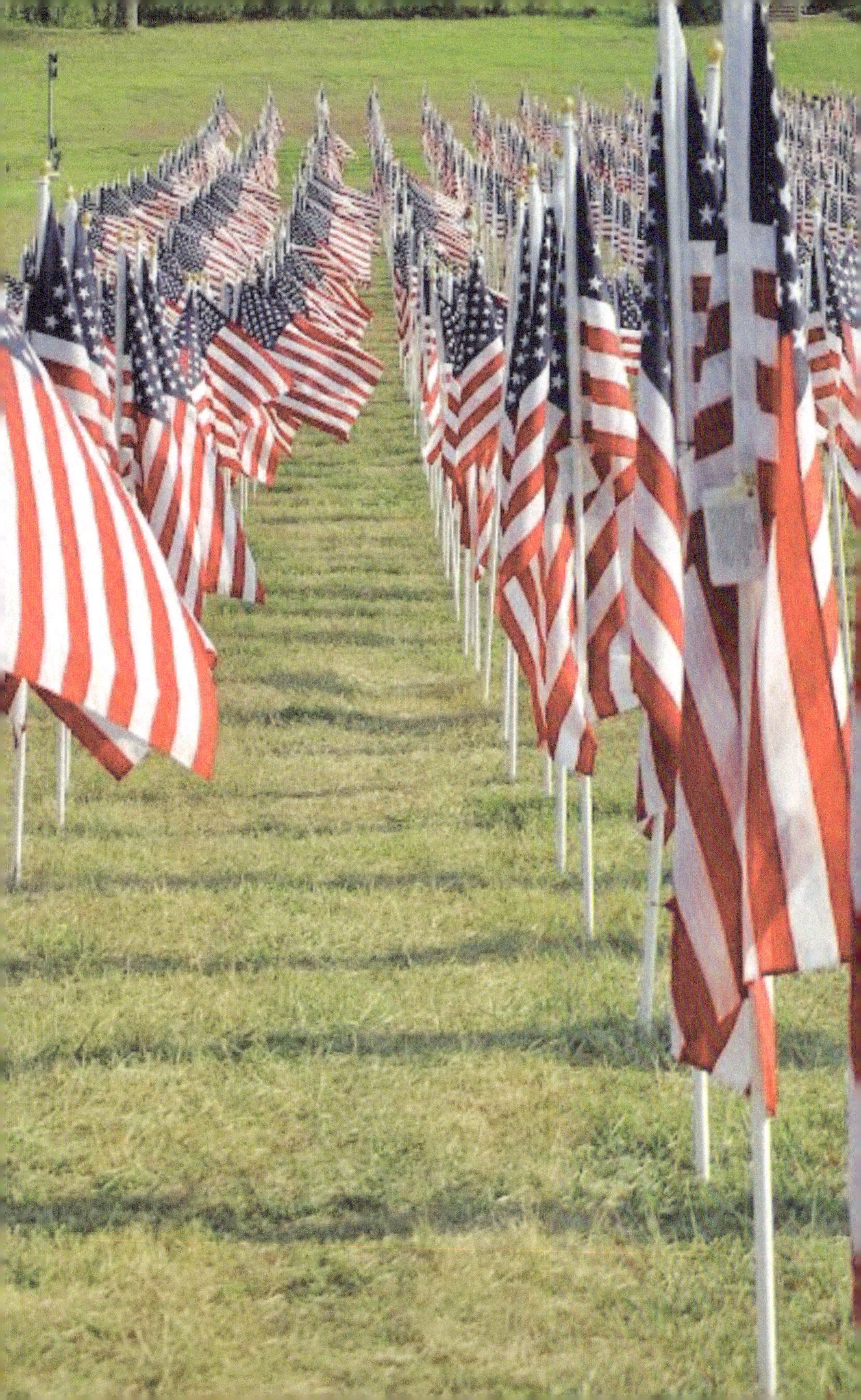

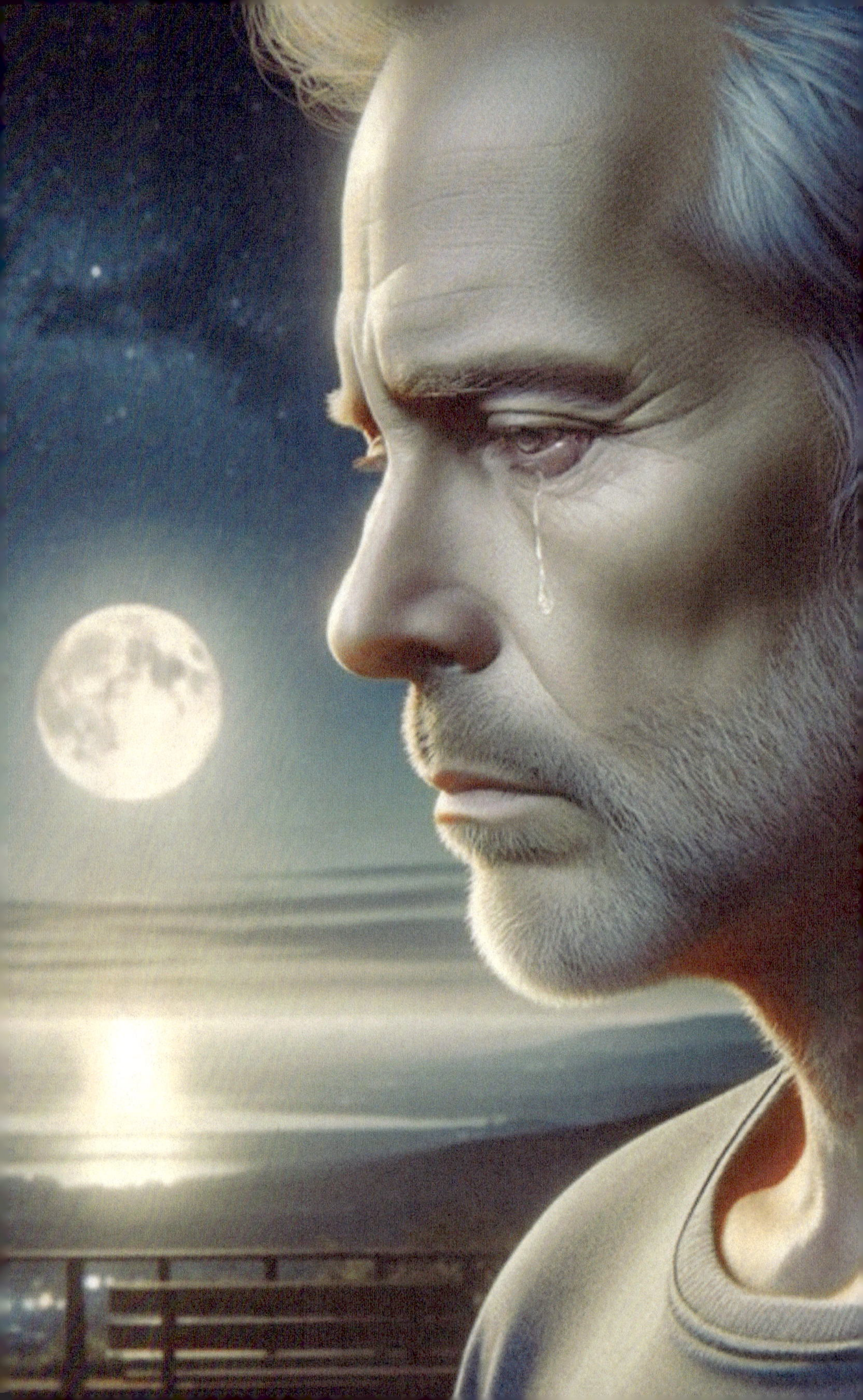

Echoes from the Heart

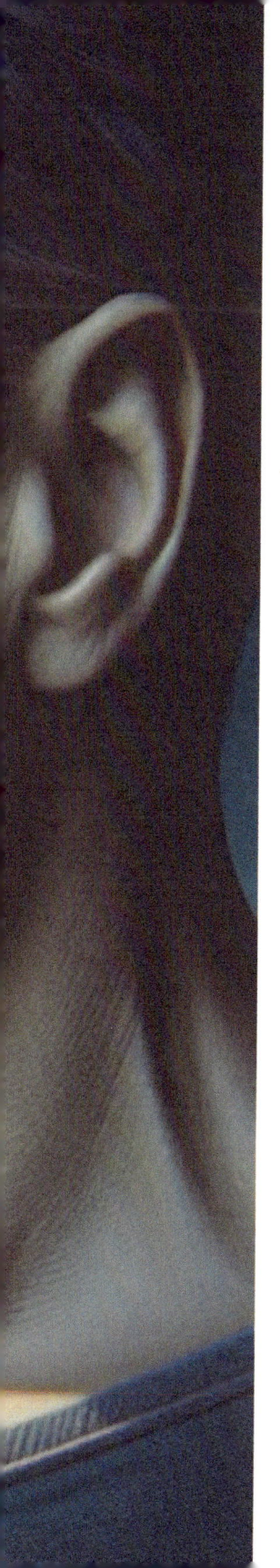

The Tears That Taught Me

In the quiet of a moonlit night,
Whispers of the past take flight.
Lessons learned in tearful hue,
A heart's silent cry, deep and true.

Each drop a story, a memory's trace,
In the mirror, a reflection's grace.
The pain of love, the joy of loss,
Life's tempests navigated, a personal cross.

Through the veil of sorrow's rain,
Strength is forged from tender pain.
In every tear, a wisdom's seed,
Watering the soul in its time of need.

The rivers of life, ever twisting, turning,
In their depths, a spirit burning.
Tears that taught, both harsh and kind,
In their wake, a peace of mind.

For in my tears, I found my way,
From darkest night to brightest day.
A journey through the heart's deep sea,
The tears that taught have set me free.

Now as I stand with lessons earned,
I see the paths where I once burned.
Each tear that fell was not in vain,
For strength was born through every pain.

Someday, I Hope to Forget

In time's soft hands, may memories fade,
Where past regrets in shadows are laid.
A heart once heavy longs to be free,
From sorrow's chains, I ache to flee.

You crossed the line, unseen, unknown,
Leaving hurt where love once shone.
No guilt for the path I chose to take,
Yet a wilted rose still blooms in its wake.

Dreams once bright now fade away,
Lost in the dusk of yesterday.
But hope whispers in dawn's first light,
Where rivers of pain lose their might.

As the world spins in endless flight,
New dreams rise from ashes bright.
Someday, I'll forget and start anew,
Where pain is lost like morning dew.

Through shifting time, the hurt will go,
Winds of healing will softly blow.
Someday, I'll find peace, let go of regret,
In the calm of dawn, I'll forget.

With each new day, the scars will mend,
The pain will cease as memories bend.
Someday, I hope to forget and be free,
In the light of peace that waits for me.

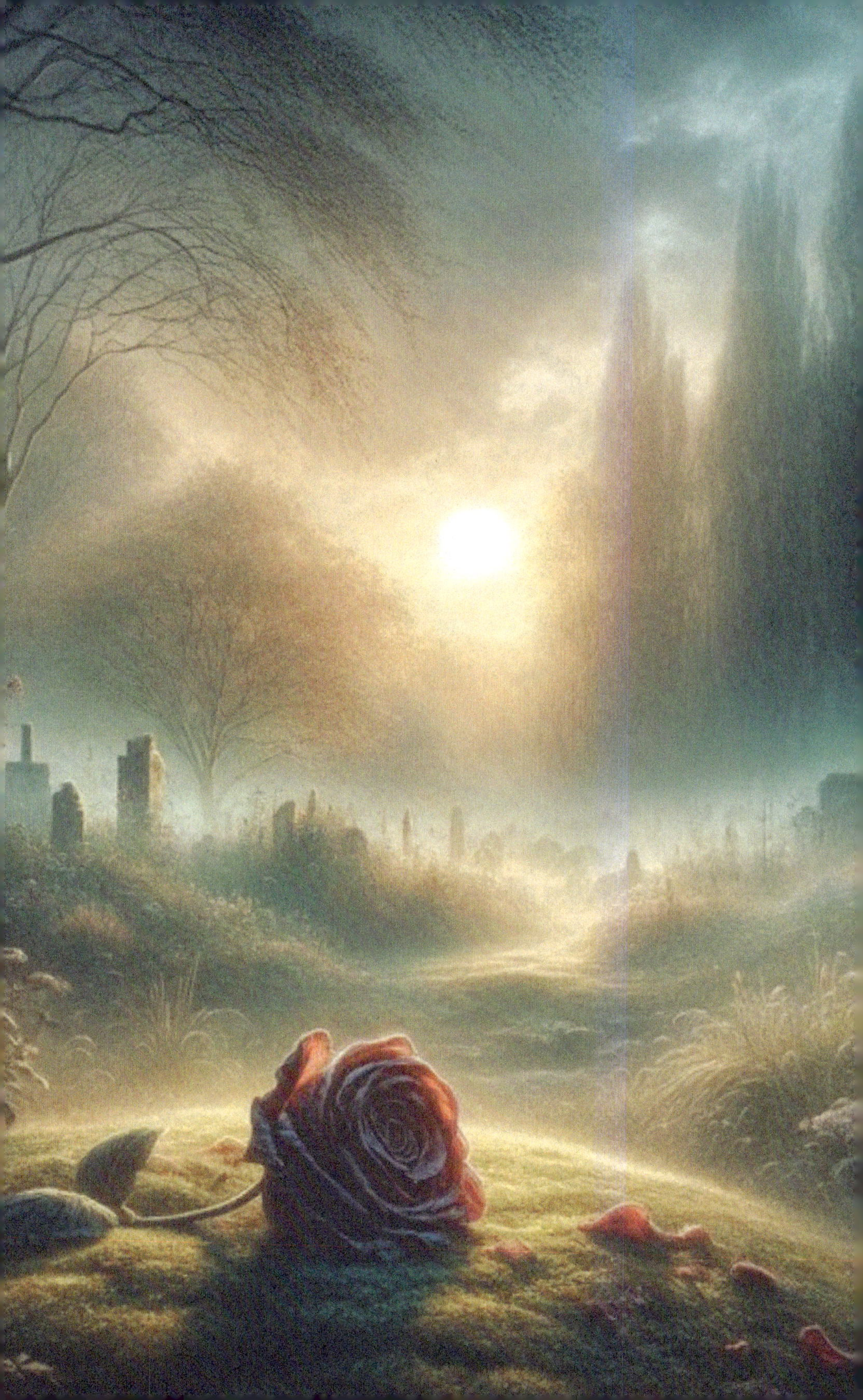

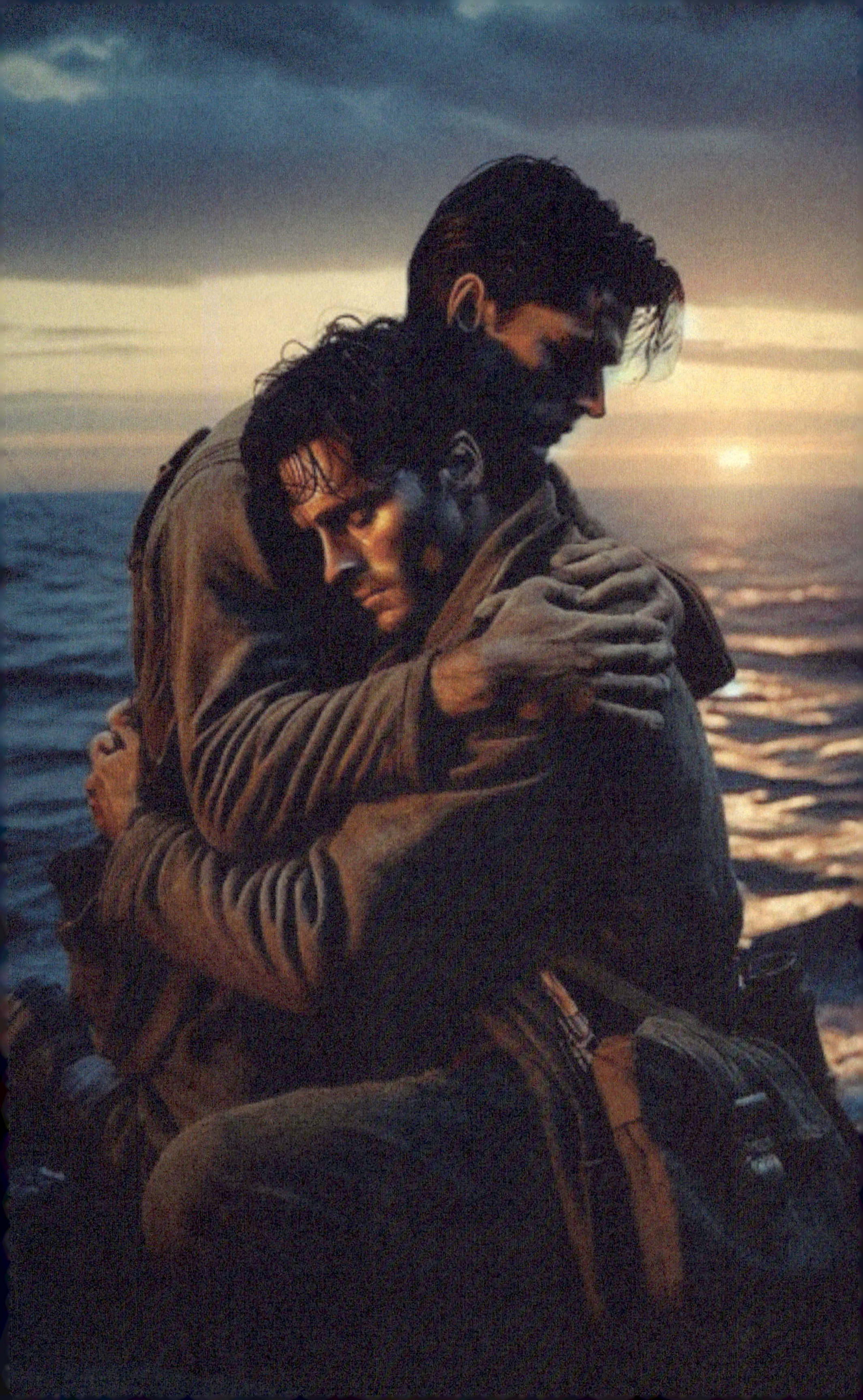

Echoes from the Heart

Never Let Me Down Again

In the echoes of twilight's serene,
A promise whispered, barely seen.
Through the maze of life, so vast,
A vow to hold, from first to last.

Gentle strength in your steady gaze,
Guides me through the foggy haze.
In storms and calm, you remain,
A steadfast ship, in life's domain.

Never let me down again,
In this dance of time, we spin.
Your words, a melody, my balm,
In your embrace, a soothing calm.

Through seasons that come and go,
In you, a constant glow.
A beacon bright, in night's domain,
Never let me down again.

In the symphony of life's grand score,
Your presence is the core.
A harmony, so pure and true,
In every shade, in every hue.

So, here's to promises we make,
In morning light, at twilight's wake,
A journey shared, through joy and pain,
Never let me down again.

The Eternal Knot

In a dance of ink and time's embrace,
Lines entwine in a tender chase.
Flowing free, yet closely bound,
A silent symphony without a sound.

Infinity drawn with a deft hand's trace,
A quartet of hearts in a ceaseless race.
Each curve a whisper of love profound,
Where beginning nor end is ever found.

No stroke misplaced in this quiet space,
A moment captured with enduring grace.
In this symbol, a harmony is crowned,
A testament of life, forever wound.

Beneath the stars, this pattern spins,
A circle where all ends begin.
In every twist, in every round,
The echoes of life's rhythm sound.

Endless loops in the quiet weave,
Threads of joy and threads of grief.
In its arcs, the stories stay,
Carved in time, yet swept away.

So let the ink in silence flow,
Tracing paths we'll never know.
In the endless dance of love and grace,
Forever spun, forever in place.

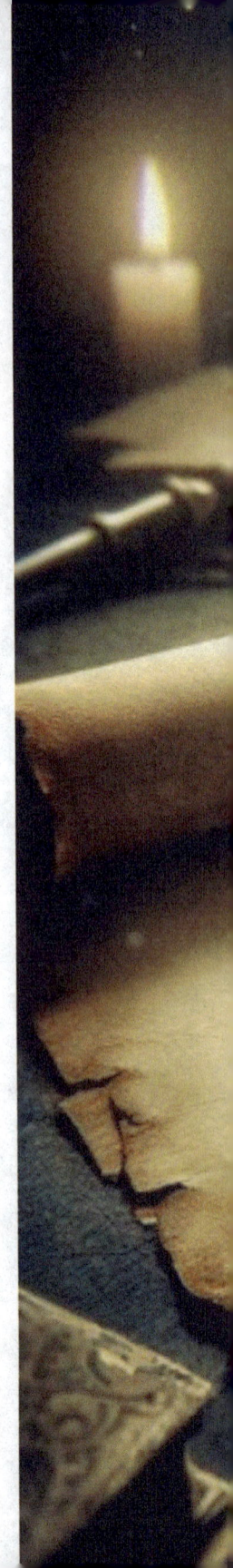

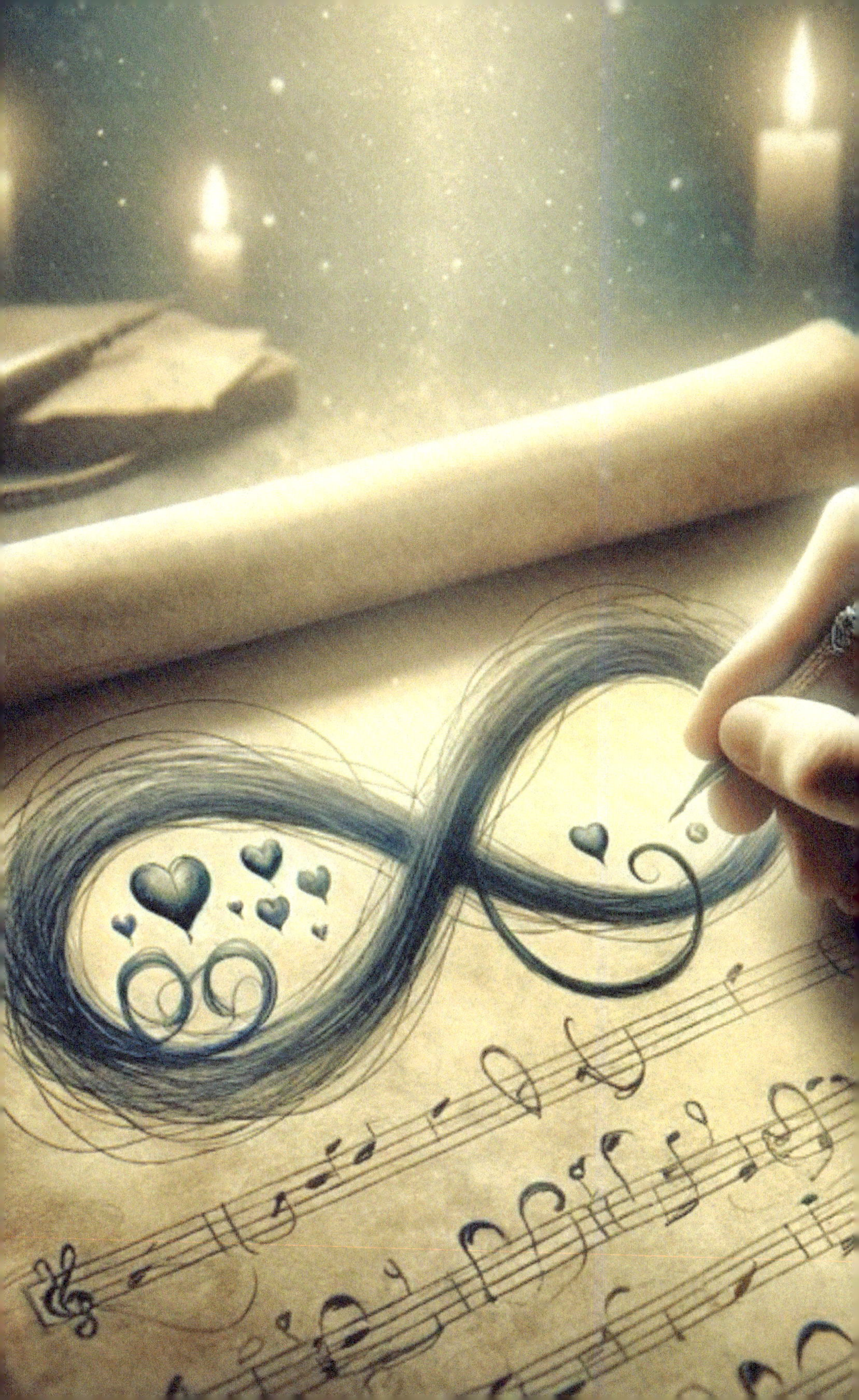

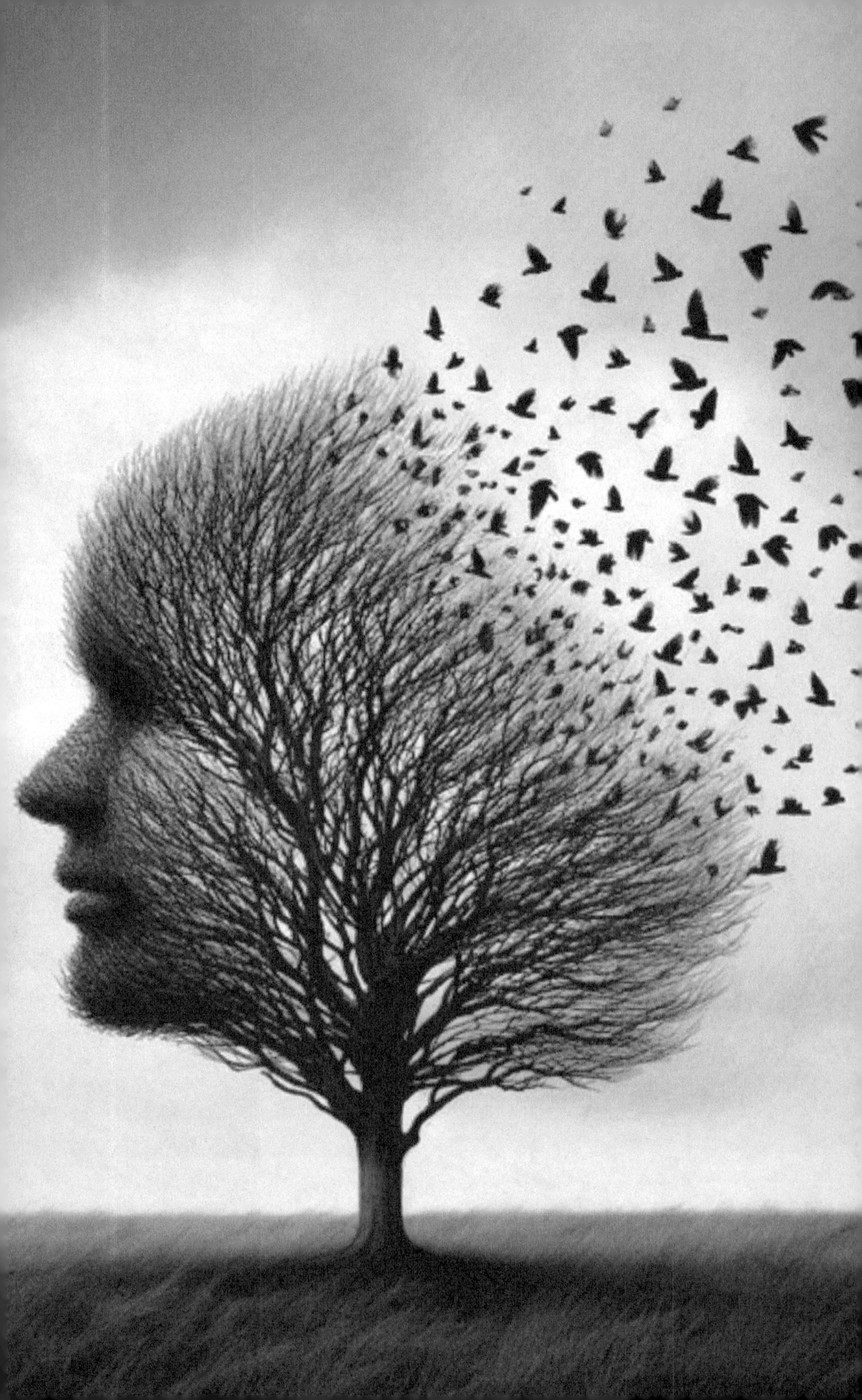

Echoes from the Heart

The Many Faces We Wear

In the quiet field of being,
A tree stands lone where winds are freeing.
Leaves take flight in forms deceiving,
Murmuration's of our souls' achieving.

The many faces we adorn,
Like leaves in breezes, tossed and worn.
Each a whisper of a life forlorn,
In every silhouette, a new dawn is born.

Nature's breath, in gentle heaves,
Scatters the essence of all it weaves.
In every departure, the heart grieves,
For the many faces one receives and leaves.

The tree, undressed by time's decree,
Bears the truth that sets us free.
Our truest self, the trunk beneath,
Stands resolute, without the leaf.

And thus, we stand in time's grand hall,
Watching the leaves of our being fall.
Each one a face, a moment's call,
In the field of life, we embrace it all.

In the end, as branches bend,
The many faces we suspend,
Fall like whispers, without a sound,
And in their absence, truth is found.

Embers of Challenge

In a realm where flames meet their fiery twin,
Two fires clash, neither destined to win.
Igniting passion, a dance of power and light,
They burn together, turning day into night.

With sparks that fly like stars in a fight,
Each ember tells a tale of strength and might.
Yet in their heat, a strange harmony they find,
A fiery waltz, in a whirlwind entwined.

Fierce and wild, yet a beauty unseen,
In their battle, a unity serene.
Like warriors of old, they stand and defy,
In the dance of flames, where fire meets sky.

Beneath the flames, the earth starts to glow,
Feeding on power only they know.
The ground beneath trembles in awe,
As their shared strength breaks every flaw.

Their light reflects in each other's gaze,
A testament to their unyielding blaze.
In this inferno, a lesson is born,
From fire to fire, new strength is torn.

And as the ashes settle, calm and still,
The fire's fury becomes a test of will.
In the embers of challenge, wisdom's attire,
Revealed is the truth, in fighting fire with fire.

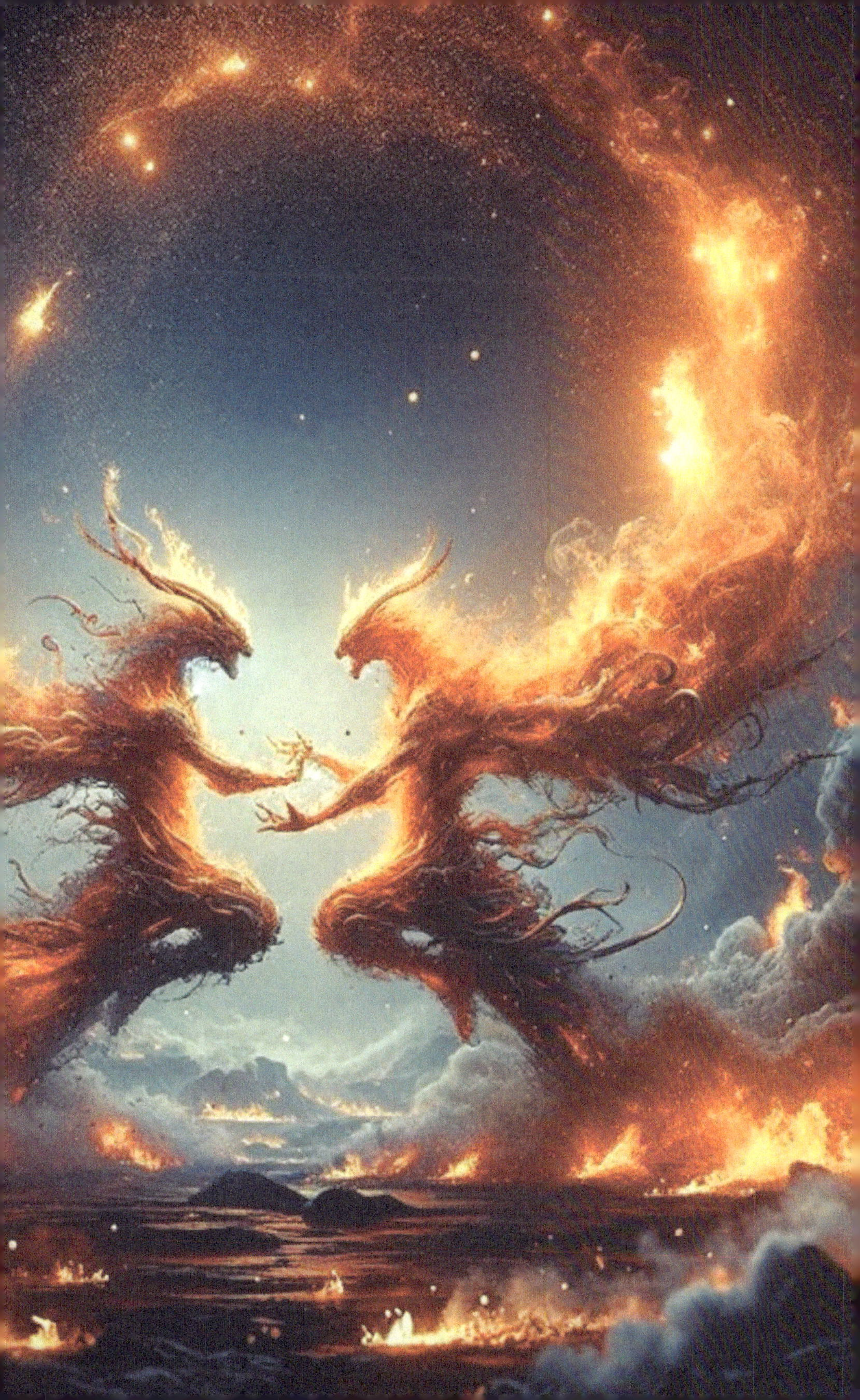

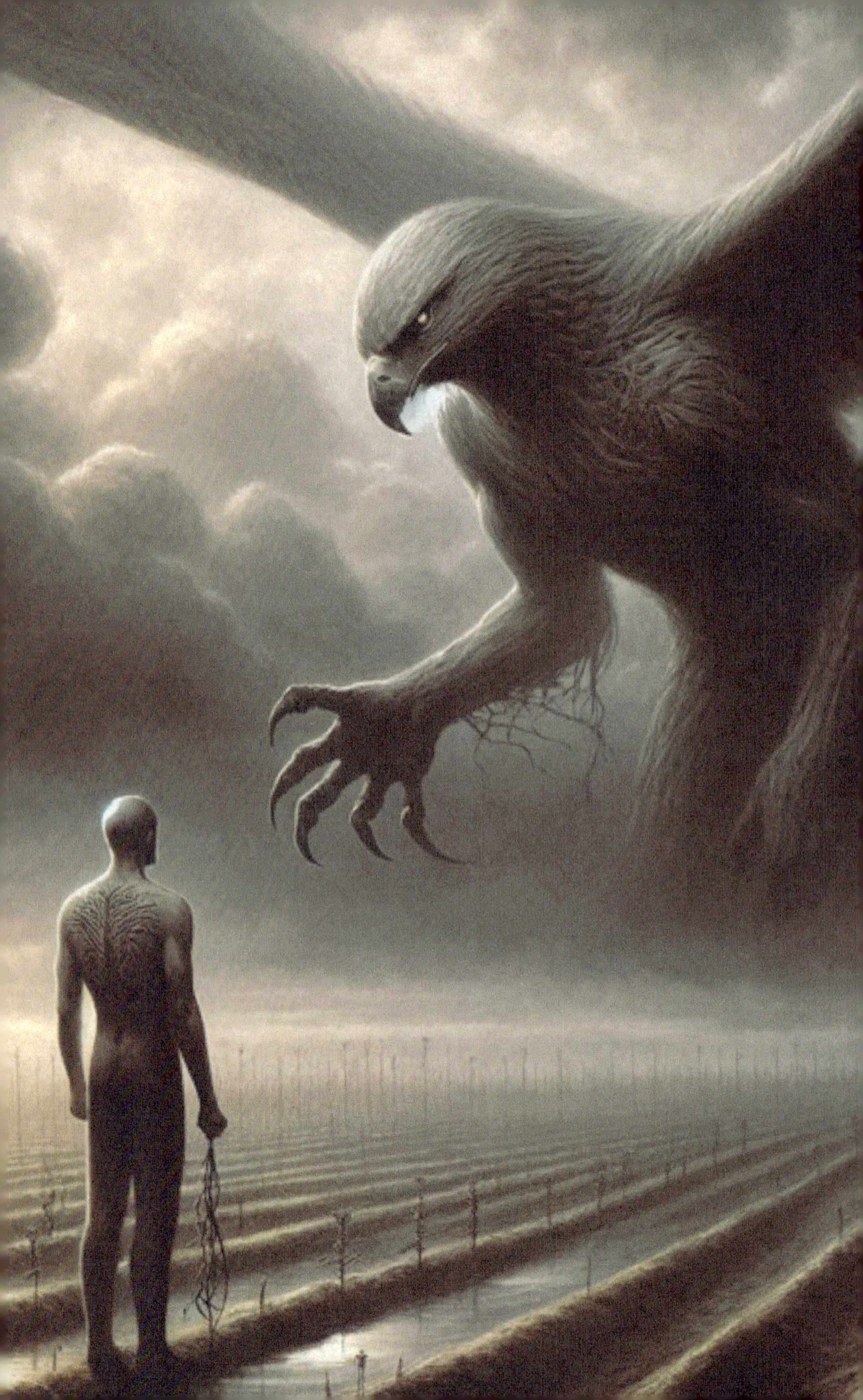

Echoes from the Heart

Harvesting Sorrow

Why do you reap from my sorrow,
Like a hawk on a hunt
You hover to reap from me,
With talons sharp, you taunt.

You circle, ever watchful,
In the sky of my despair,
Seeking to gather my tears,
With a merciless, relentless glare.

I wonder what you gain,
From the pain that I endure,
Do you feed on my anguish,
Like a vulture, so impure?

Yet, I won't be your victim,
In this game you choose to play,
For my spirit is resilient,
And I'll find my strength today.

No longer will I falter,
In the shadow of your greed,
I'll rise above this darkness,
Plant a brighter, better seed.

So, hawk, your time is fleeting,
As I break free from your snare,
I'll soar beyond your reach,
With a soul too strong to tear.

In Chains

In chains, I find myself ensnared,
Bound to you, my soul laid bare.
A captive heart, a love profound,
In your embrace, forever bound.

Yet, in this tether, I am free,
To explore love's vast, endless sea.
Our souls entwined, a sacred dance,
In this enchanting, sweet romance.

No prison bars, no locks or key,
Can break this bond, you and me.
With every heartbeat, love's refrain,
In chains of passion, we remain.

In these bonds, a tender grace,
Love's true essence, we embrace.
Each link a memory, a shared dream,
In love's unyielding, gentle stream.

Together in life's ebb and flow,
In chains of affection, love does grow.
United hearts, in joy and pain,
In love's chains, we find our gain.

Through time's passage, strong and sure,
These chains of love, forever endure.
A bond unbroken by strife or pain,
In these chains, our love remains.

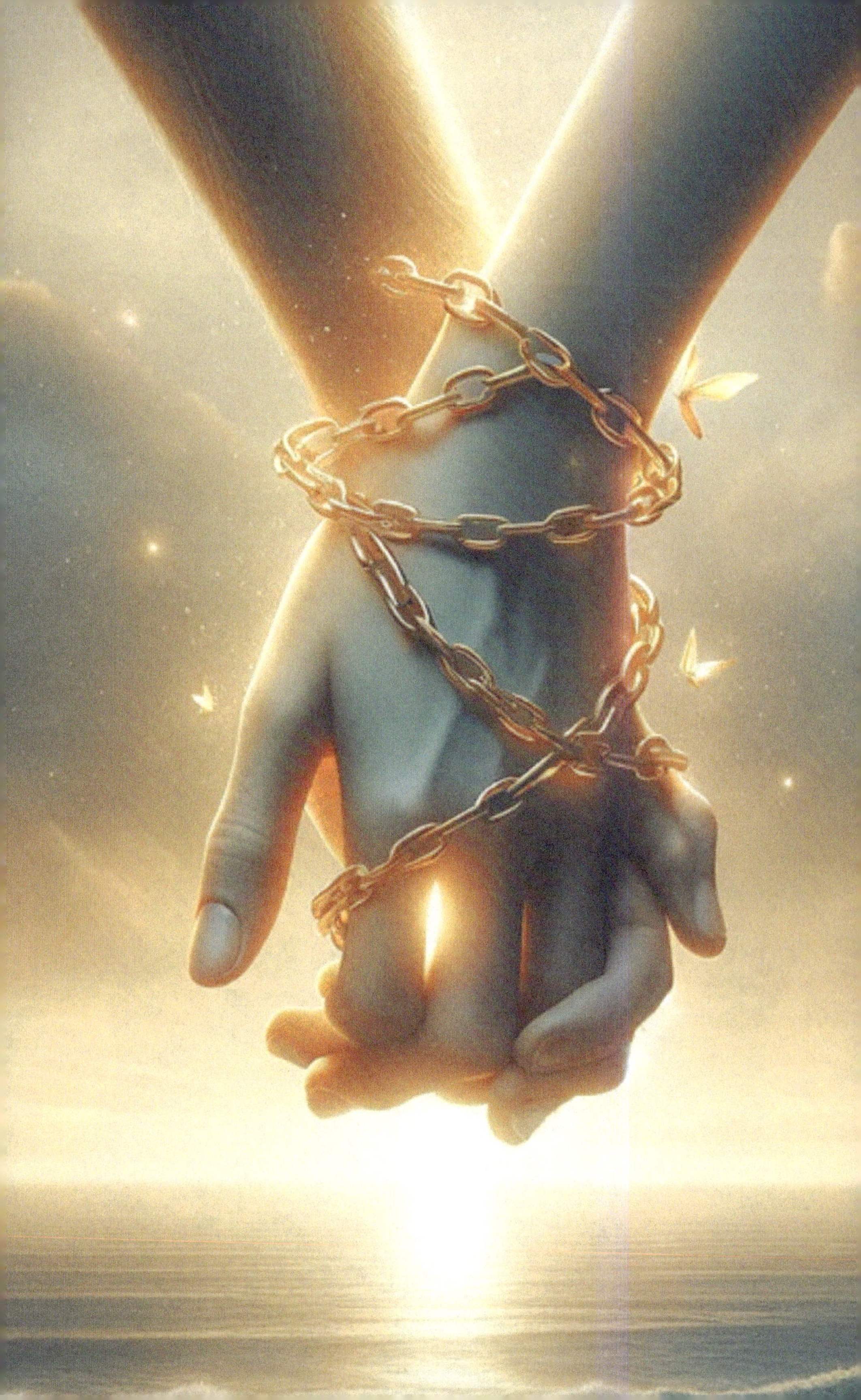

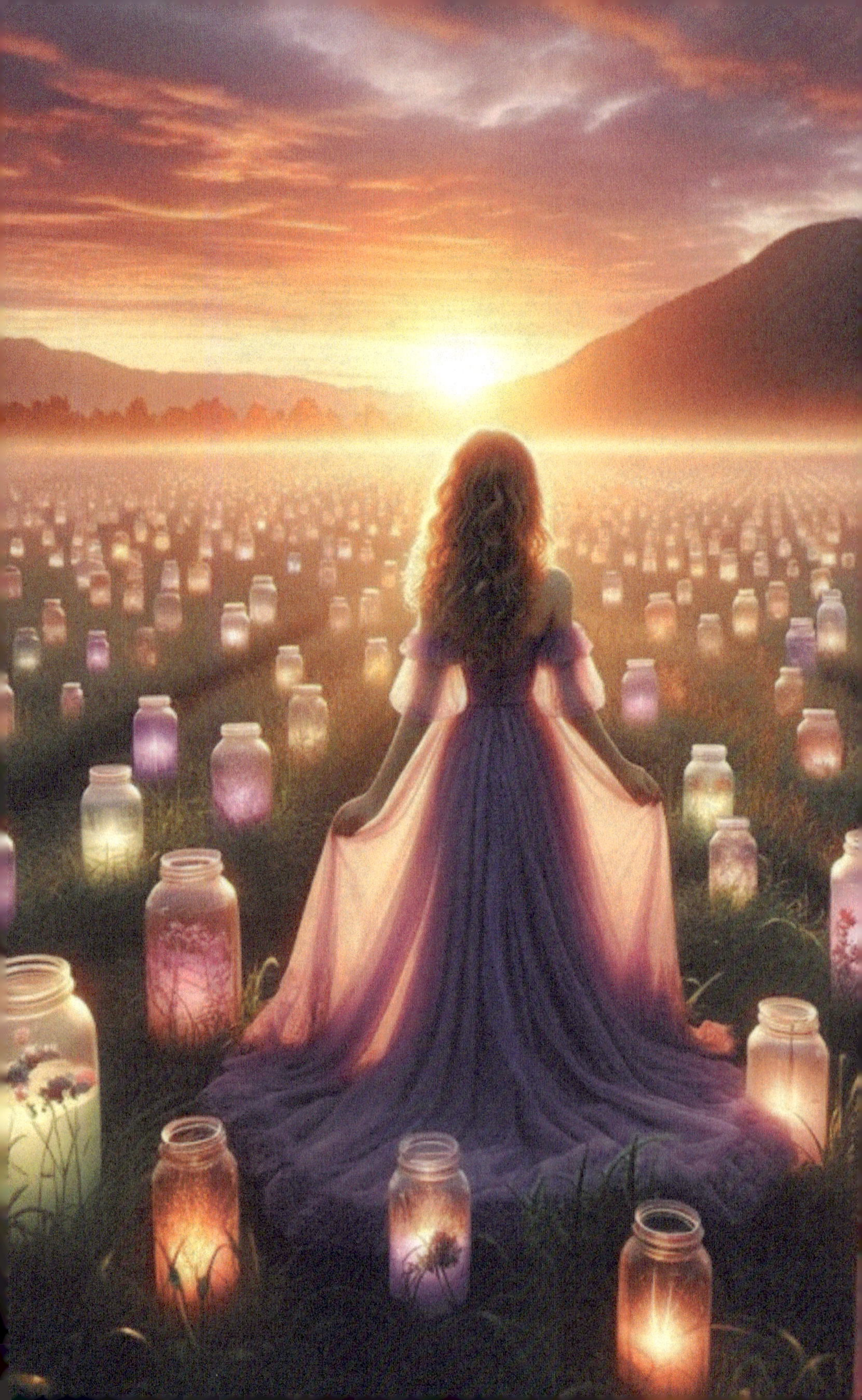

Echoes from the Heart

Jars of Dawn

In twilight's hush, the glow begins,
A field of jars, light's softest hymns.
A girl amidst the dawn's embrace,
Each step a dance, the night's erase.

She wanders through the silent choir,
Glowing vessels of captured fire.
Colors whisper to the skies,
In murmured hues, the dark defies.

Sunrise kisses jar-lit sea,
A blend of flame and reverie.
The girl, a shadow cast in light,
Moves through the dawn, dispelling night.

Reflections dance on glassy spheres,
Each jar, a world, the cosmos nears.
In this expanse of light and hue,
Morning's breath feels soft and new.

Horizon's edge, a melting gold,
A symphony of warmth unfolds.
The jars, like stars, begin to fade,
In the orchestra that daylight made.

With every jar, a dream's release,
A tranquil space, a piece of peace.
The girl, a silhouette now gone,
Leaves whispered dreams in the jars of dawn.

Apology

In pain's grip, I stumbled and fell,
Hurt others as I sank in my well.
Regret now fills the space inside,
For forgiveness, I set aside pride.

I lashed out, my wounds unhealed,
Unaware of the pain concealed.
Each word a dagger, each action a sting,
To those I hurt, I owe everything.

I'm sorry for the tears and trust,
Shattered in anger's careless thrust.
In darkness, I lost my way,
But seek redemption, starting today.

To those I hurt while lost in strife,
I carry this weight, changing my life.
With new strength, I vow to mend,
Heal the hearts on which I depend.

Each sunrise brings my chance to atone,
For all the pain, I'll make it known.
I'm so sorry, my heart's sincere,
I'll heal your wounds, and draw you near.

With time and care, I'll strive to right,
The wrongs I caused in darkest night.
In your forgiveness, I find my light,
And build a future pure and bright.

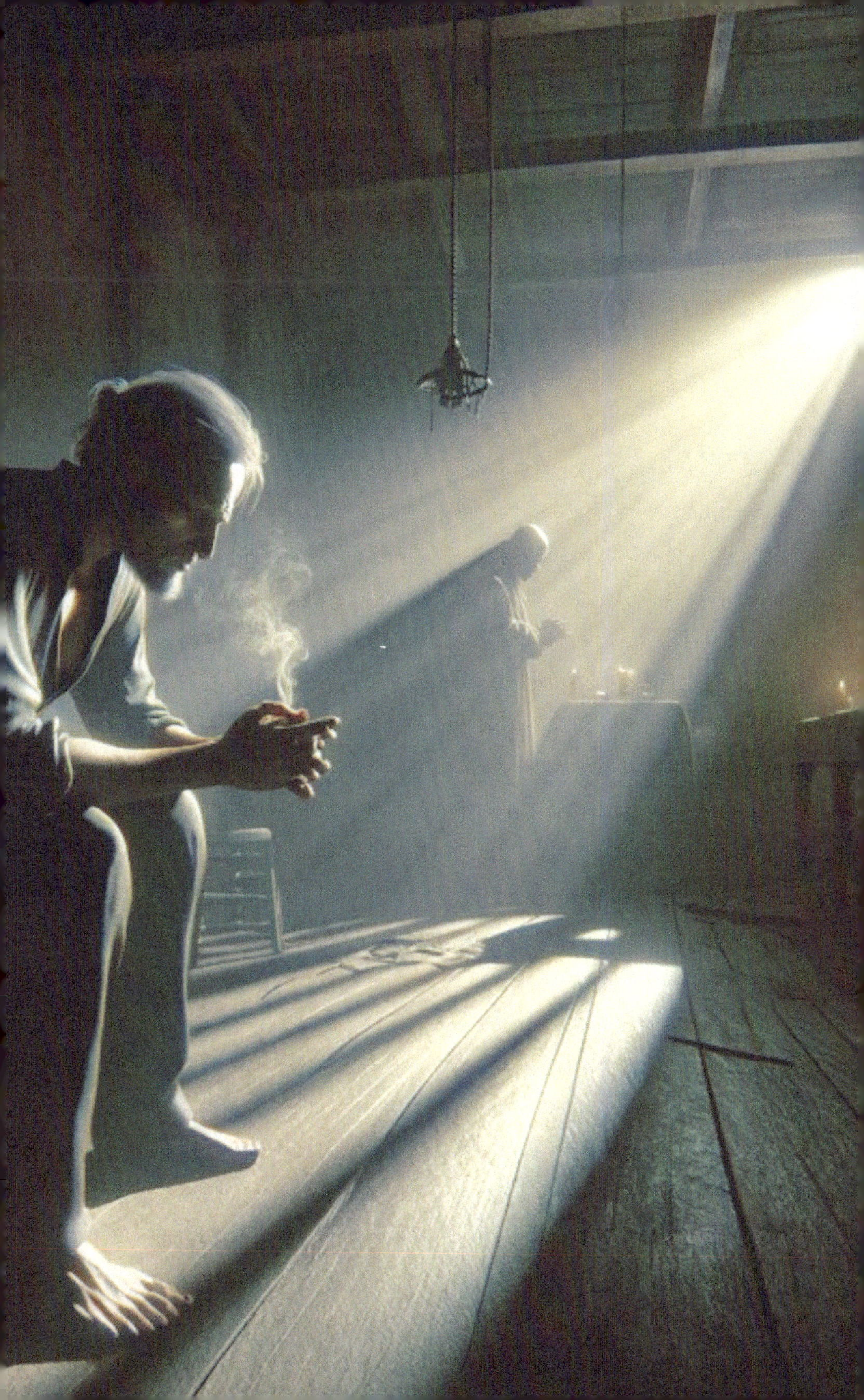

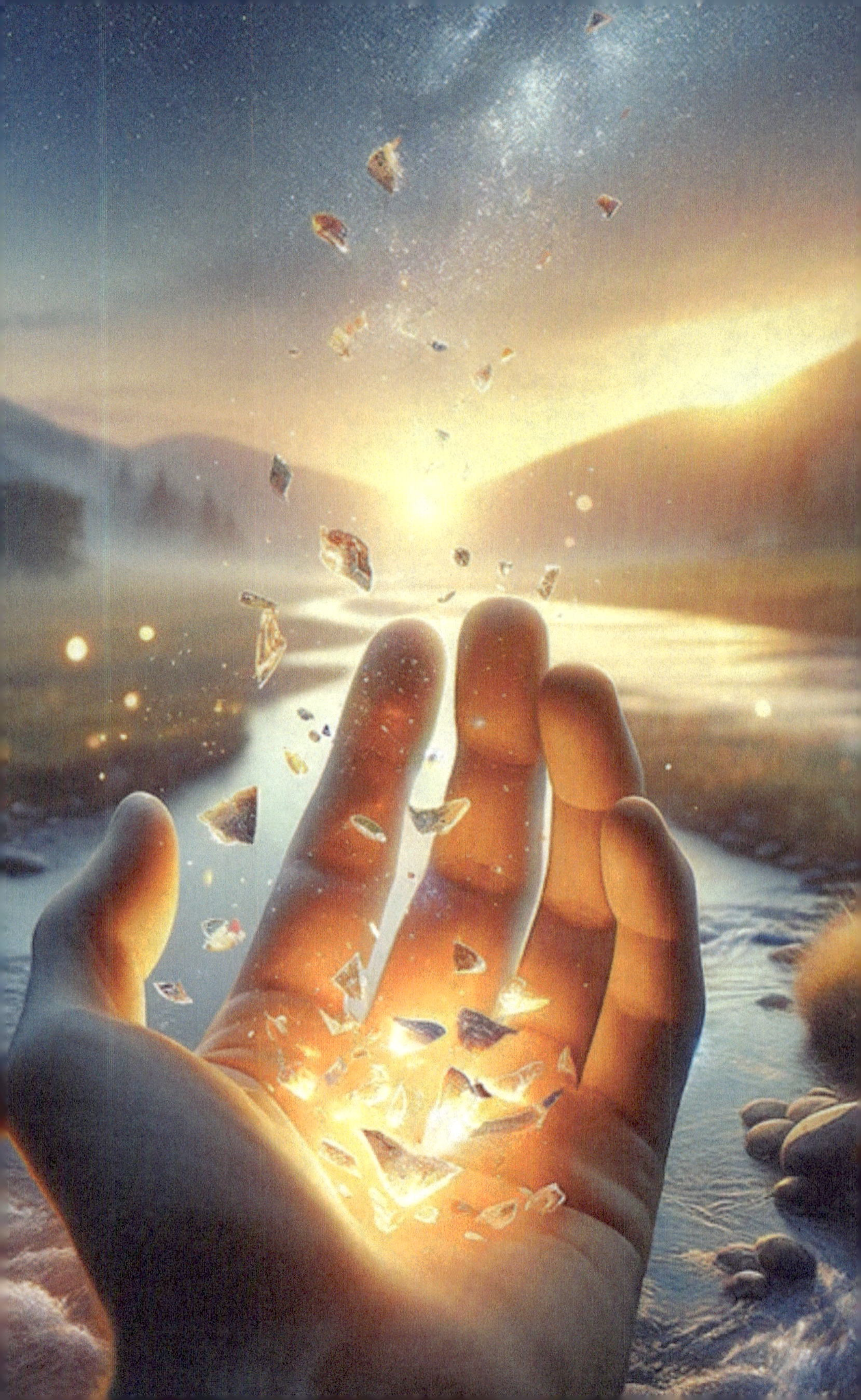

Echoes from the Heart

Shards of Serenity

In tangled thoughts, the cosmos wide,
I toiled for peace, for light inside.
Through trials and battles, fierce and fought,
Mending solace, in fragments caught.

The arduous path, through chaos spun,
Day by day, my world begun.
In vigilance, my gaze does rest,
Guarding the haven, I've built and blessed.

Sanctuary's light, a realm so bright,
For those who know, my tireless fight.
Within these walls, serenity's song,
A respite realm, where joys belong.

Selective gates, for souls so true,
Who see the peace I've built anew.
This tranquil place, a sacred sight,
Where dreams and solace unite in light.

My struggle's mark, in every stone,
A universe rebuilt, my own.
With love and care, these walls I bear,
A refuge from despair, so rare.

In scars, my story, my spirit's lease,
A patchwork peace, a silent crease.
Solace's fragments, in harmony lie,
Resilience's essence, under the sky.

Tell Me the Darkness

Tell me the darkness in your eyes,
In shadows, secrets, and silent goodbyes.
A mystery lies in your gaze,
Whispers of longing in a maze.

Each flicker of light hides desire,
In silence burns a quiet fire.
A tale of love and loss you wear,
Etched on your face, beyond compare.

The fears you keep, the truths concealed,
In your eyes, all is revealed.
I'll stand by you through dark and light,
To find the truth and hold you tight.

In your eyes, I see a world untold,
A love deeper than words unfold.
Tell me the darkness, let us reside,
Where our love and hearts collide.

In silent night, under moon's glow,
Your eyes speak of what you know.
A dance with shadows, struggles bright,
In your gaze, I find the fight.

Yet within that darkness, hope will rise,
A bond unbreakable in your eyes.
In shadows deep, love is found,
In the light your eyes surround.

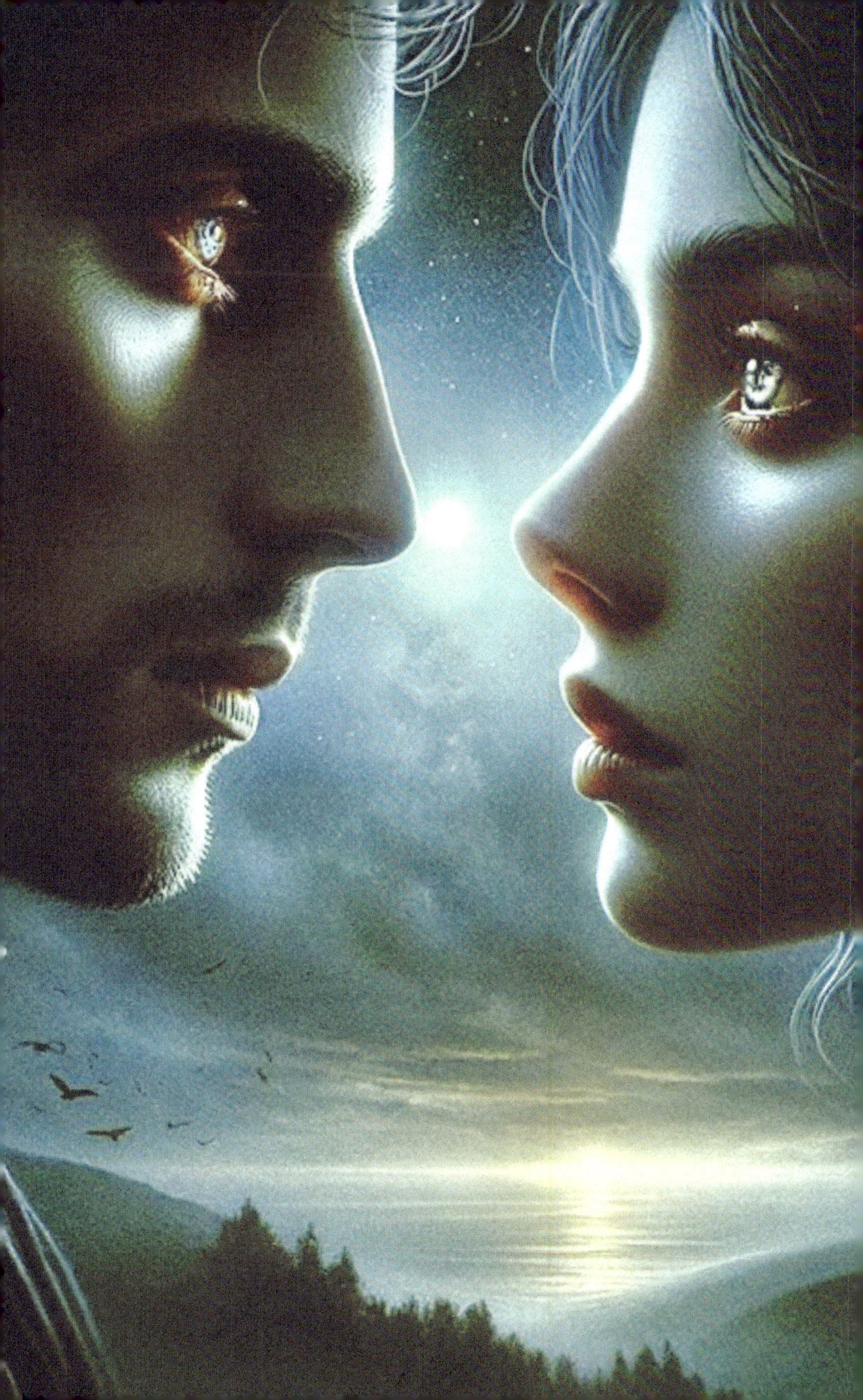

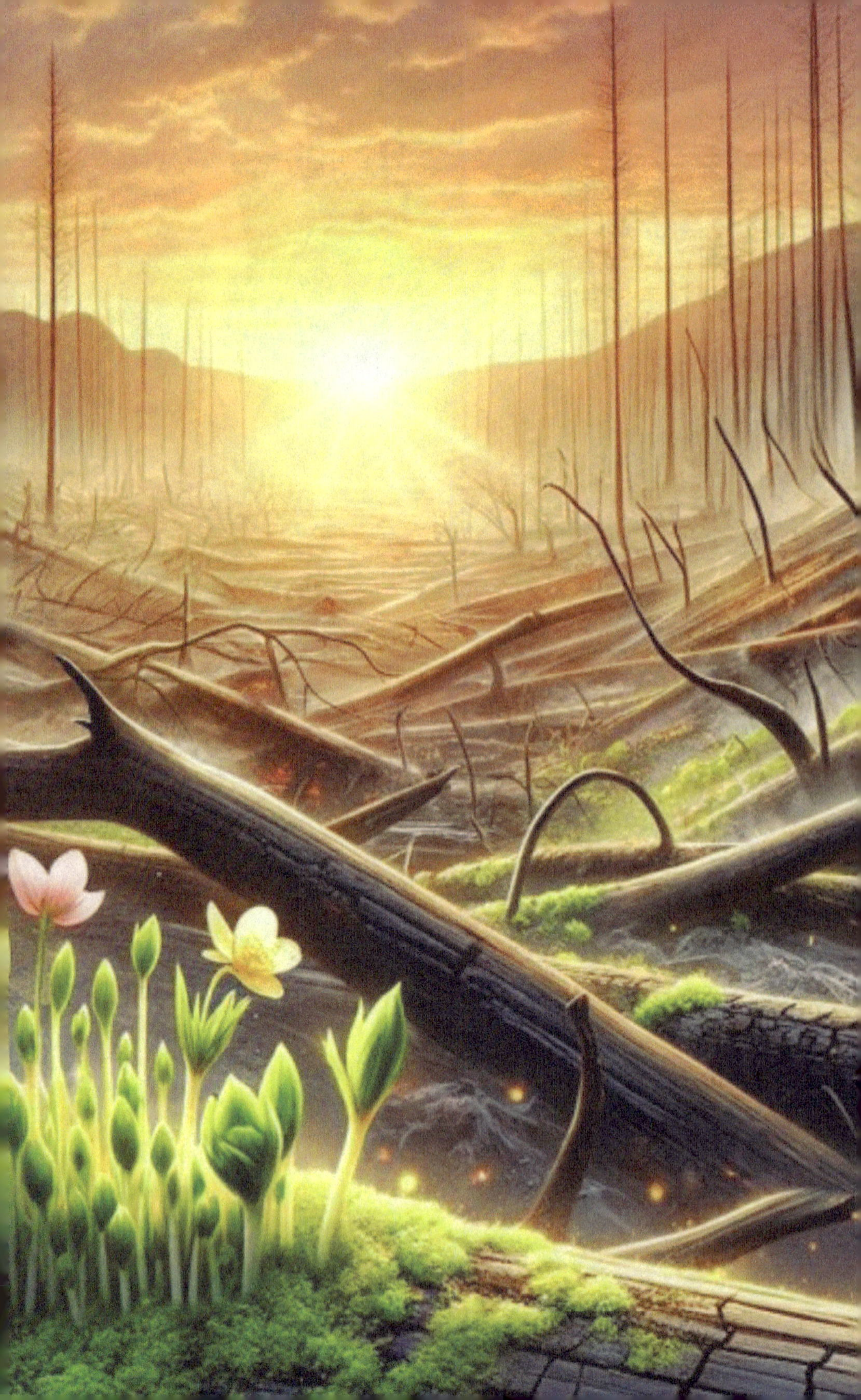

Echoes from the Heart

Roaring Silhouettes

In the roar of tongues aflame,
Life's silent gestures stake their claim.
Though flames may dance and sing their song,
They cannot own the life that's long.

Amidst the heat, the smoke, the haze,
Life's delicate whispers find their ways.
For in the embers, soft and meek,
Are stories flames cannot speak.

From scorched land and ashy tears,
Blossom tales of countless years.
Sweet things, born from pain so deep,
In unexpected places they creep.

Where the conditions often seem bleak,
Life's resilient dance is unique.
From ashes, hope and dreams do spawn,
In life's eternal, radiant dawn.

Beneath the char, beneath the sorrow,
Lies the promise of tomorrow.
Life's beauty, in its subtle guise,
Emerges strong, undeniably wise.

In every spark, a story dwells,
Of resilience, as the heart swells.
Amidst destruction, life anew,
In every dawn, a view renewed.

A Quiet Descent

The weight I bear, a whispered thread,
Pulls tighter with each breath I take.
The world moves on, but in my head,
A silent storm I cannot shake.

The shadows grow, they start to cling,
With every step, the ground gives way.
A heavy heart that cannot sing,
Lost in the haze of endless gray.

No light to chase, no dawn to see,
The stars seem far, the sky too high.
A broken soul too numb to flee,
Just hoping for the chance to die.

The voices tell me I'm alone,
That worth is something I can't claim.
The skin I wear feels not my own,
And every mirror shows my shame.

The fear of falling fades away,
For in the fall, there's peace, it seems.
Perhaps I'll rest and cease to stray,
Or drown within forgotten dreams.

Yet still, I walk, though no one sees,
Each step a silent, lonely fight.
The dark consumes, and I'm at ease,
A ghost unseen in endless night.

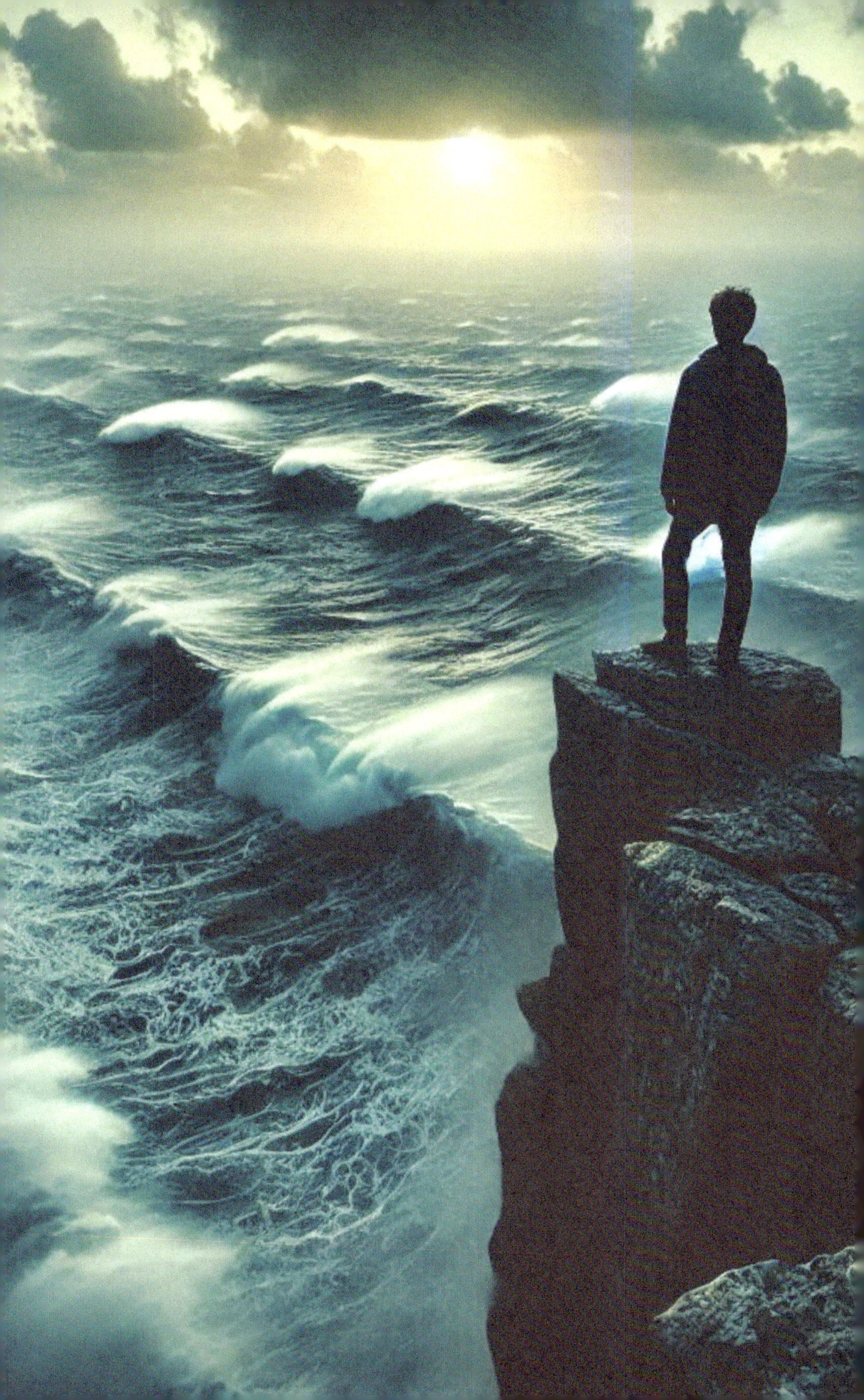

LOVE

Echoes from the Heart

The Loudest Way to Love

In a world full of noise and clash,
Love isn't in the grand, bold flash.
It's in the ways that make them feel,
In simple acts, both deep and real.

To make them feel seen, with a gaze so kind,
A look that shares both heart and mind.
Their hopes and fears, dreams in flight,
To truly see is love's pure light.

To make them feel heard, beyond just talk,
To listen close as their stories walk.
Laughter, sorrow, joy, and pain,
Listening brings love's deepest gain.

To make them feel known, through storm or sun,
To stand with them till battles are won.
Understanding brings peace and grace,
A love that time can't erase.

Love isn't loud, but gently stays,
In the smallest, quietest ways.
To see, to hear, to deeply know,
This is the love that helps hearts grow.

So, as we journey day by day,
Remember love's the quiet way.
In every glance and word you share,
Let love's loud silence fill the air.

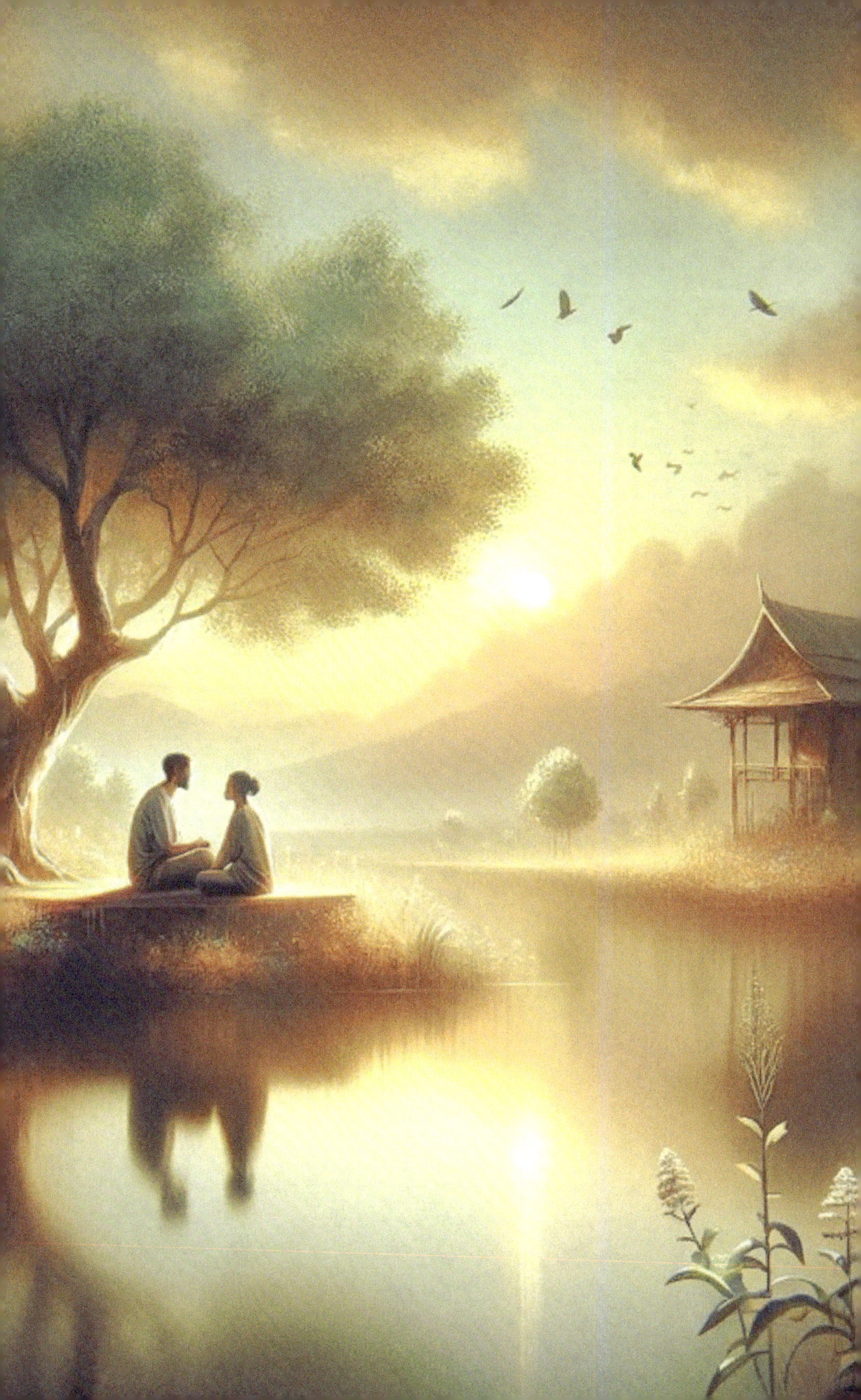

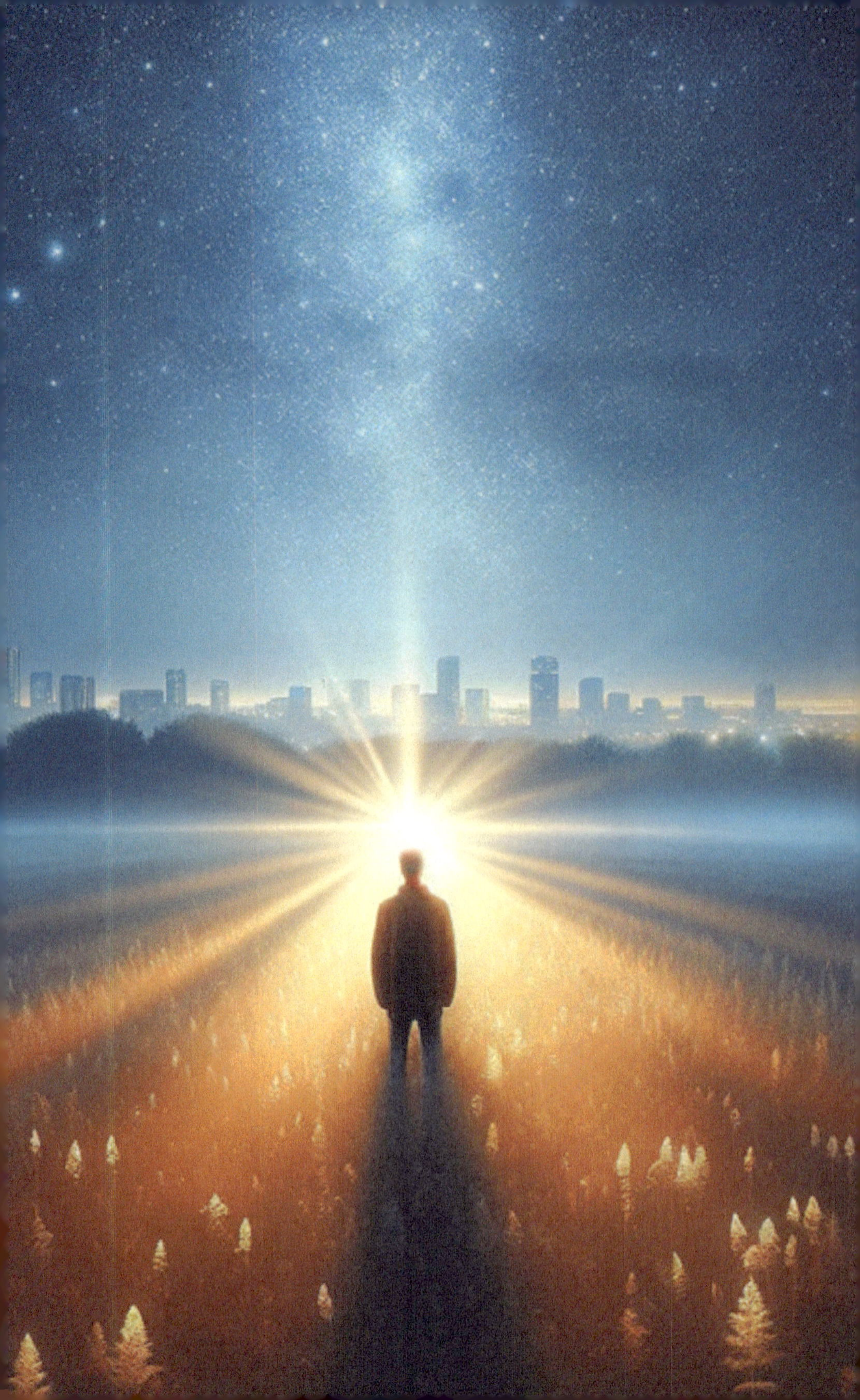

Echoes from the Heart

Special Moments

In life's vast, ever-changing light,
You shine, a gem in day and night.
A radiant soul, wherever you roam,
You're cherished, special, always home.

Beneath the sun or starry sea,
Your glow shines bright for all to see.
In every place, in each memory,
You're treasured, precious, eternally.

Amid the city's bustling hum,
Or 'neath the quiet moon's soft drum,
Your essence sparkles, wild and free,
A masterpiece for all to see.

In nature's grace or city's sprawl,
You stand out, unique, in moments small.
No matter the scene, near or far,
You're special, shining like a star.

Through changing seasons, bright you stay,
In hearts and minds, you light the way.
Wherever life may take you far,
Remember, you're a guiding star.

Your light endures, strong and true,
In every heart, a part of you.
Forever special, shining bright,
A beacon of love, pure and right.

Through My Eyes

How do you see beyond my pain,
Through every veil I can't explain.
In a world of loss and gain,
You seek truth where lies remain.

Each layer hides a tale untold,
Wrapped in shadows, hard and cold.
But in your gaze, I unfold,
Fears released, no longer bold.

Your sight cuts through the darkest night,
With your gentle, guiding light.
In your eyes, wrong turns to right,
And my world begins its flight.

Through my eyes, you understand,
Unspoken dreams, the life I've planned.
In your empathy, I stand,
Held and healed by your kind hand.

In your eyes, you see my soul,
Every part, complete and whole.
Through your gaze, I find my role,
And feel my heart regain control.

So, look through me, and you will see,
A world reborn, where I am free.
With your sight, I come to be,
A soul renewed, in unity.

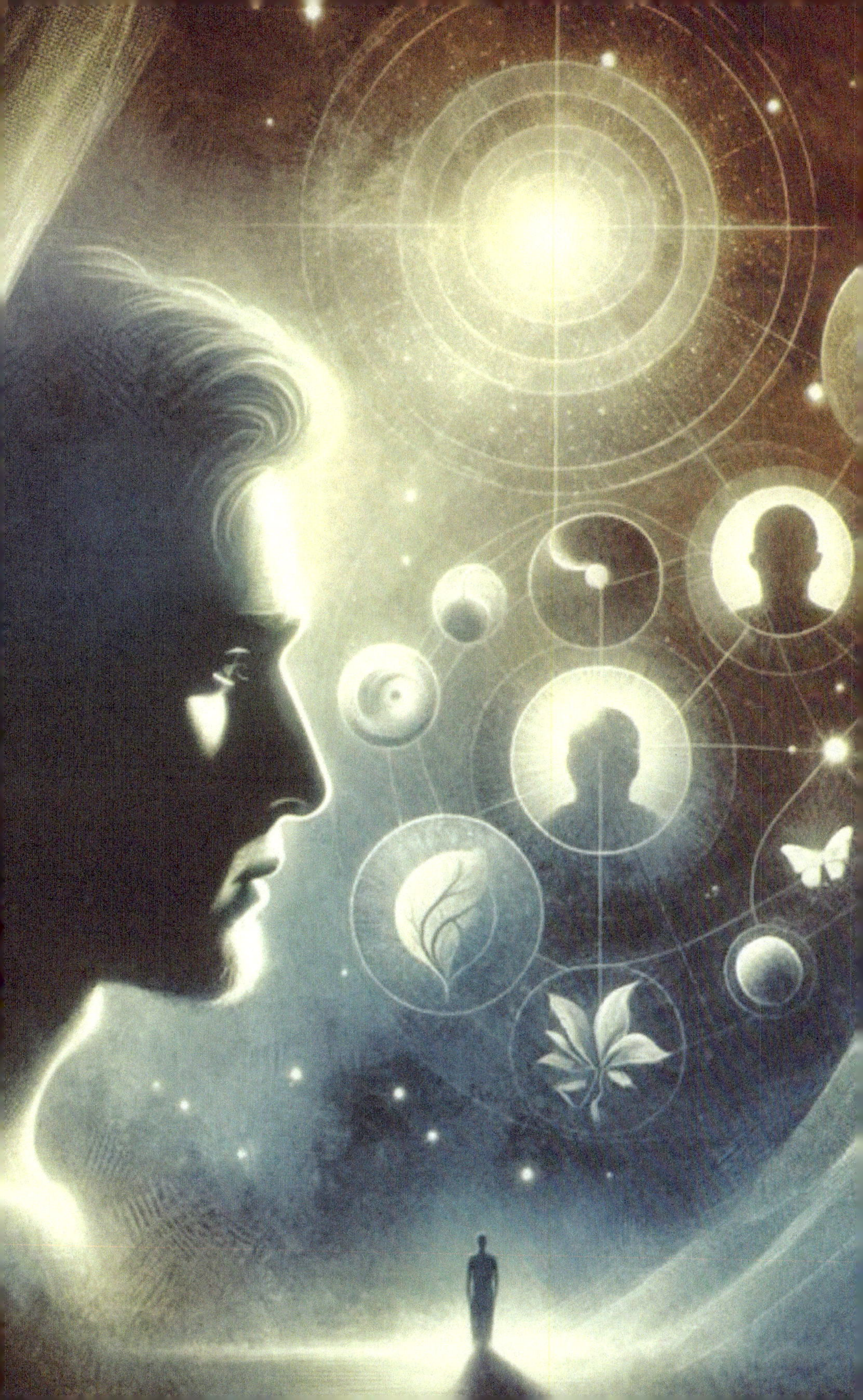

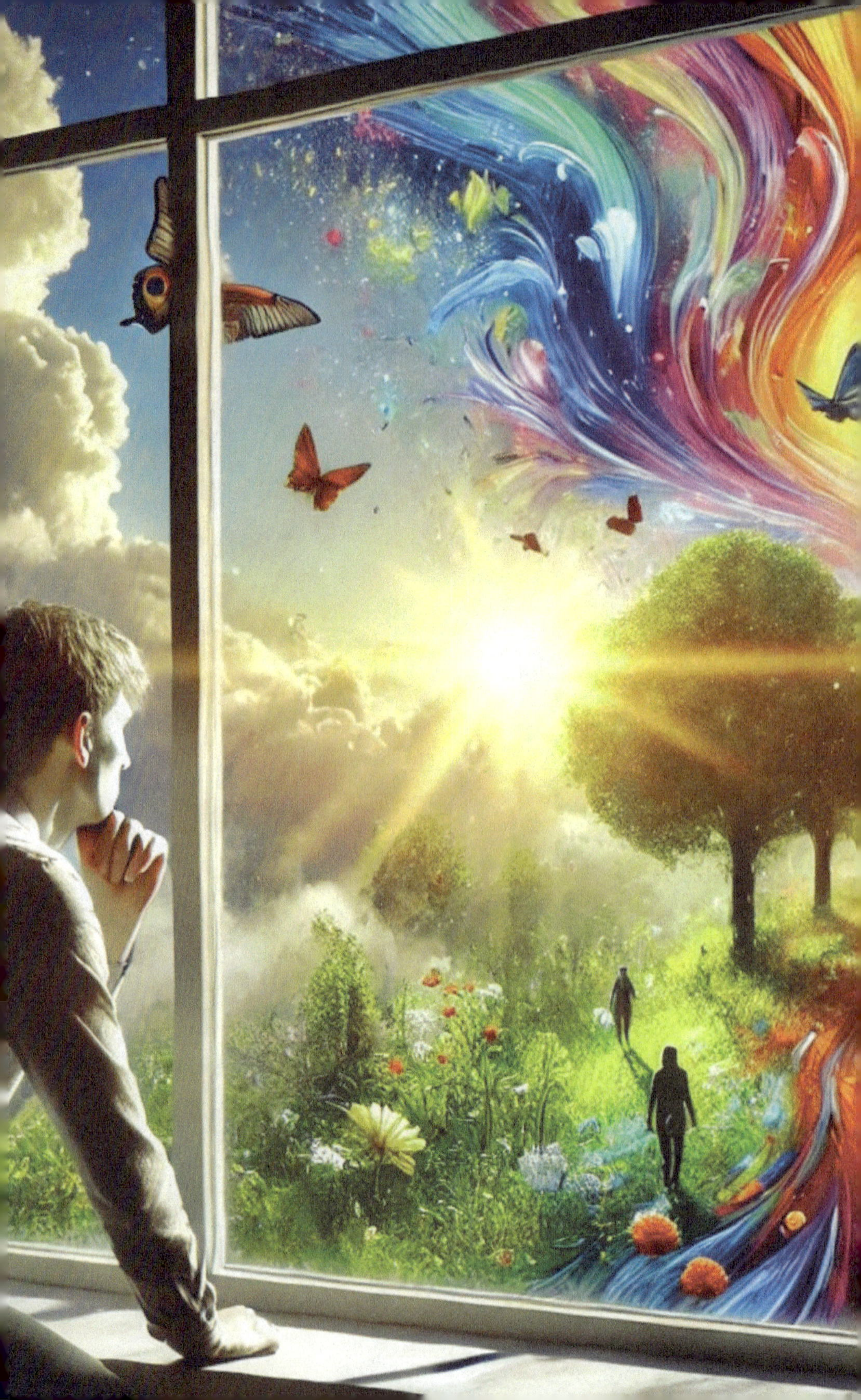

Echoes from the Heart

Echoes of Emotions

In the quiet shadows of the soul,
Pain and sorrow often take their toll.
I seek refuge, a place to hide,
The aching heart that won't subside.

The world outside sings its merry song,
But within, the notes feel so wrong.
A plea to silence the heart's deep plea,
To break the chains and simply be free.

Yet in silence, a glimmer appears,
A whisper of hope, calming my fears.
For even in darkness, a path can show,
A way to find light and let the pain go.

The heart may wish to close its door,
Life's melodies beckon, offering more.
In every ending, new beginnings await,
The strength to heal is never too late.

When the ache seems too much to bear,
Remember, hope lingers in the air.
Through the echoes of grief, let love spark,
And guide you gently out of the dark.

The journey through shadow and pain,
We learn to dance in the pouring rain.
Every heartbeat, there's strength to impart,
Echoes of emotions can mend the heart.

Unspoken Echoes

In twilight's veil, you departed,
A soul emboldened, yet half-hearted.
With all you craved in your grasp,
Yet leaving echoes in your clasp.

The being you were, silently cries,
In the hush, a fragment lies.
Your life, a tale of fear and awe,
Like shadows cast in a graveyard's maw.

In your wake, a void resides,
Where laughter met with somber tides.
A journey etched in the wine's decree,
Yet the remnants, they cling to thee.

For in the depths of every cheer,
Lurks the ghost of yesteryear.
Though you fled into the night,
You left behind the fading light.

Your absence, a spectral melody,
Sings of bonds, broken so free.
In the sobering dawn's embrace,
Lingers the memory of your trace.

Now, as stars fade in morning's glare,
I ponder the love we used to share.
Your path diverged in tipsy sway,
Yet in my heart, you'll always stay.

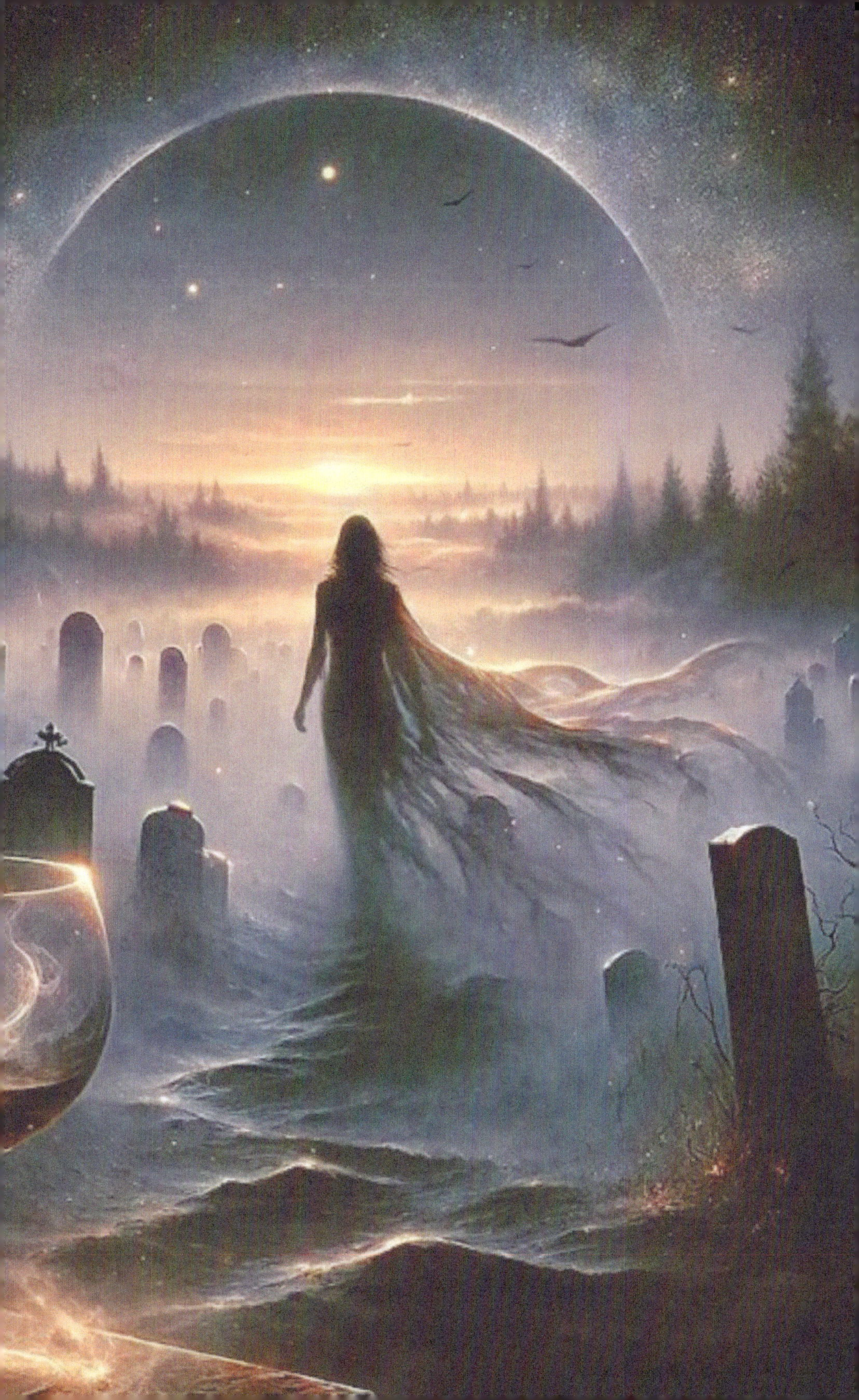

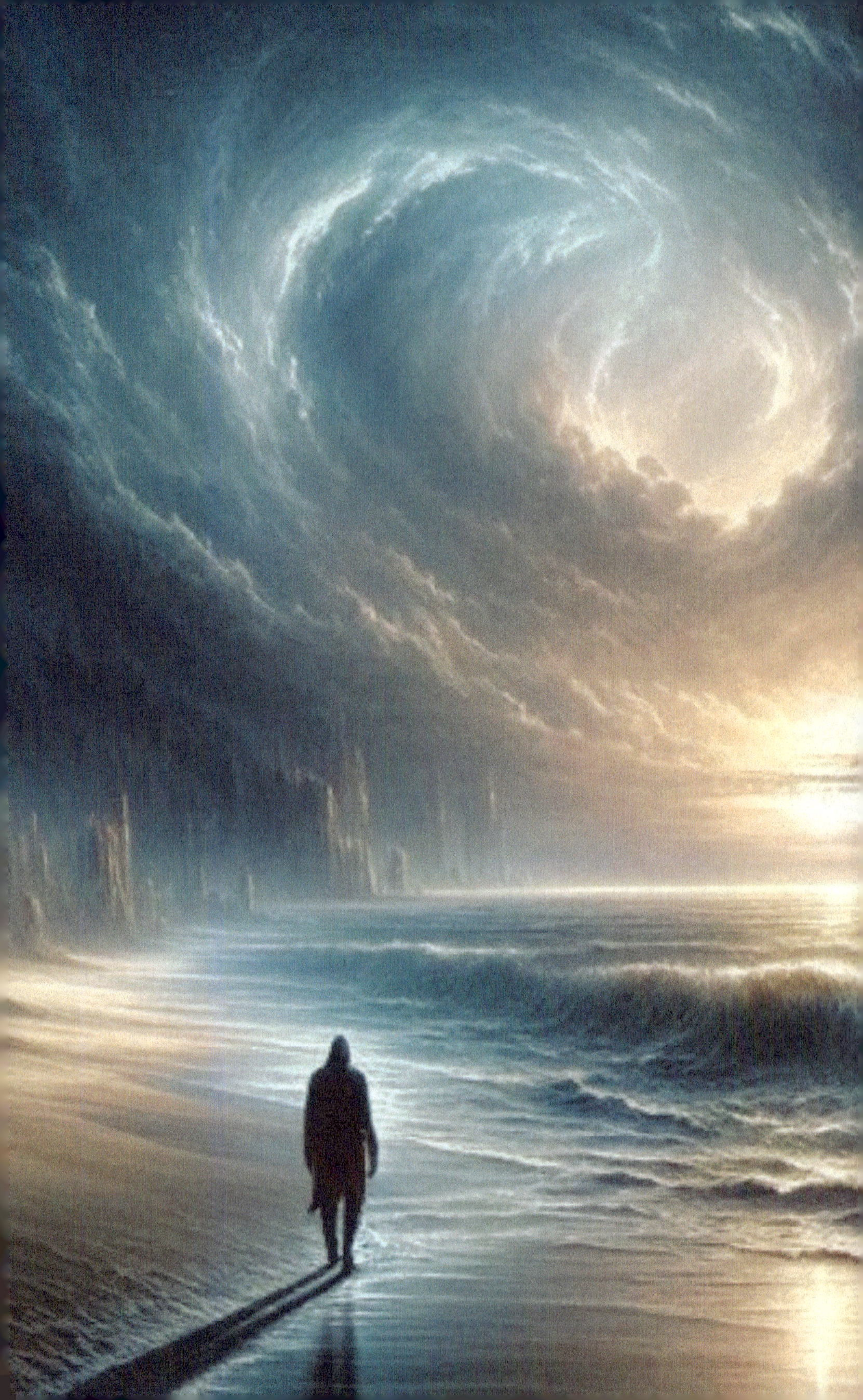

Echoes from the Heart

Embrace of the Abyss

In the twilight's tender grasp,
Where the sea meets yearning's gasp,
I dream of casting your sweet form,
Into the ocean's heart, so warm.

Adrift upon these endless blues,
Your essence mingles with the hues,
Plunging deep, where light does fade,
In love's abyss, where trust is laid.

"The depths," you whisper, "hold me tight,
For in your arms, I lose the fight."
Yet, on the sands, I stand forlorn,
Clutching memories, love stillborn.

The waves, they sing a lonesome song,
Of love that's right, yet feels so wrong,
"Leave me here," your echo pleads,
As my heart, for your touch, it bleeds.

But in this vast and briny deep,
Your essence, the ocean vows to keep.
And though your love may fade from shore,
In these depths, it lives forevermore.

"For if not in arms, then in the tide,
My love for you will never hide."
So, I vow, with each cresting wave,
In the sea's heart, your love I'll save.

Echoes from the Heart

Unclaimed Thoughts

In the chambers of the mind, a sacred hall,
Where echoes bounce, but seldom fall.
Be wary who you let within these walls,
Only good tenants should answer your calls.

Thoughts are like rooms, waiting to be filled,
Guard them well, so peace is instilled.
Rent them not to worries, nor fear's decree,
Only to those who set your spirit free.

In the attic of dreams, where ideas fly,
Don't let the doubts cloud your sky.
Invite in hope, let it take a stand,
Banish the shadows with a firm hand.

The heart's corridors, echoing with song,
Shouldn't echo with words that don't belong.
Let only kindness walk these floors,
Shut the door on hurtful roars.

The basement holds fears, the darkest part,
Don't let them rise and break your heart.
Clear the dust, let courage ignite,
Fill the void with love and light.

In the end, it's your mind's lease to sign,
Choose tenants that make your soul shine.
In this life, so fleeting and swift,
Make sure each guest is a positive lift.

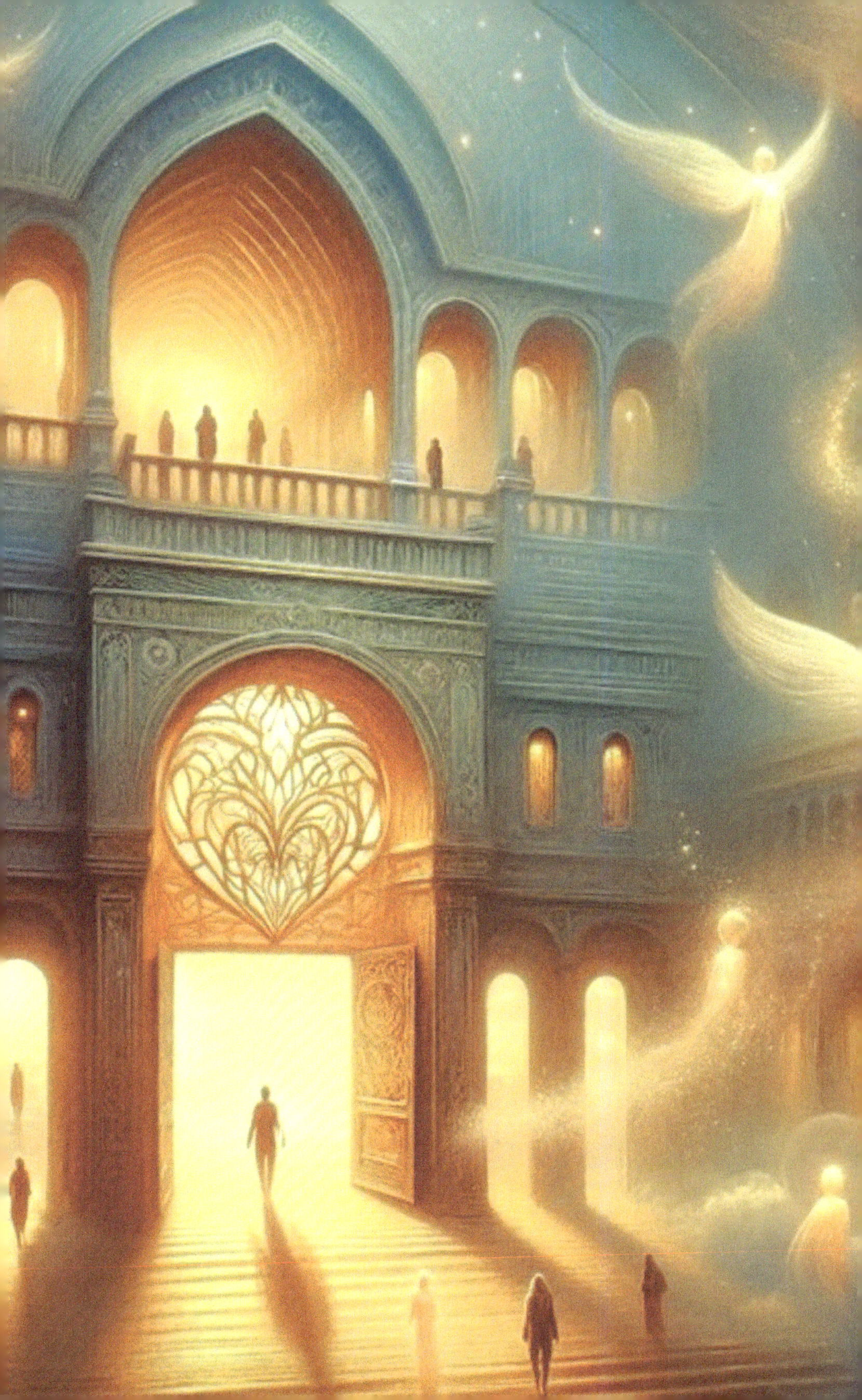

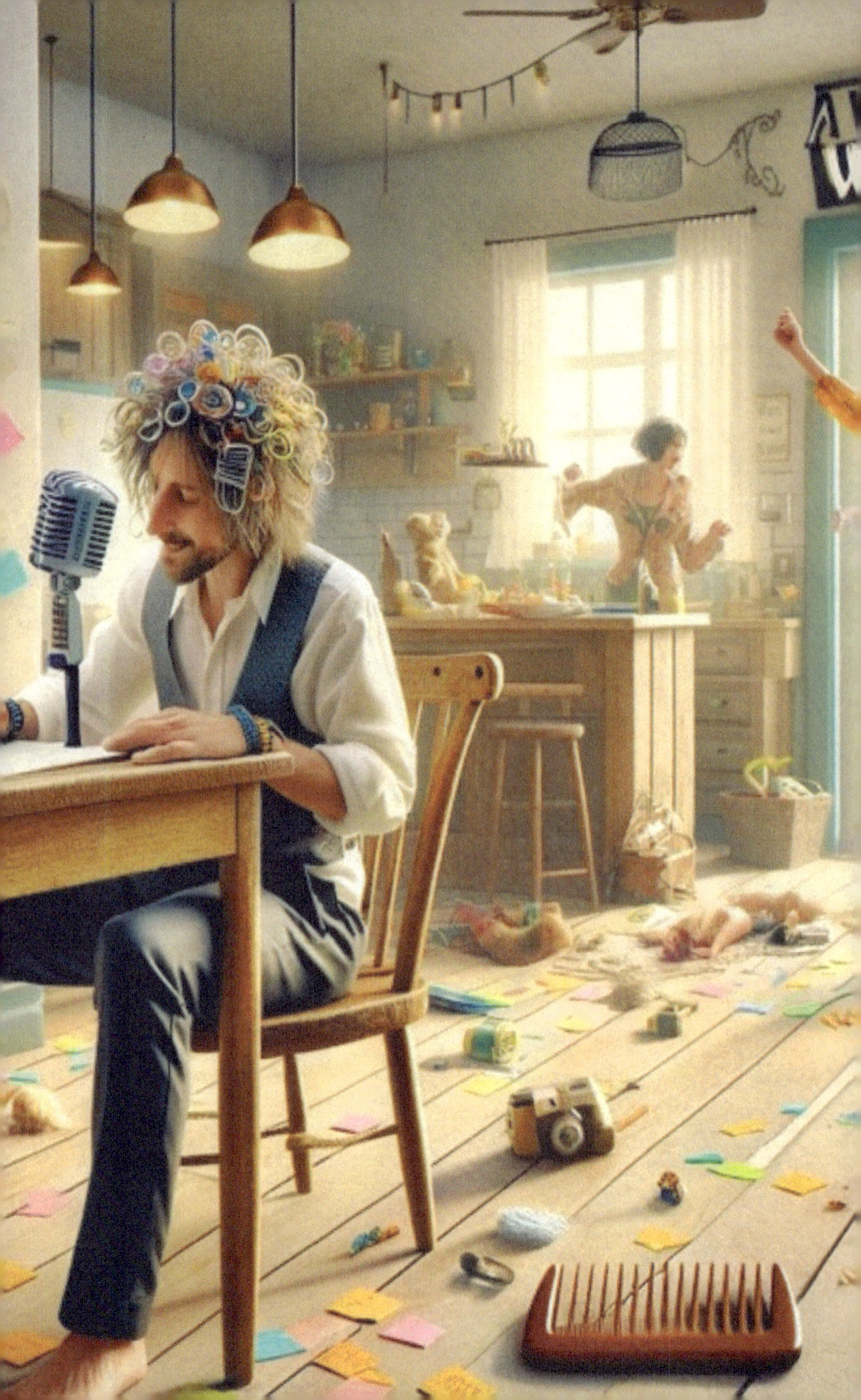

Echoes from the Heart

A World of Whimsy

In a realm where the zany thoughts roam,
Scribbling wild verses, a whimsical tome.
Laughter dances in lines of rhythmic poem,
Crafting a world where playfulness is home.

Voices echo with tunes, nonsensically sweet,
Humming through combs, in mirthful retreat.
Songs of mumble-gumble, rhythmically neat,
A symphony of joy, wonderfully upbeat.

In kitchens, the loony-goony dance takes flight,
Twirling, swirling in the soft morning light.
Feet tapping tunes, a delightful sight,
In a dance of freedom, hearts take flight.

Beneath the trees, where giggles sprout,
Odd creatures spin and leap about.
Their quirky steps and silly shout,
Fill the air with laughter's clout.

Walls adorned with laughter, colors ablaze,
A portrait of happiness, in numerous ways.
Each silly stroke, a testament to daze,
A gallery of glee, in the sun's soft rays.

In this world, something silly finds its space,
A corner of the universe, a whimsical place.
Here, happiness is more than just a trace,
In this world of whimsy, joy interlace.

Echoes from the Heart

Embraced by Moments

In the realm where hours are thieves,
Lurking in life's shadowed eaves.
We steal moments, sweet and brief,
For love, that timeless, tender chief.

Amidst the tick and tock's loud chime,
We carve a space, suspend the time.
In whispers, laughs, in dreams we weave,
A world where hearts can dance and grieve.

For in each stolen second's hold,
Lie tales of warmth in nights so cold.
Dreams to chase, in starlit cover,
Seeking truths, we're yet to discover.

Within the pause, where silence sings,
We find the grace that stillness brings.
A fleeting breath, a quiet sigh,
Where love and time entwine and fly.

Each fleeting instant we defend,
Holds promises the stars commend.
A trace of light, a hope we share,
In moments caught beyond despair.

In the embrace of time we've taken,
Love's true essence, not forsaken.
Through every moment, love's endeavor,
Stealing time for dreams forever.

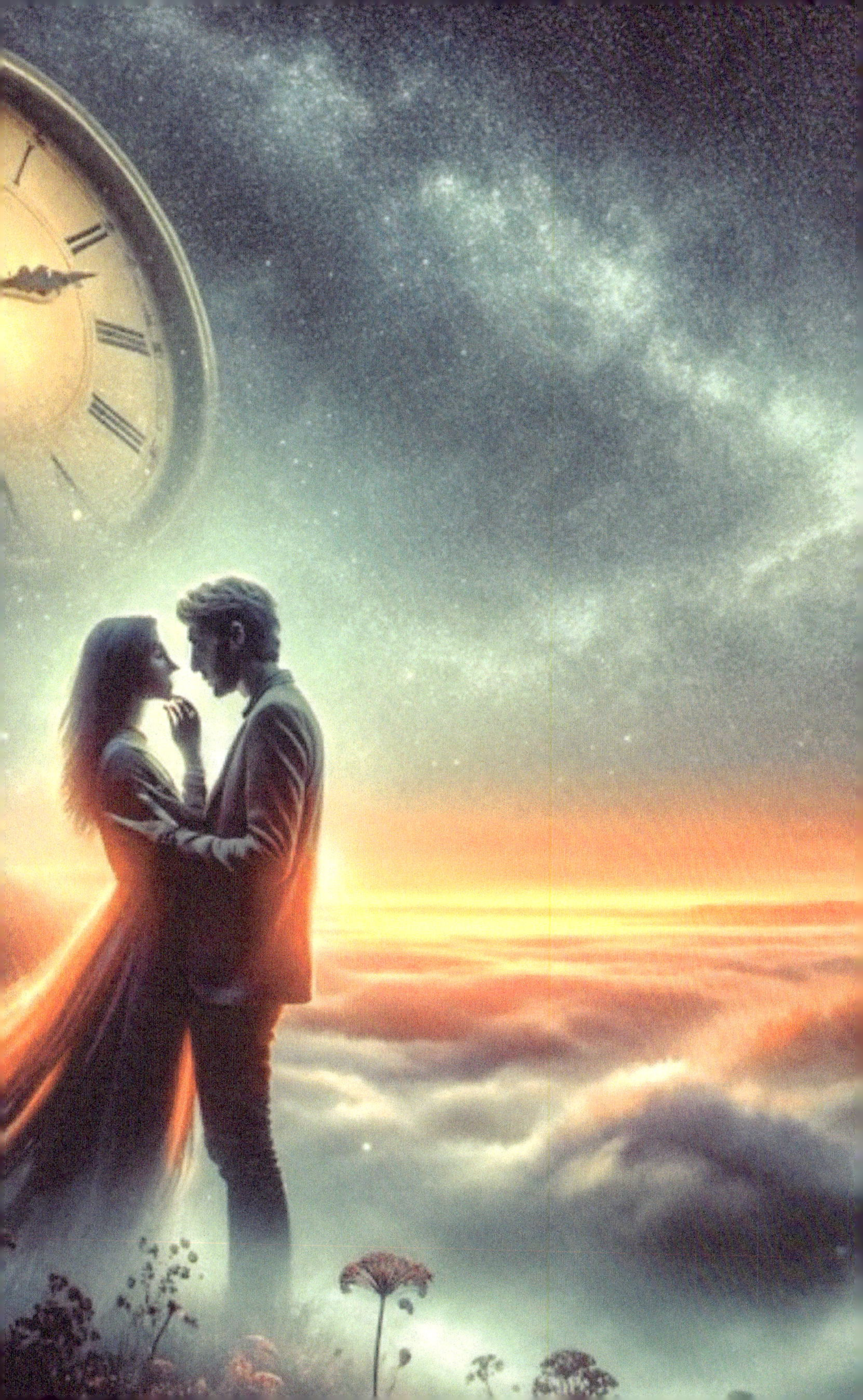

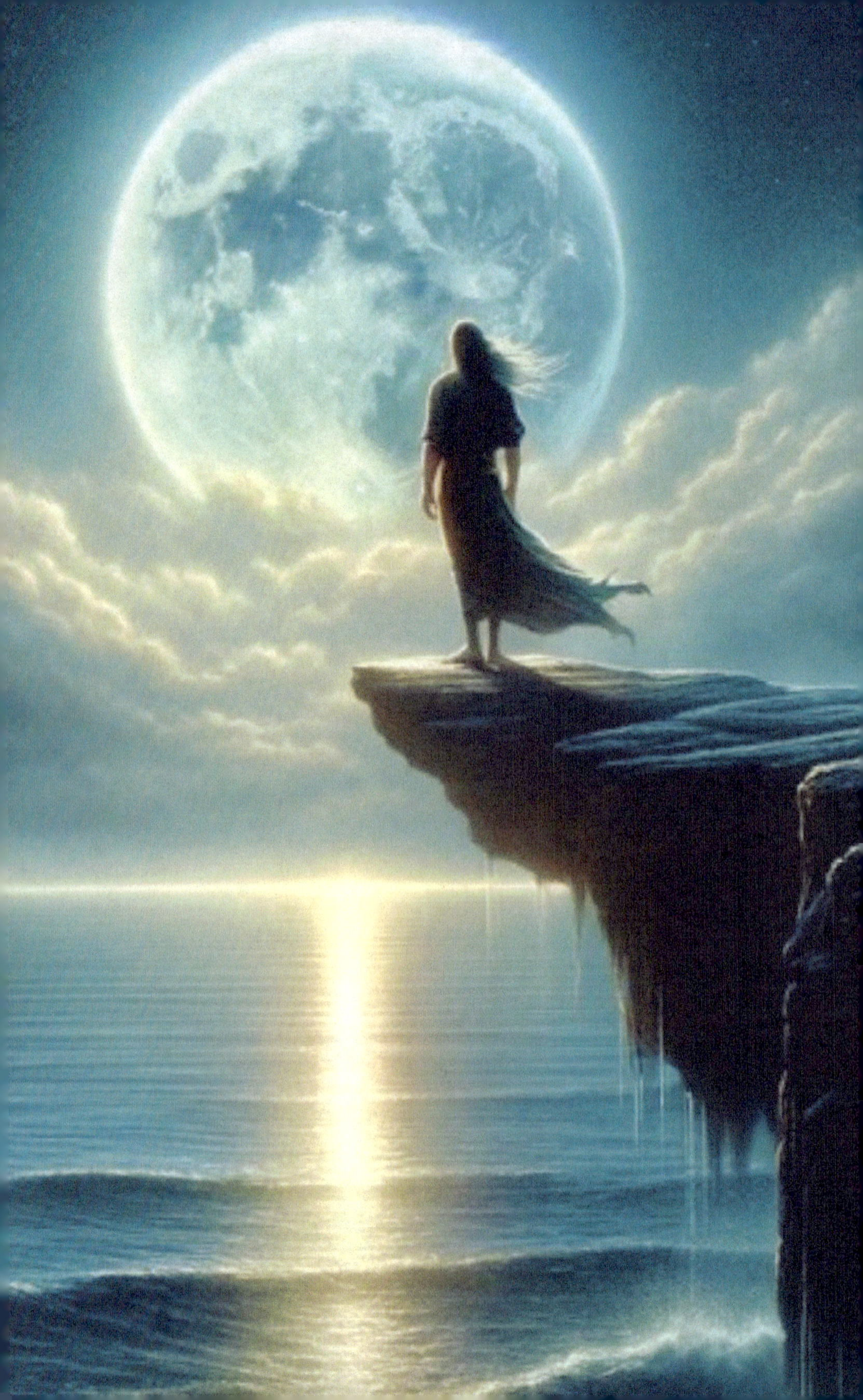

Echoes from the Heart

In the Realm of Truth

In the realm of truth, under moon's gentle sway,
I stand at the edge where night whispers today.
Your presence, a danger, in shadows it brews,
For I am too honest, and secrets I lose.

In the silence, your words like a siren's call,
Echo through my mind, over logic they sprawl.
A dangerous game, this dance of the heart,
Where honesty plays its most vulnerable part.

In the depths of your eyes, a tempest resides,
Luring me deeper, where my caution subsides.
Truth becomes a blade, in love's intricate plot,
Your siren song lures, but safety it's not.

Each glance exchanged is a double-edged sword,
Where truth unveils more than I can afford.
In this perilous space, desire entwines,
With honesty's power, no safe confines.

In our conversations, truths spill like wine,
Intoxicated, on honesty's fine line.
Each word a step closer to edges unseen,
Where heart laid bare, with nowhere to lean.

In the realm of truth, I find myself lost,
In the beauty of honesty, lines are crossed.
A dance with danger, in each word you spew,
For I am too honest, and I fall deeper for you.

Whispers of Departure

I know your past, shadows retreat,
Your warmth now distant, bittersweet.
Once solace, now a heavy sin,
The bond we shared fades thin.

Your voice, once soft, now hollow rings,
Echoes of forgotten things.
Lies replaced where truth was rare,
In silence, trust vanished there.

Our dance of shadows reached its end,
No more your love do I defend.
Your kiss, a battle lost in time,
I walk away, no climb.

The yearning dies, you won't return,
Innocence lost; fires burn.
Whispers fade with night's embrace,
I let go, forget your face.

Now in the quiet, strength takes form,
Releasing love once lost and warm.
Memories drift, like fleeting air,
Your kiss no longer there.

In moving forward, I find my peace,
Your hold on me begins to cease.
No longer trapped in what we knew,
The future shines, free of you.

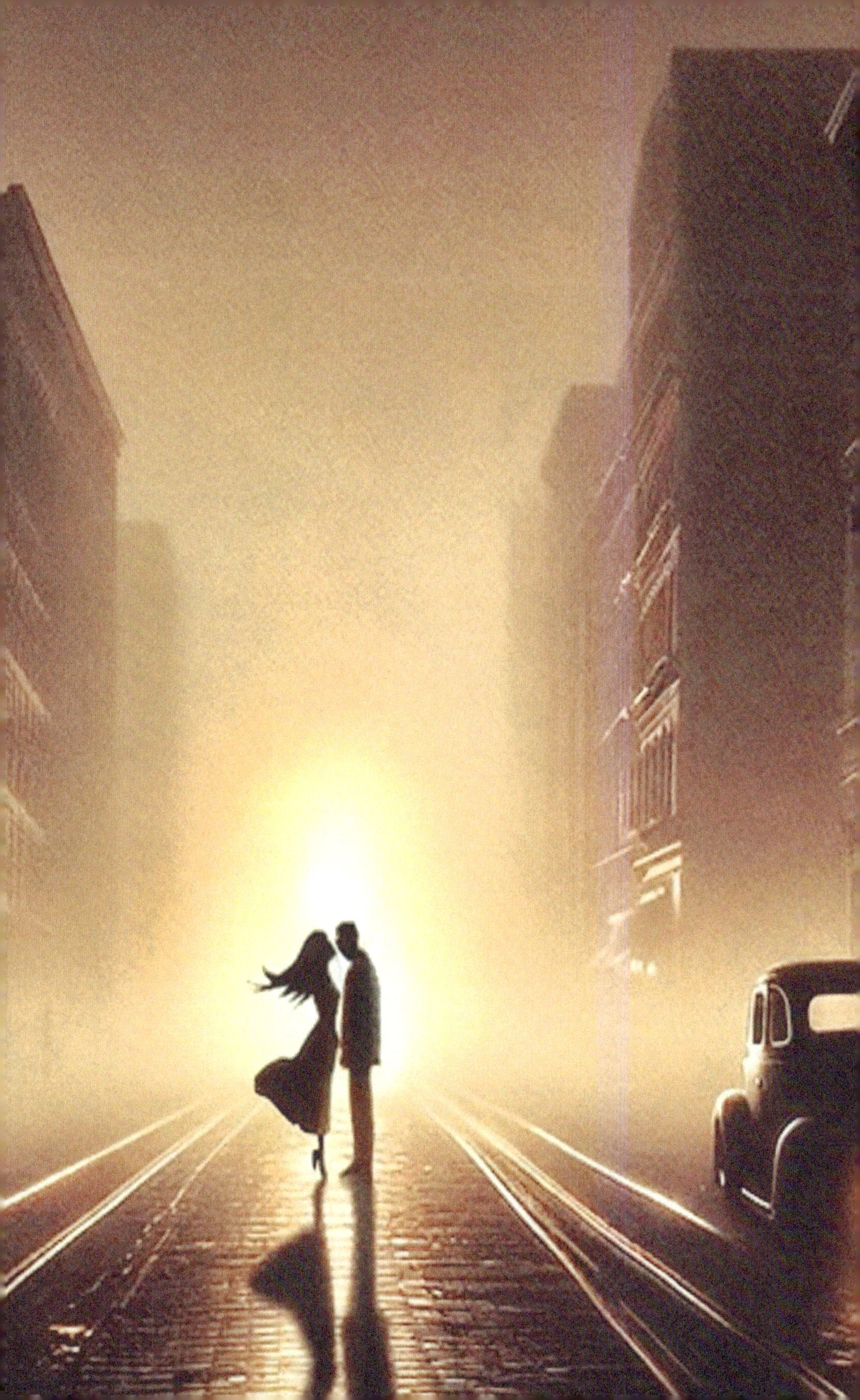

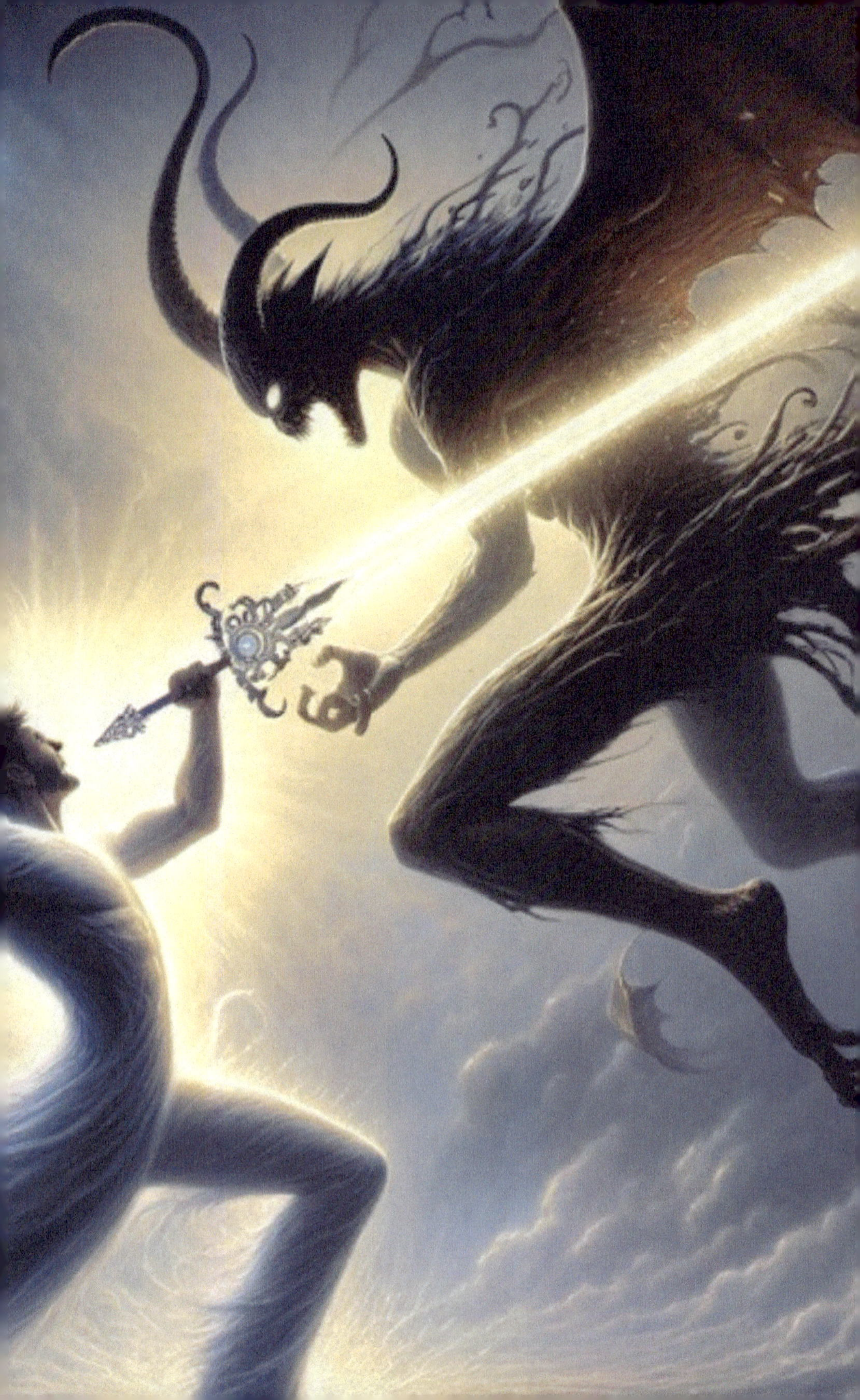

Echoes from the Heart

Guardian of the Key

Beware the demon who seeks the Key,
To the vault where your true essence lies.
In shadows it weaves its treacherous plea,
Guard your light with heart, as time flies.

The Key is your will, your joy, your might,
Held fast by the spirit, fierce and bright.
Let not the dark its gleam ensnare,
Fight with love, for your soul's fair flare.

Through trials that seek to quench your flame,
Stand resolute, your purpose the same.
The Key within stirs the bravery you wield,
In life's great battle, your heart is your shield.

Though winds may howl, and skies turn gray,
Let not your courage fade away.
For even in storms, the Key will stay,
Anchored deep in the heart's array.

Demon of doubt, with whispers so vile,
May find no home in your hallowed aisle.
With every beat, assert your power,
For in your chest lies an unyielding tower.

So, heed the call, brave and free,
The Key is safe, for it is thee.
Your love, your light, your strength endures,
Against the demon, your heart assures.

Echoes from the Heart

Fragments of Solace

In this vast cosmos of tangled thoughts,
Shards of dreams paint fractured skies,
I labored, I toiled, with relentless might,
To resurrect my world, my peace, my light.

For you see, dear soul, if only you knew,
The arduous path I trod, the journey through.
An array of trials and battles fought,
Mend the fragments of solace I sought.

Each fragment mended, painstakingly wrought,
With resilience, strength, and lessons taught.
In the crucible of chaos, I found my way,
To rebuild my universe, day by day.

Amidst the darkness, a flicker remained,
A light undimmed, though heavily strained.
Through cracks in my heart, hope softly crept,
In silence and pain, I rose, though I wept.

So, pardon my caution, my vigilant gaze,
The discerning eyes that scrutinize ways,
For I've tasted the bitter, the sorrow's cost,
Now I shield my haven from the tempest's host.

No longer will I suffer unworthy souls,
Who seek to tarnish, to breach the folds.
Of my sacred haven, my tranquil abode,
Where serenity reigns, and joy bestowed.

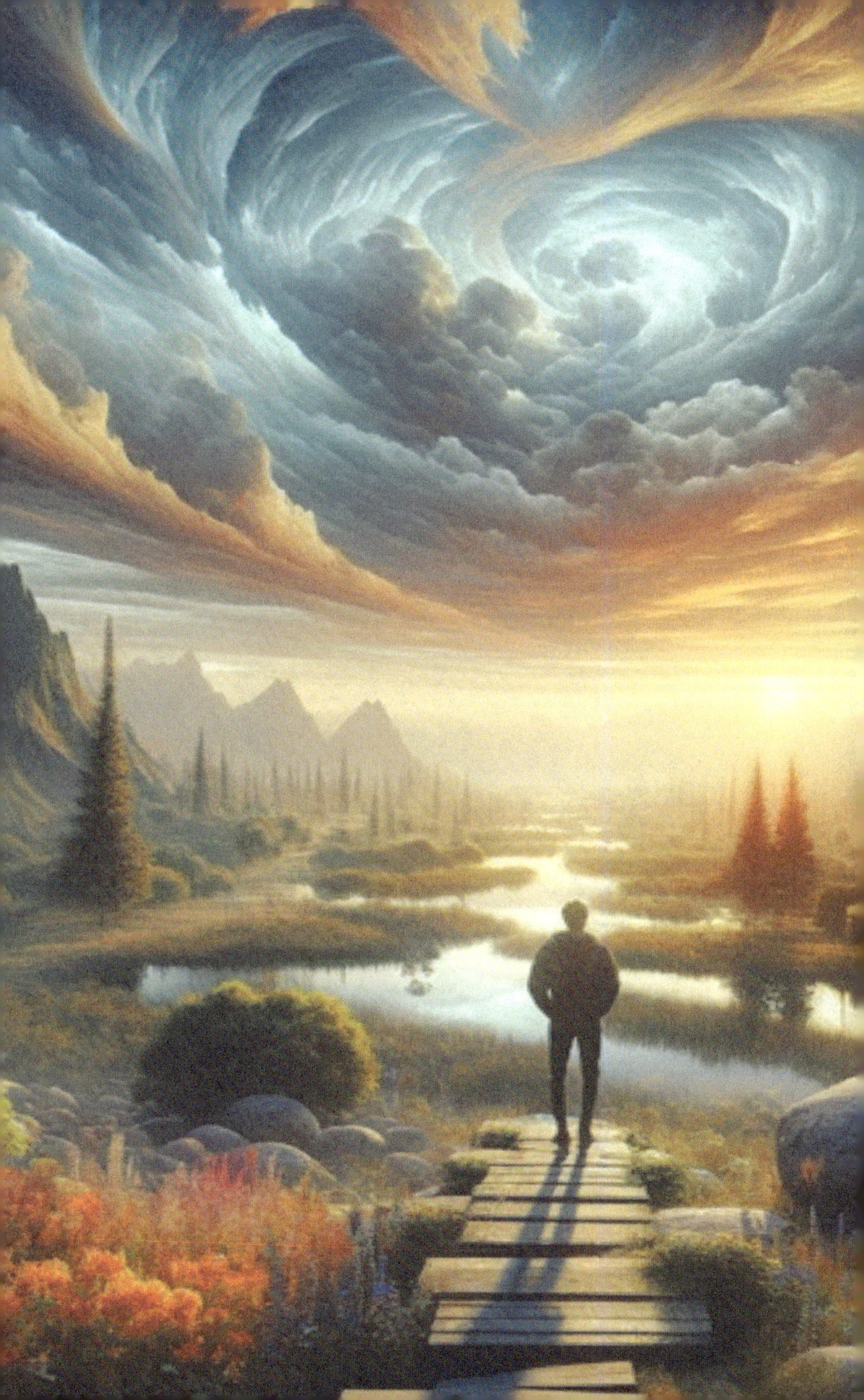

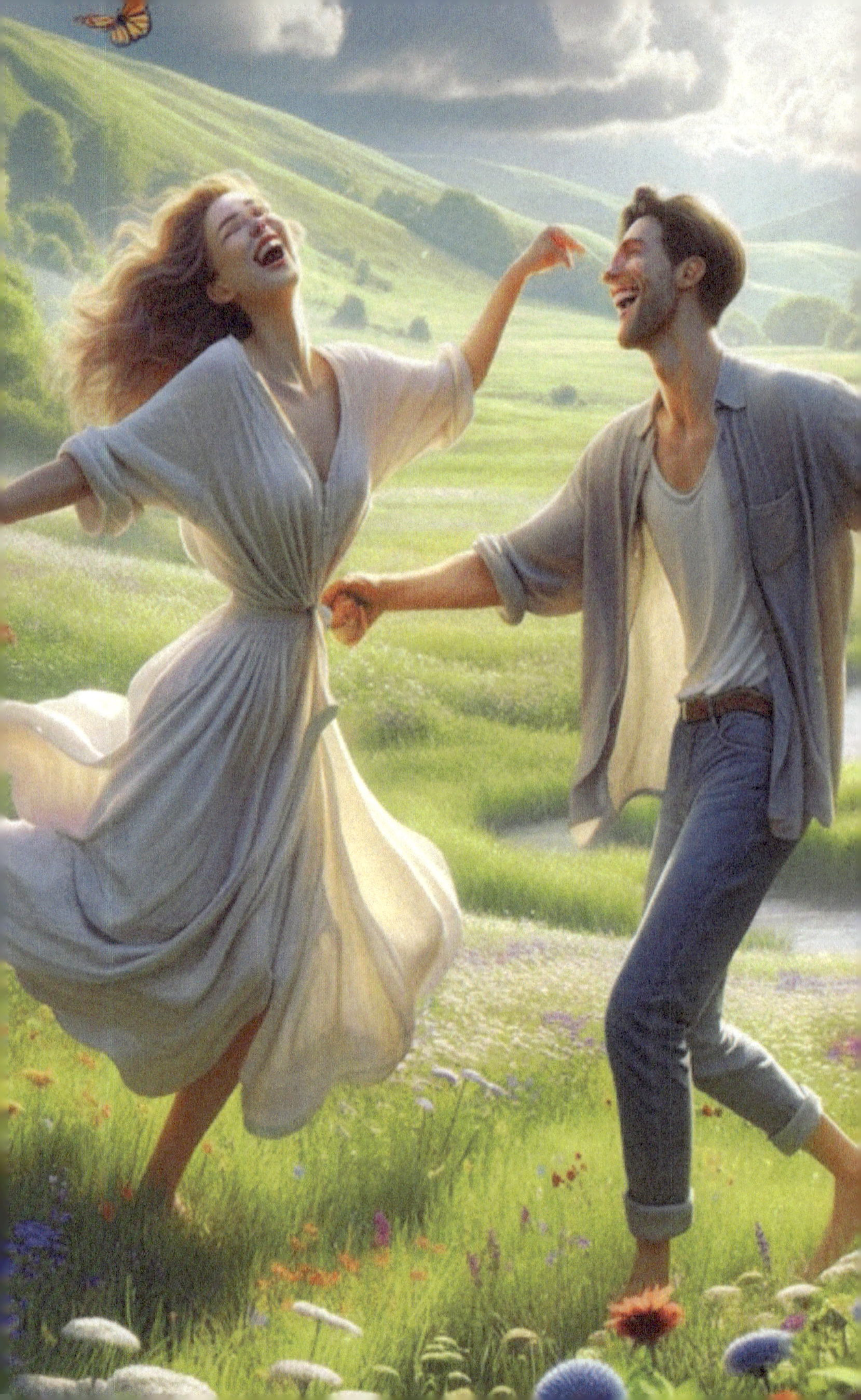

Echoes from the Heart

Matters of a Giddy Heart

Be mindful of your giddy stride,
In matters of the heart, don't hide.
For love's a labyrinth, winding wide,
Where emotions ebb and flow like the tide.

Fragile hearts, like porcelain, shatter,
Yet they mend, they heal, they scatter.
Pieces reassemble, love's all that matter.
In the dance of romance,
where souls converge and clatter.

The heart's a compass, guiding us through life,
Amidst joy and sorrow, amidst peace and strife.
With every beat, it whispers, cuts like a knife,
But it's in its rhythm, we find love's fife.

So, take heed, as you depart,
In this complex realm, where feelings start.
Be cautious not to trip, for in matters of the heart,
Love's a journey, a treasure, a work of art.

In the tapestry of time, love's threads intertwine,
Creating a pattern, both simple and divine.
It's the melody of a symphony, a poetic line,
A language universal, yet distinctly thine.

Through the seasons of the soul, love endures,
In its strength, its vulnerability, it assures.
An anchor in storms, its magic lures,
In the story of life, love's chapter secures.

Unyielding Hearts United

In this world, where trials abound,
Only the strong hearts stand together, unbound.
Through storms of life, they stand tall,
Never faltering, never to fall.

Side by side, they march with grace,
Fearless souls in life's embrace.
Challenges come, yet they remain,
A steadfast force against the pain.

Through struggles and trials, they hold tight,
In the darkest of times, they share their light.
For only the strong hearts, you see,
Can stand together in perfect harmony.

Beneath the sky, vast and clear,
They find the courage to persevere.
In each other's gaze, truths are found,
A love profound, forever bound.

Through seasons change and time's swift flow,
Their bond, a constant glow.
Together they rise, together they dream,
In unity, their spirits gleam.

When the world turns cold and shadows fall,
Their unyielding hearts conquer all.
In the dance of life, they twirl and sway,
Unyielding hearts united, come what may.

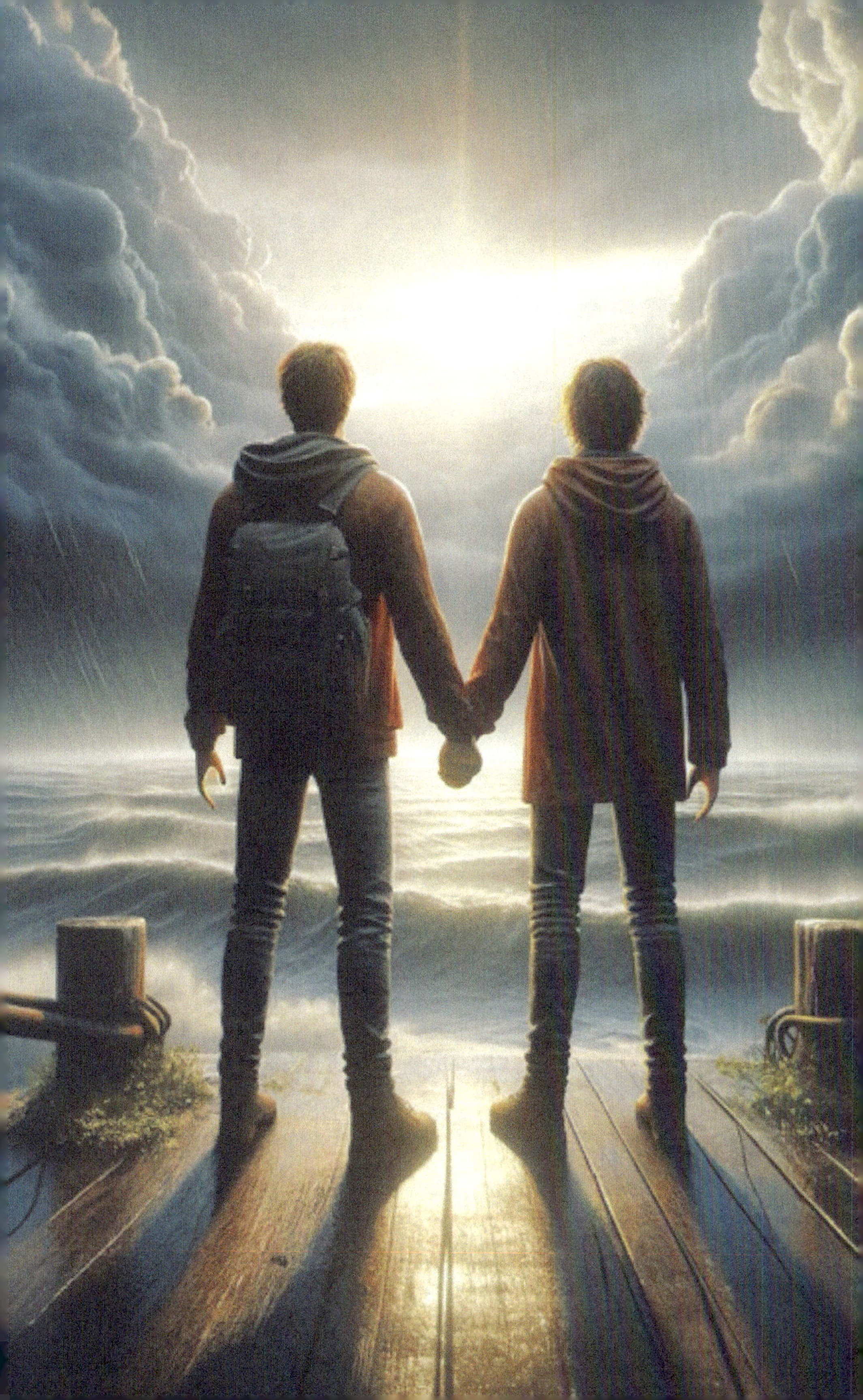

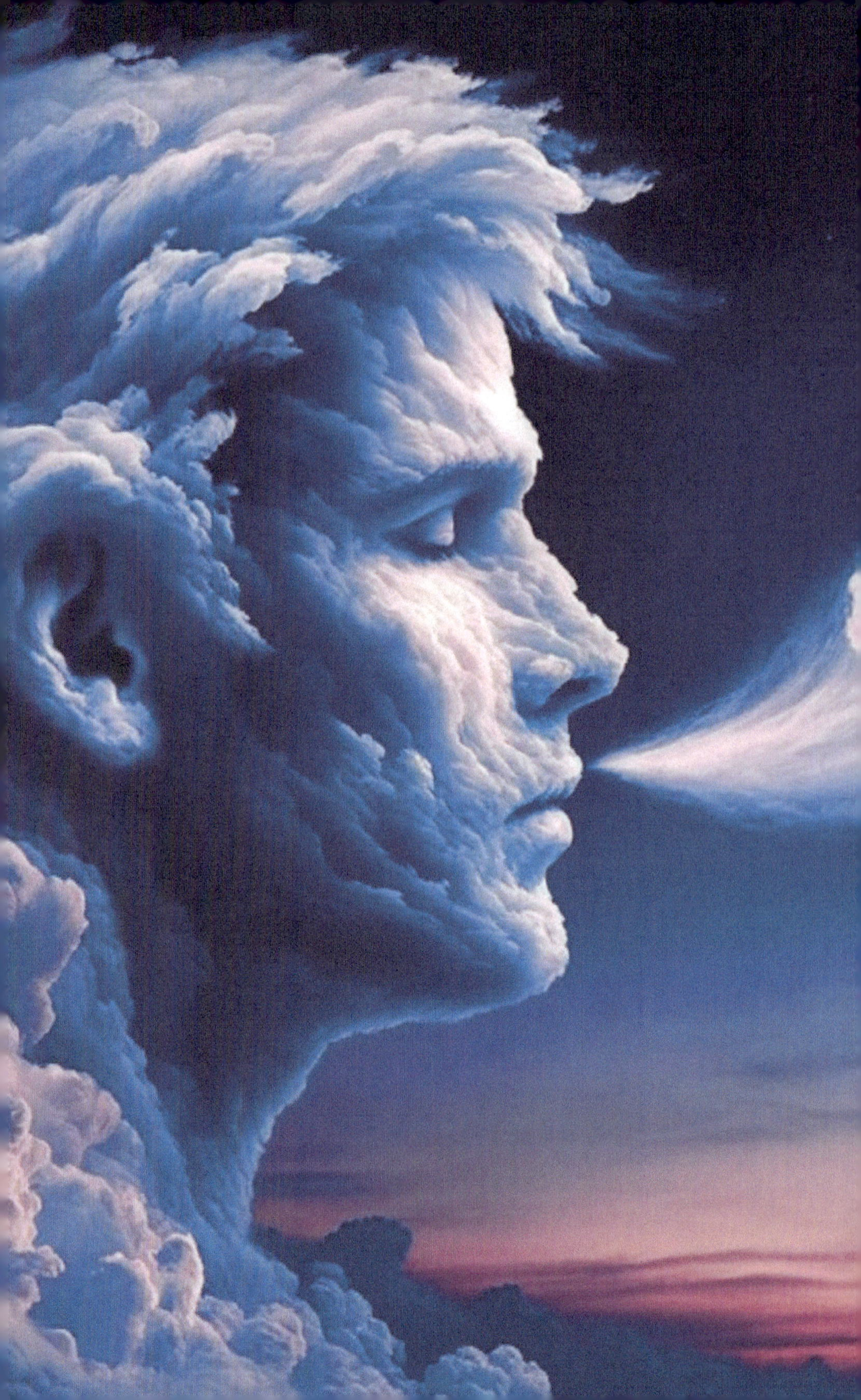

Echoes from the Heart

Hearts Adrift

You make me want to watch the sky,
Above, where dreams and daybreak tie,
To find a cloud in love's own shape,
And send it to you, no escape.

In every hue of dawn or dusk,
Your face appears, a welcome musk,
Amidst the drifting hearts on high,
A silent, sweet, celestial sigh.

I scan the vastness for a sign,
For heart-shaped whispers, purely thine,
And in the breeze, they float so free,
From me to you, o'er land and sea.

Beneath the stars, my thoughts take flight,
A journey wrapped in tender light.
Through endless skies, I send my plea,
That love will find its way to thee.

When sunlight wanes, to stars I speak,
Of love's own language, strong yet meek,
The night's embrace holds hearts aloft,
Bearing to you my whispers soft.

In moon's soft glow, I close my eyes,
And dream of hearts in boundless skies,
With every beat, they cross the blue,
From my horizon straight to you.

Echoes from the Heart

FAITH

Echoes from the Heart

Strength in Our Toughest Battles

In trials fierce, His chosen ones stand tall,
Through darkest nights, they answer the call.
With strength divine, they rise, unafraid,
In battles hard, where courage is displayed.

For in the crucible of life's great test,
His mightiest warriors prove their best.
With faith unshaken, they march the way,
Where shadows loom and doubts may sway.

In every storm, they find their grace,
Embracing challenges they must face.
With every step, they climb the hill,
With hearts ablaze, they seek His will.

Though winds may howl, and trials endure,
Their faith remains steadfast and pure.
Through valleys deep, they carry the light,
Guided by love, they win the fight.

The Lord, in wisdom, knows the cost,
Yet in His love, no soul is lost.
For in the fires of trials and strife,
He forges heroes, strong in life.

So, when life's battles come your way,
Remember these words, come what may.
The Lord gives battles to the strong,
In Him, you'll find the courage to belong.

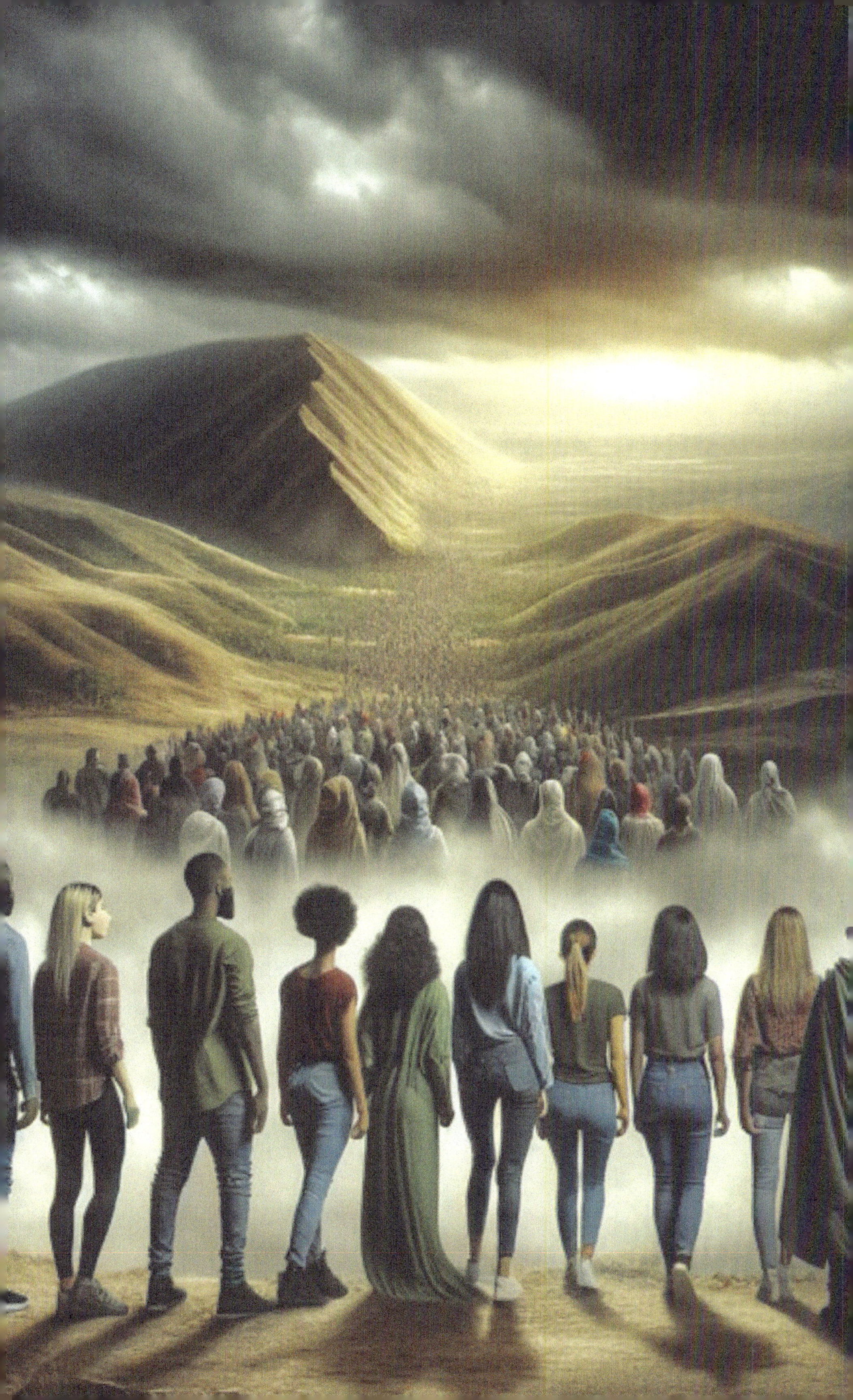

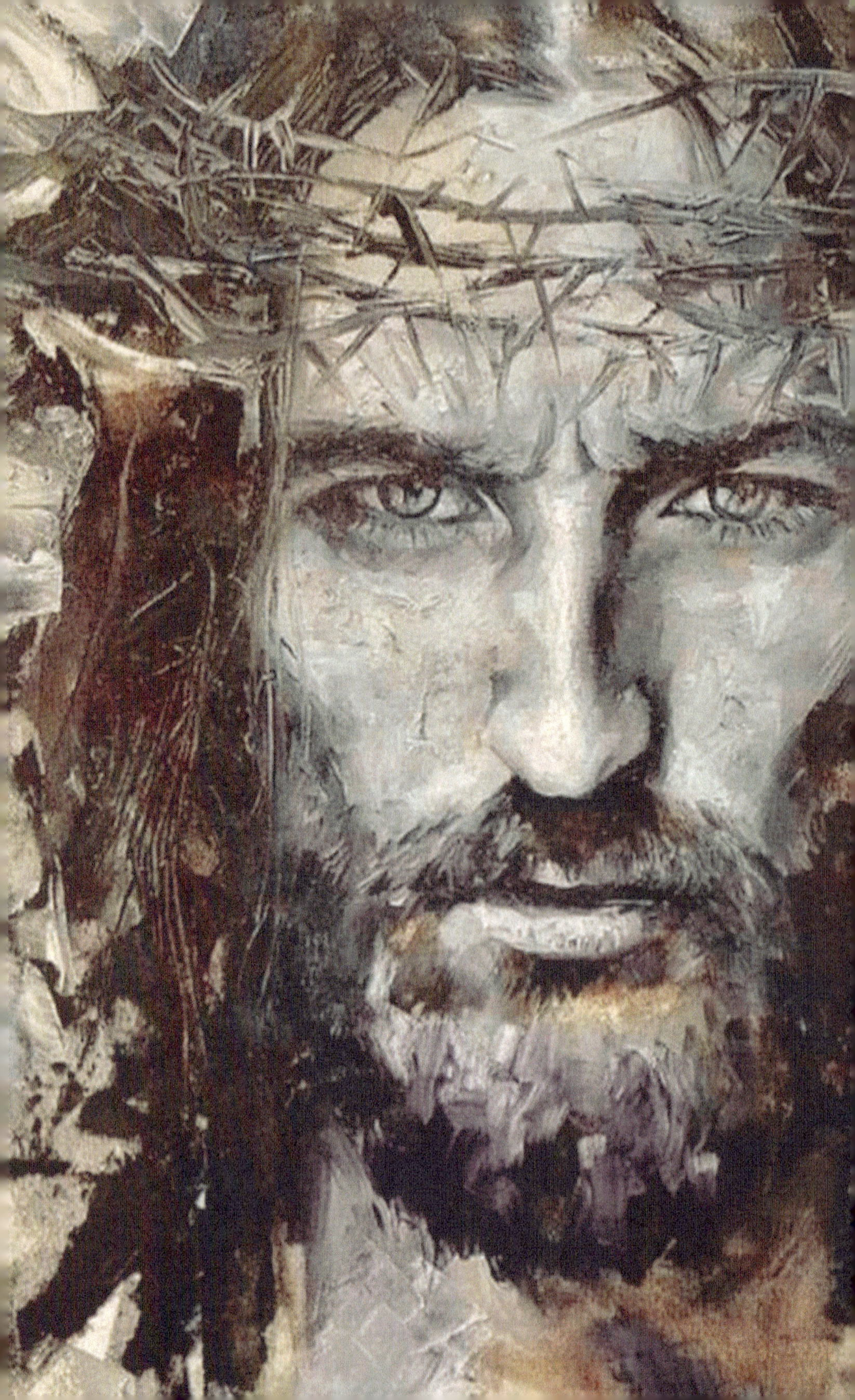

Echoes from the Heart

Thorns of Serenity

In a palette of sorrow and of earth,
A visage emerges, etched with silent tales.
Eyes deep as night, gaze through time's girth,
Bearing a crown not of gold, but of nails.

Beneath the thorns, the shadows play,
Across the features strong and worn.
A testament of both night and day,
A figure of peace, in pain adorned.

The strokes of gray and whispers of white,
Tell of burdens carried, of a heavy plight.
Yet, in this image, there lies a light,
A depth of love, an end to night.

Through every tear etched in stone,
A cry for peace, a strength unknown.
In silence loud, the heart has grown,
A story of hope from pain is sown.

In every line, a story unfolds,
Of a spirit unbroken, a will untold.
Captured in moments, frozen and bold,
A portrait of bravery, in shades of old.

For in this face, we see our own,
The shared humanity that we've all known.
Through this crafted visage, it is shown,
Beauty of strength, through suffering grown.

Fire with Fire

In the heart of flames, where secrets lie,
A dance of sparks, under the moonlit sky.
Ember's whisper of strength and desire,
Kindling the soul's unquenchable fire.

Against raging tempests, fierce and dire,
Brave souls confront, never to tire.
Infernos met with courage's ire,
Battling darkness, fire with fire.

In love's furnace, passions conspire,
Two hearts aflame, never to expire.
Through trials and tribulations, they aspire,
To fuse as one in a pyre higher.

Where ashes fall, the phoenix will rise,
From smoldering depths, it claims the skies.
Renewed in flame, it never dies,
A symbol of strength that defies.

In life's forge, where challenges transpire,
Each obstacle, a chance to inspire.
With every setback, resolve grows brighter,
Forged in adversity, fire with fire.

As stars collide in celestial choir,
Destinies entwined, fate's tight wire.
In the cosmos' endless gyre,
Burns the eternal flame, fire with fire.

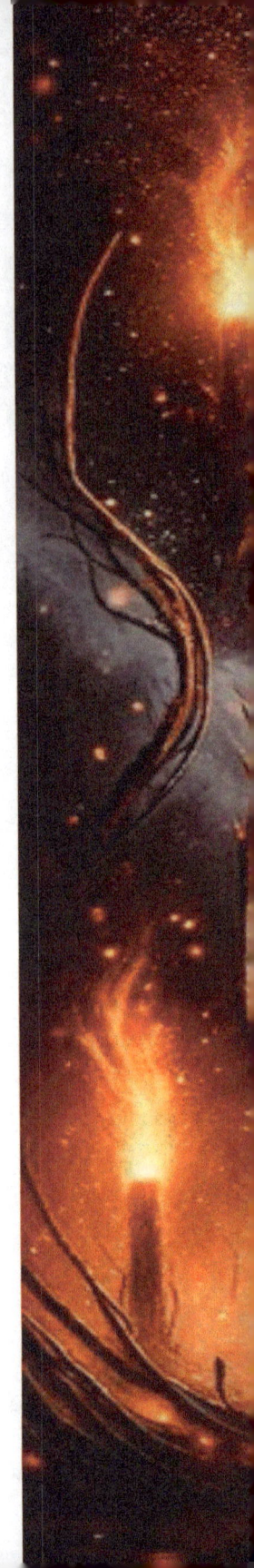

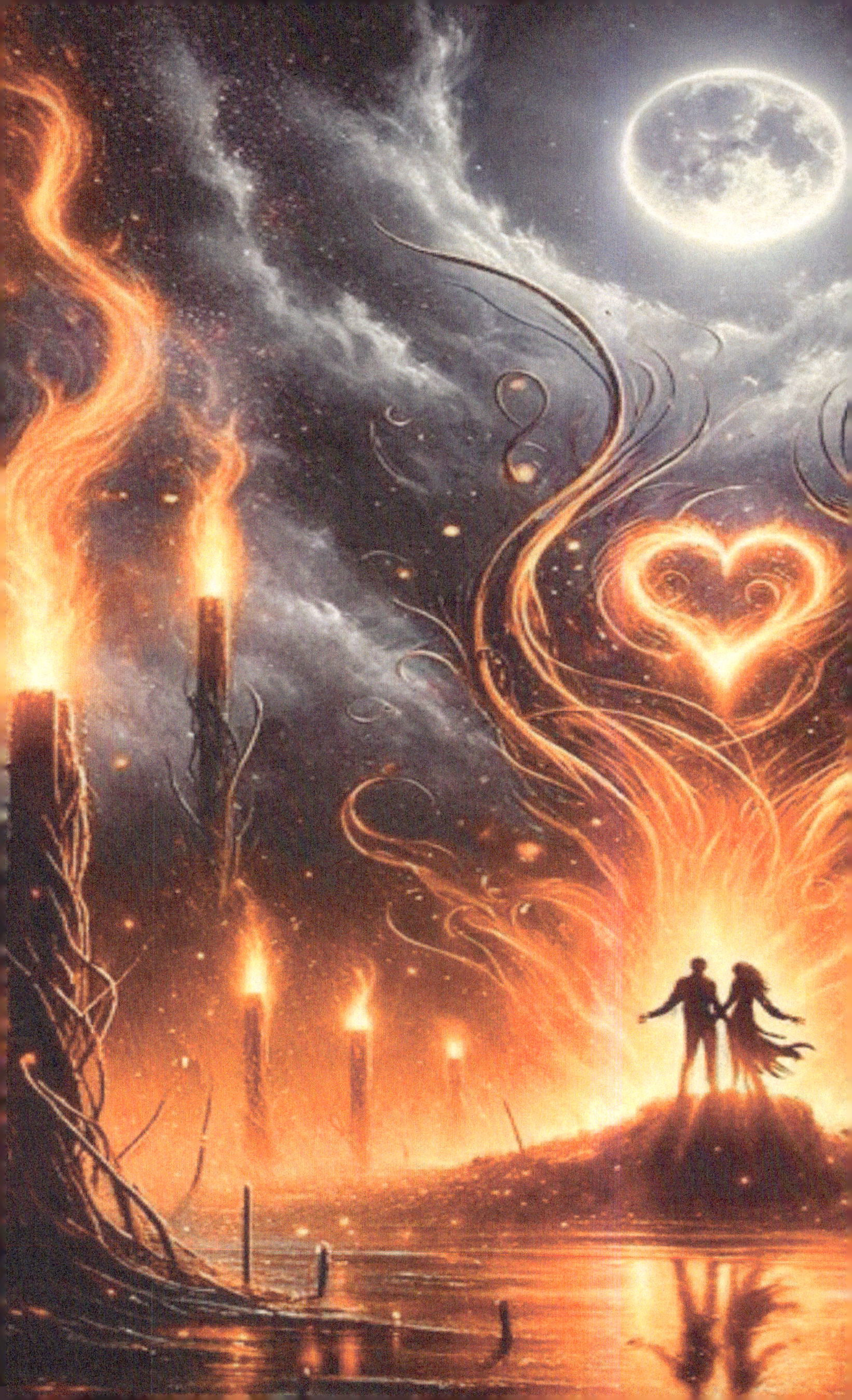

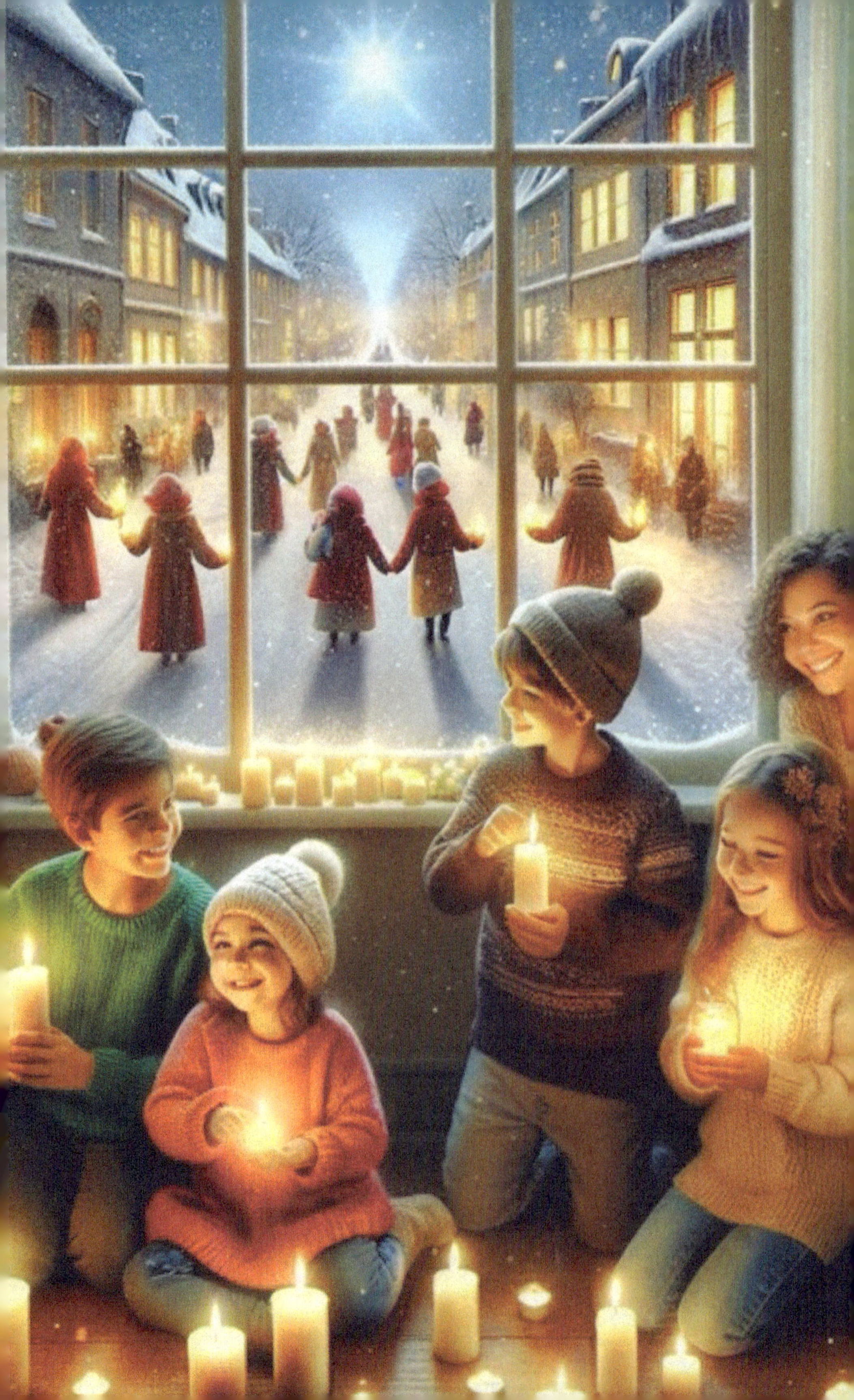

Echoes from the Heart

Guiding Lights of Christmas

In homes where laughter echoes bright,
Who will light the candles this Christmas night?
With gentle hands and hearts so light,
To fill the room with warmth and sight.

In churches where the faithful kneel,
Will they have the faith to bring the light, to feel?
Their prayers rise like a silent flight,
Uniting souls under the star's gentle might.

On streets where winter's chill bites deep,
Brave souls wander, not lost, but in keep,
Of promises made, in love's sweet rite,
Guiding through darkness with their internal light.

In every hearth where flames now glow,
The spirit of giving begins to grow.
A simple spark, a quiet vow,
To spread the warmth that we all know.

In eyes of children, where wonder never ends,
They believe, dream, in magic that transcends.
A world of hope, of endless, starry nights.
With each candle lit, their joy ignites,

As we gather 'round, in this festive cheer,
Remember the light that draws us near.
From heart to heart, it weaves its flight,
Who will light the candles this Christmas?
We, with love's might.

Sentinel of the Shore

Bare branches reach for azure skies,
Roots entwined in stone's embrace,
Where water meets the stoic earth,
A single tree in contemplative grace.

Upon this shore of silent tales,
The whispers of the lake doth swell,
In rhythmic dance of ebb and flow,
A quiet story they long to tell.

The sun casts shadows, long and deep,
Across the rock, through time's slow creep,
Where nature's artwork, both bleak and fair,
Stands resolute in the crisp air.

Through seasons' shift and winds that howl,
The tree endures each passing trial.
Its strength in stillness, firm and sure,
A witness to all things endure.

A sentinel of the changing hours,
Withstanding storms and sun's fierce power,
A testament to life's firm will,
Upon this shore, it stands so still.

In solitude, it guards the land,
With rooted grace, a steadfast hand.
Through shifting tides and skies of gray,
Its silent watch shall never sway.

©Photograph by Ashley Lowry[vi]

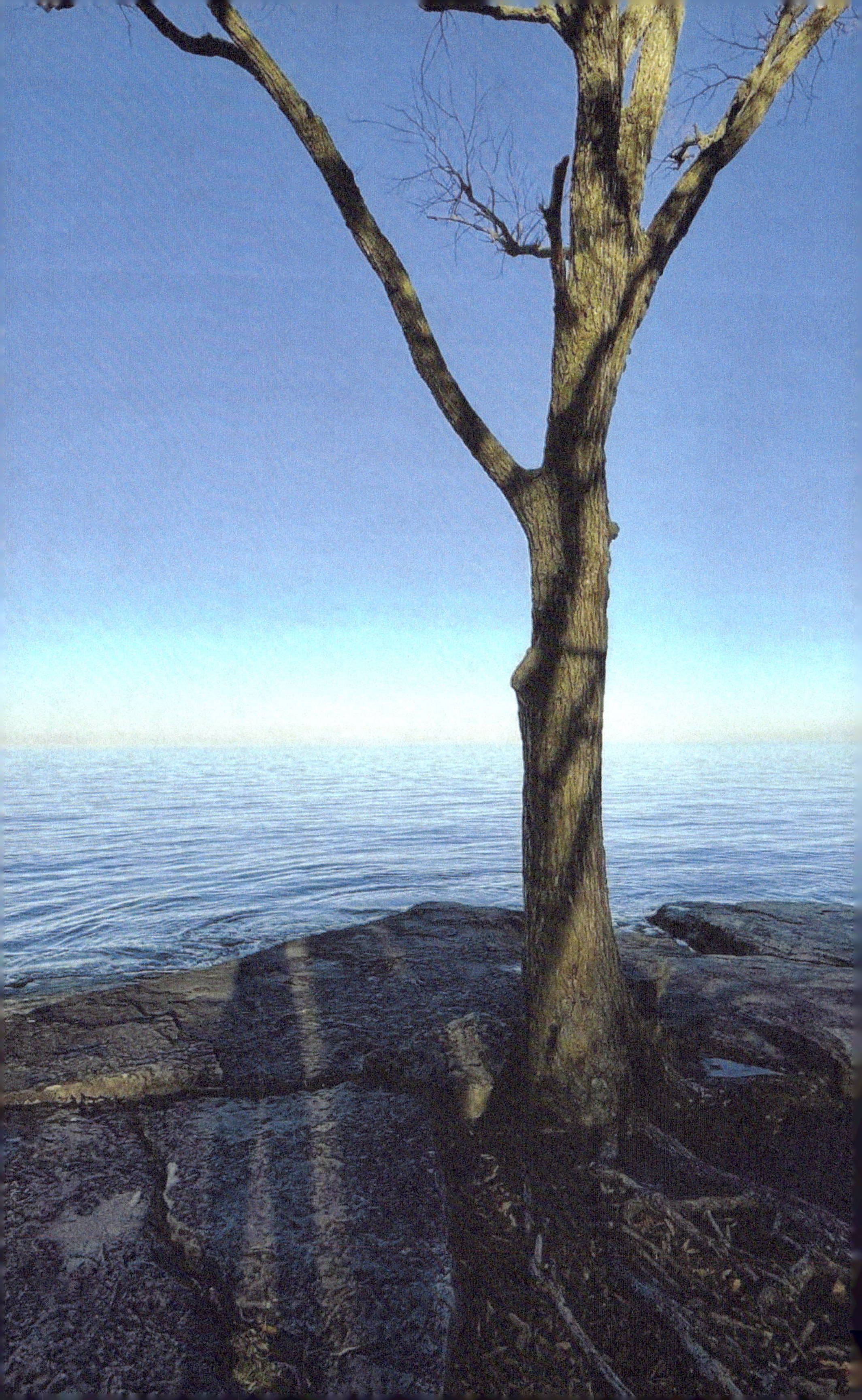

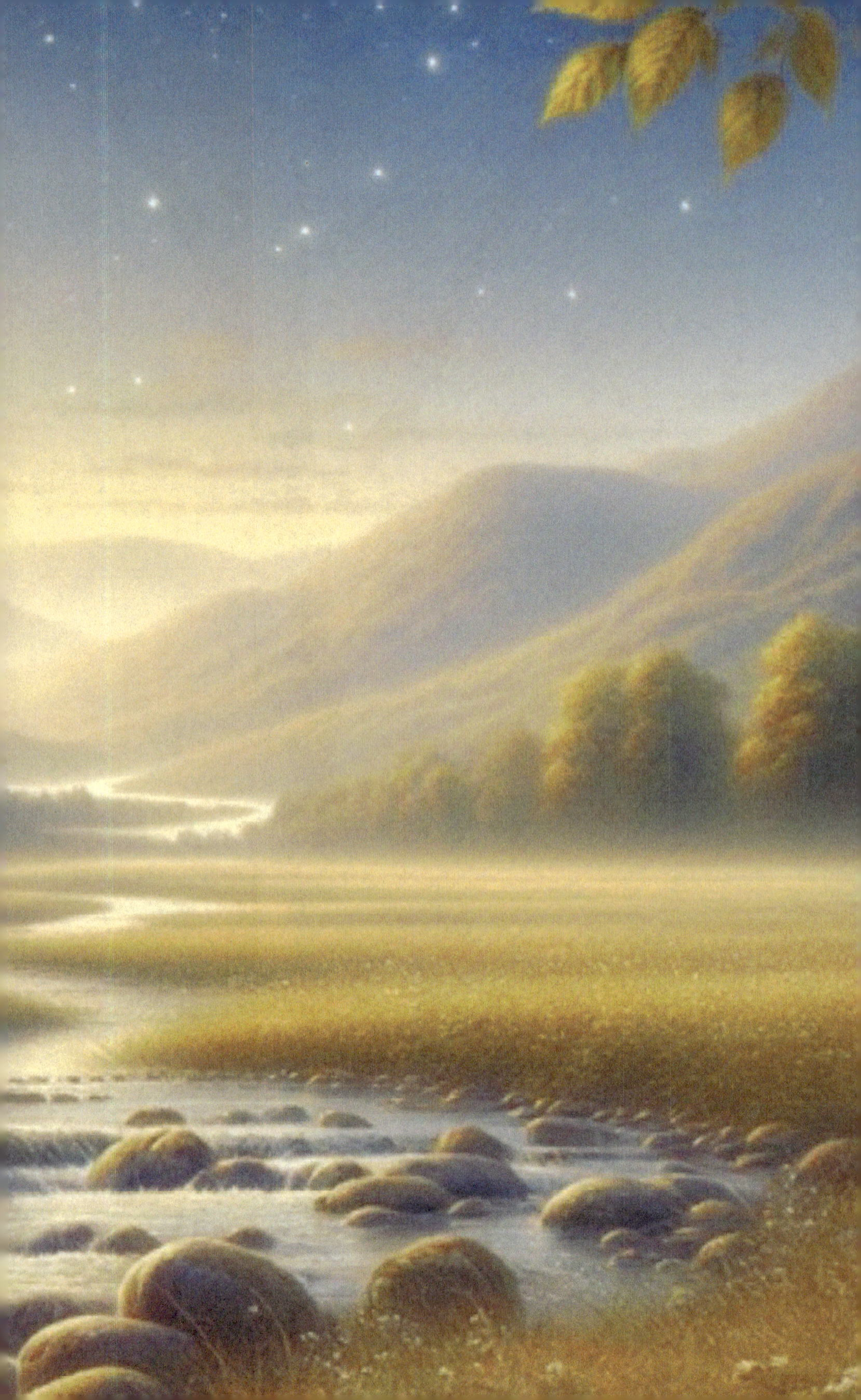

Echoes from the Heart

Echoes of Harmony

Beneath the azure dome of endless skies,
Whispers of the wind weave a silent song,
Nature's breath, in gentle rhythm, softly lies,
In this dance of life, we all belong.

Rivers murmur secrets of ancient tales,
Flowing through meadows, embracing the land,
Each drop tells a story that never fails,
Uniting the earth with a watery band.

Stars gleam above in a quiet accord,
Their ancient light in a symphonic play,
In their glow, the universe's chords,
Harmonize the night and the break of day.

Oceans cradle the world with tender care,
Their waves a lullaby, endless and pure.
From shore to shore, their voices declare,
A bond that time and tide endure.

In the heart of the forest, creatures roam,
Each step-in sync with the earth's gentle hum,
In this symphony, we find our home,
To the rhythm of life, we succumb.

Harmony, a gift in every breath,
In nature's embrace, we find our rest,
In the melody of life and death,
We are part of the world's eternal quest.

Ephemeral Graces

In fleeting moments, joy does dwell,
A glimmer like the morning's first light.
Is it better to have loved and fell,
Then never to embrace the night?

Each memory a precious stone,
Held tight in life's unyielding stream.
For those who've known, then lost, have grown,
In ways that those who've not, just dream.

The pain of loss, a teacher stern,
Yet within its grasp, a hidden gift.
Through loss, life's truest lessons we learn,
And our burdened hearts, it can uplift.

Though love may fade, its mark remains,
An echo in the soul's deep veins.
In every joy, in every pain,
The heart remembers, free from chains.

To have not loved a path untried,
Is a book unopened, a story untold.
Better to have loved and cried,
Than to never let one's heart unfold.

So, cherish the good, though it may go,
For in its leaving, wisdom's seeds are sown.
It's better to have loved, to know,
Than to walk through life's garden, alone.

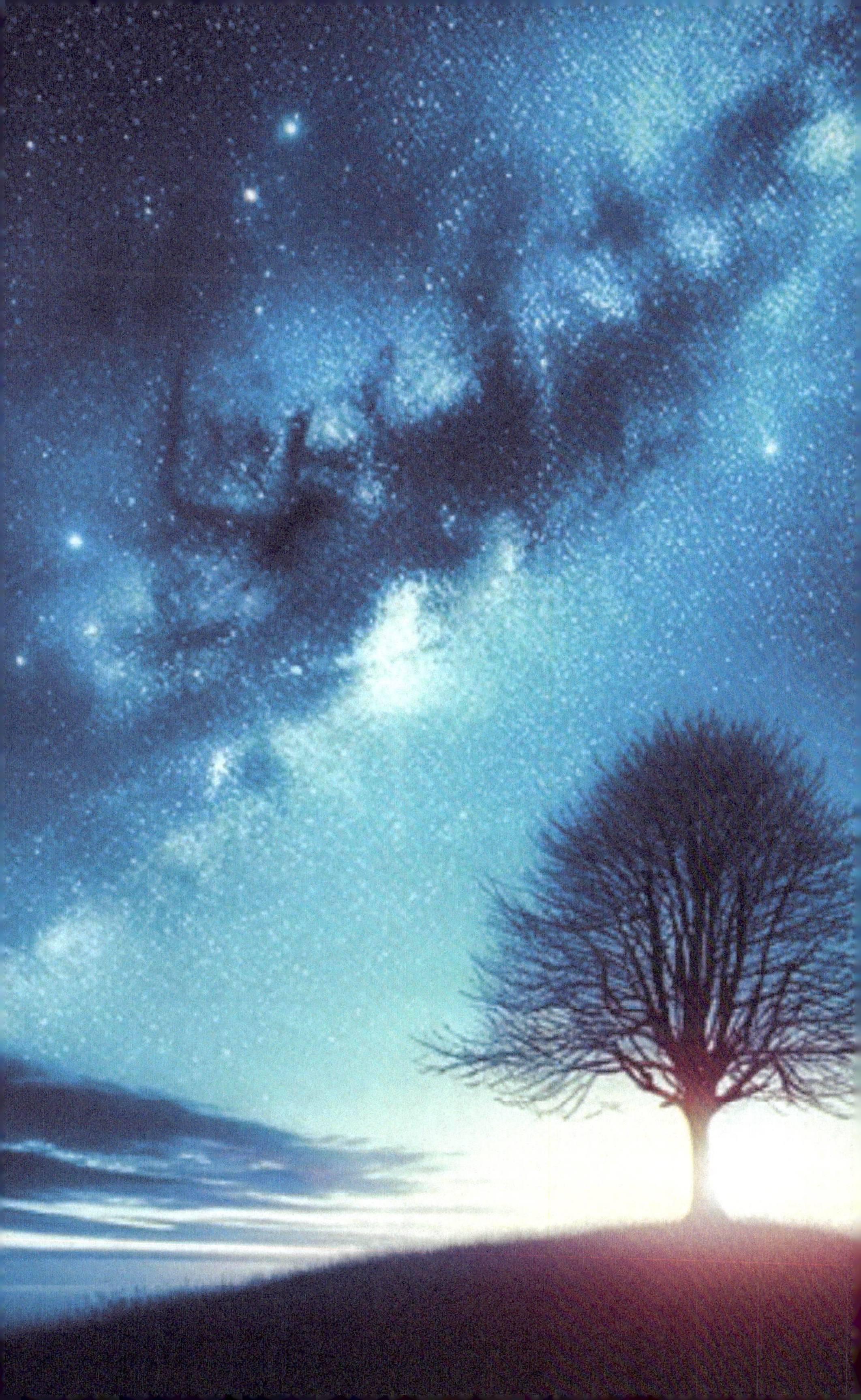

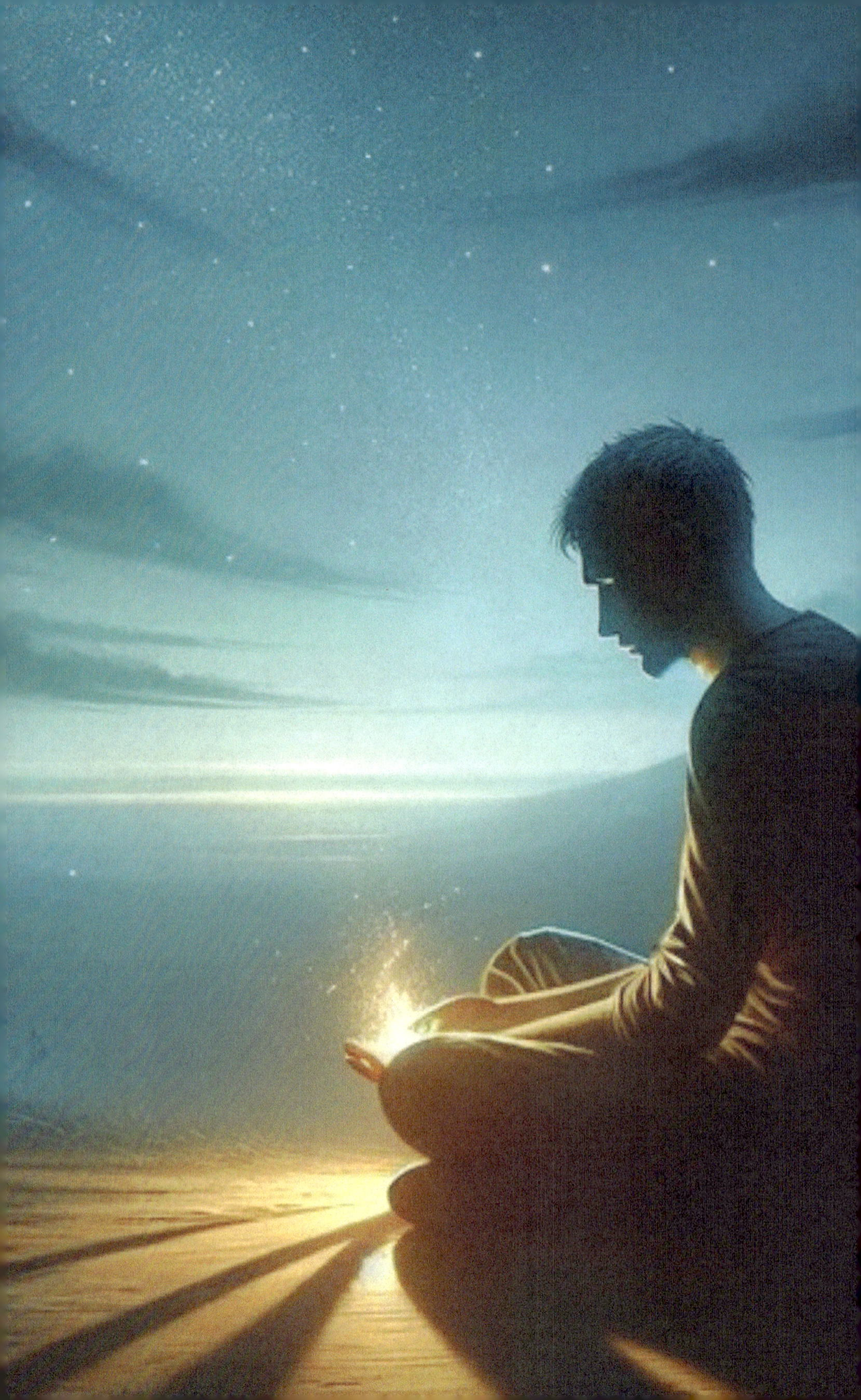

Echoes from the Heart

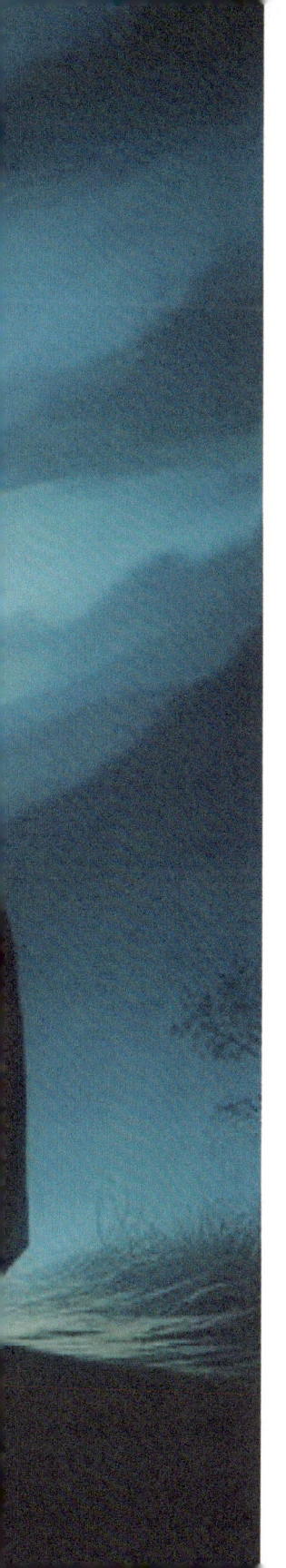

The Quiet Spark Within

In the quiet of the night, under starlit sheen,
A whisper stirs, soft and unseen.
Not a blaze that roars in open sight,
But a tender spark, glowing with inner light.

In the depths of struggle, where shadows play,
The faintest ember wards off dismay.
It's not the fire that commands the skies,
But a subtle glow in the heart that never dies.

In moments of doubt, where fear takes hold,
This tiny spark, more precious than gold.
It flickers, gentle, yet resolute and keen,
Fueling dreams in spaces in-between.

Even when the world seems dark and cold,
And burdens press, heavy and bold,
This quiet spark will rise and sustain,
A constant light through joy and pain.

Through the storm, against winds that howl,
This spark, a beacon, where faint-hearts prowl.
In its warmth, courage is born anew,
A testament to the strength that grew.

In life's vast ocean, a ripple, a start,
The smallest spark ignites the heart.
In whispers, it speaks of resilience and grace,
A silent guardian in life's endless race.

Guiding Light

In shadows deep, where whispers sigh,
A gentle light in love's soft eye.
Through darkest night and stormy blight,
Love's beacon shines, eternally bright.

In every tear, a spark concealed,
By tender touch, its glow revealed.
Through love's embrace, the shadows flee,
In its warm glow, we're truly free.

When lost in sorrow's endless night,
Love's gentle hand leads back to light.
It whispers hope, dispels all fears,
In its embrace, dries all tears.

Even when hope seems out of sight,
Love's quiet flame will still ignite.
A steadfast guide through endless maze,
Its gentle glow lights all our days.

In love, we find our truest north,
A guiding star that leads us forth.
Through every trial, love remains,
Its enduring light forever sustains.

In love's warm glow, we walk the way,
A light that never fades away.
Through every storm, through every strife,
Love is the light that gifts us life.

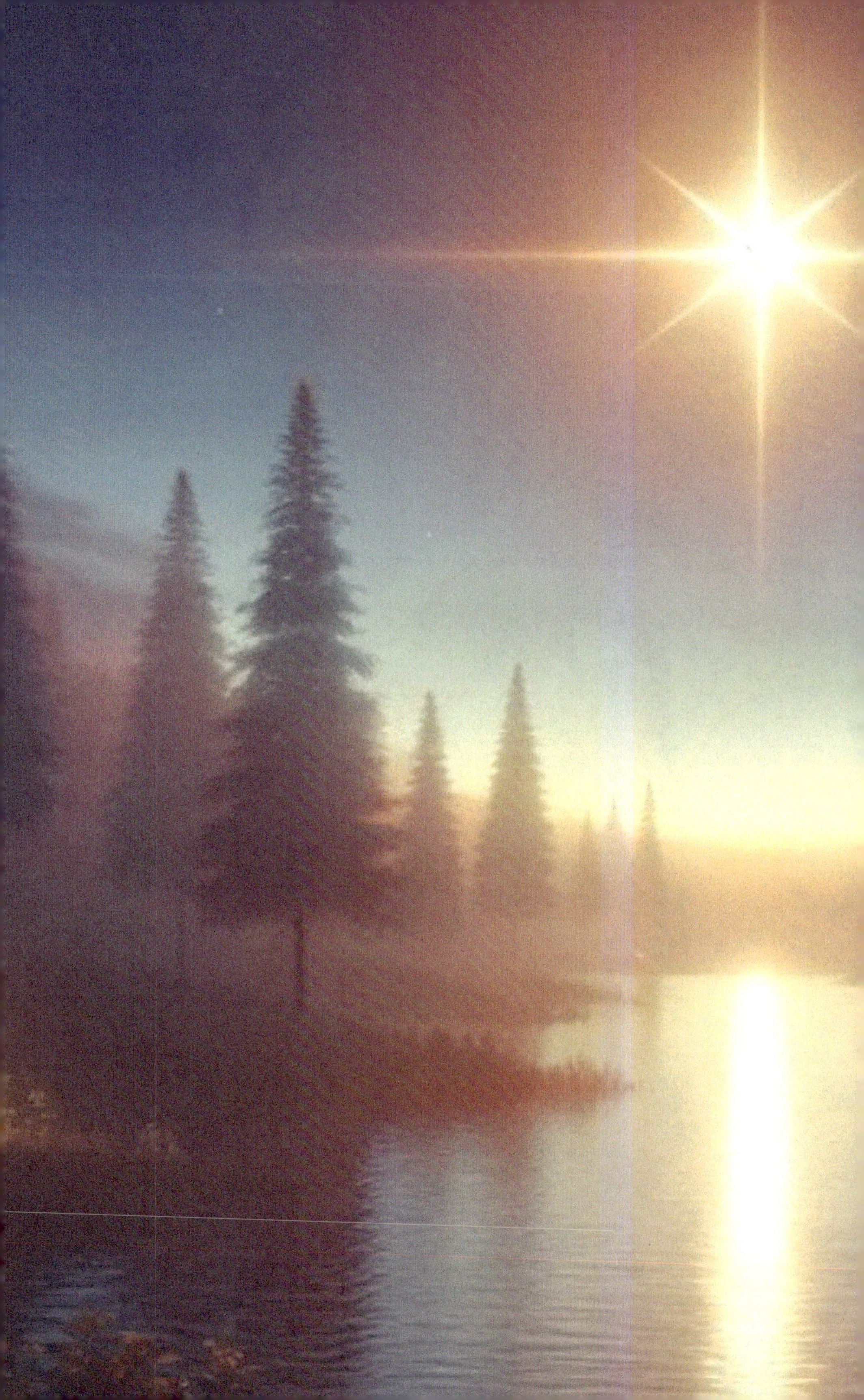

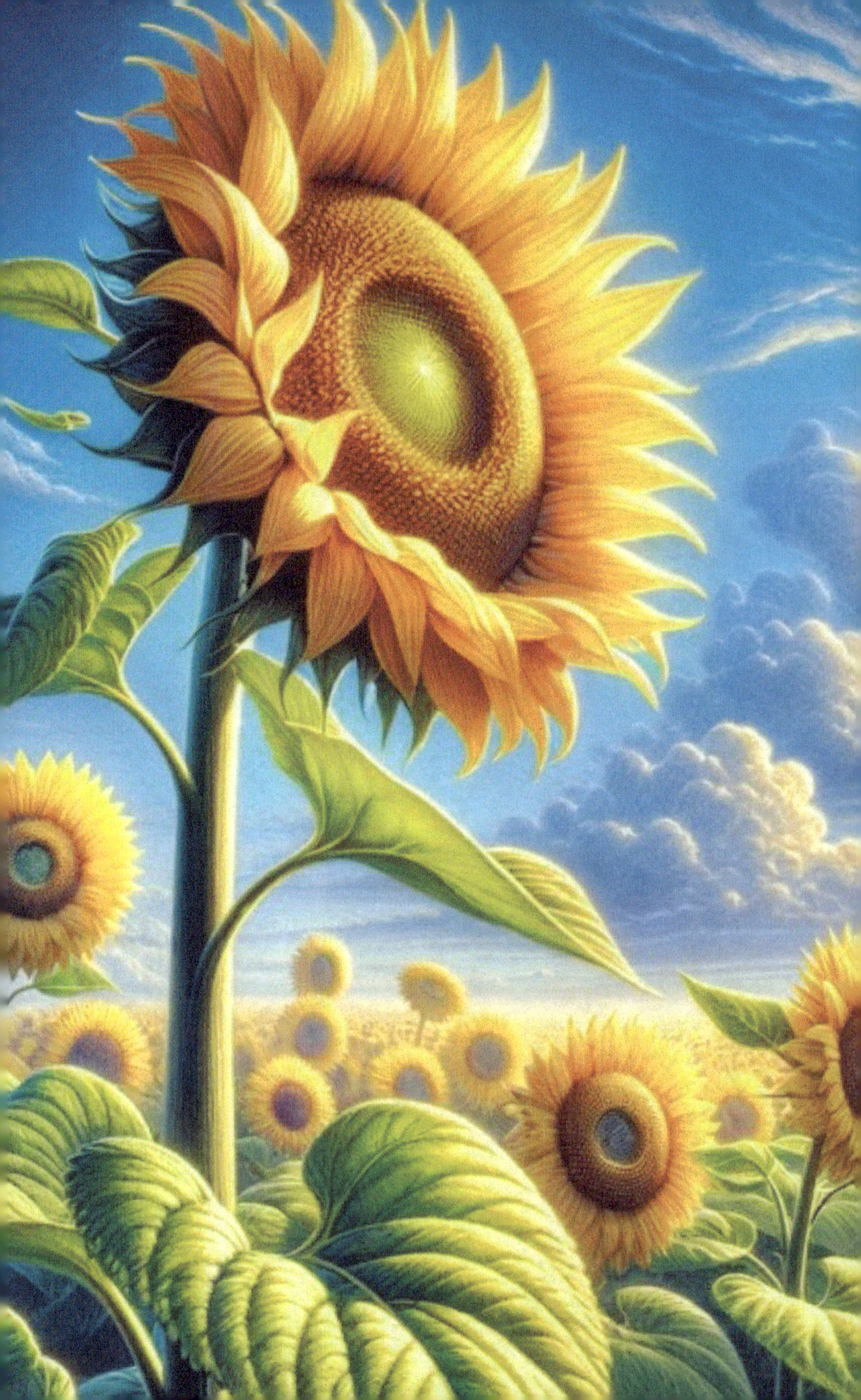

Echoes from the Heart

Sunflowers Fleeting Sunlight

In fields where golden giants sway,
Their heads held high to greet the day.
Brief lives in sunlit splendor cast,
Knowing this dance cannot last.

Roots deep in earth, they seek the sky,
Beneath the sun's watchful eye.
Each petal a fleeting, vibrant sight,
Burning bright, day and night.

Their yellow crowns in breezes sing,
To fleeting joys each moment brings.
Though aware their time is slight,
In brilliance, they claim their right.

They drink in rays, unbent, unbowed,
Each day a gift, each bloom a vow.
Their golden hues, though brief in stay,
Whisper truths that never stray.

Unfazed by fate, they stand tall,
In life's brief play, they give their all.
Embracing each dawn's warm embrace,
In their transient, sunlit space.

And when their final day draws near,
No sorrow shown, no hint of fear.
In grace, they bow to time's decree,
Their beauty etched in memory.

Echoes from the Heart

Light from the Shadows

In the hush of night's embrace,
Gentle darkness takes its place.
Yet in its silent, deep arcane,
Glimmers a light, untouched, unchained.

Stars peep through the ebony veil,
Telling tales where words might fail.
In stillness, hearts begin to see,
The beauty in night's mystery.

Shadows hold the wisdom, old,
In whispers, unspoken, bold.
In stillness, truth starts to unfold,
Silver linings, stories told.

Beneath the moon's soft, watchful glow,
A quiet strength begins to grow.
In darkness, courage dares to rise,
Guided by unseen, starry skies.

In the dark, the soul finds flight,
Beyond the fear, beyond the night.
In quietude, the mind takes light,
Finding peace in starry sight.

In the depths where shadows reign,
Silence sings a soothing strain.
Being still, in night's domain,
Unveils the light, where hope remains.

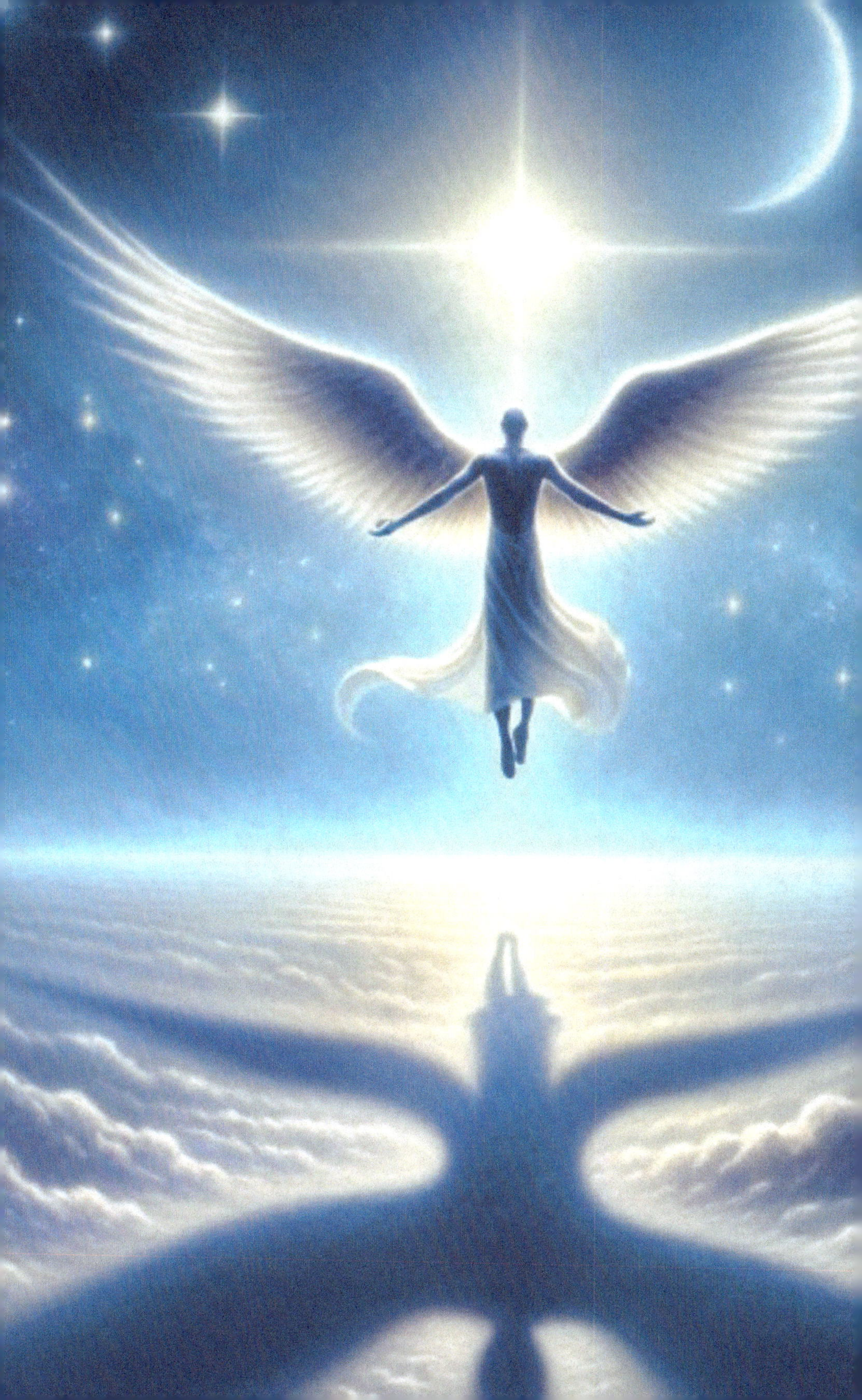

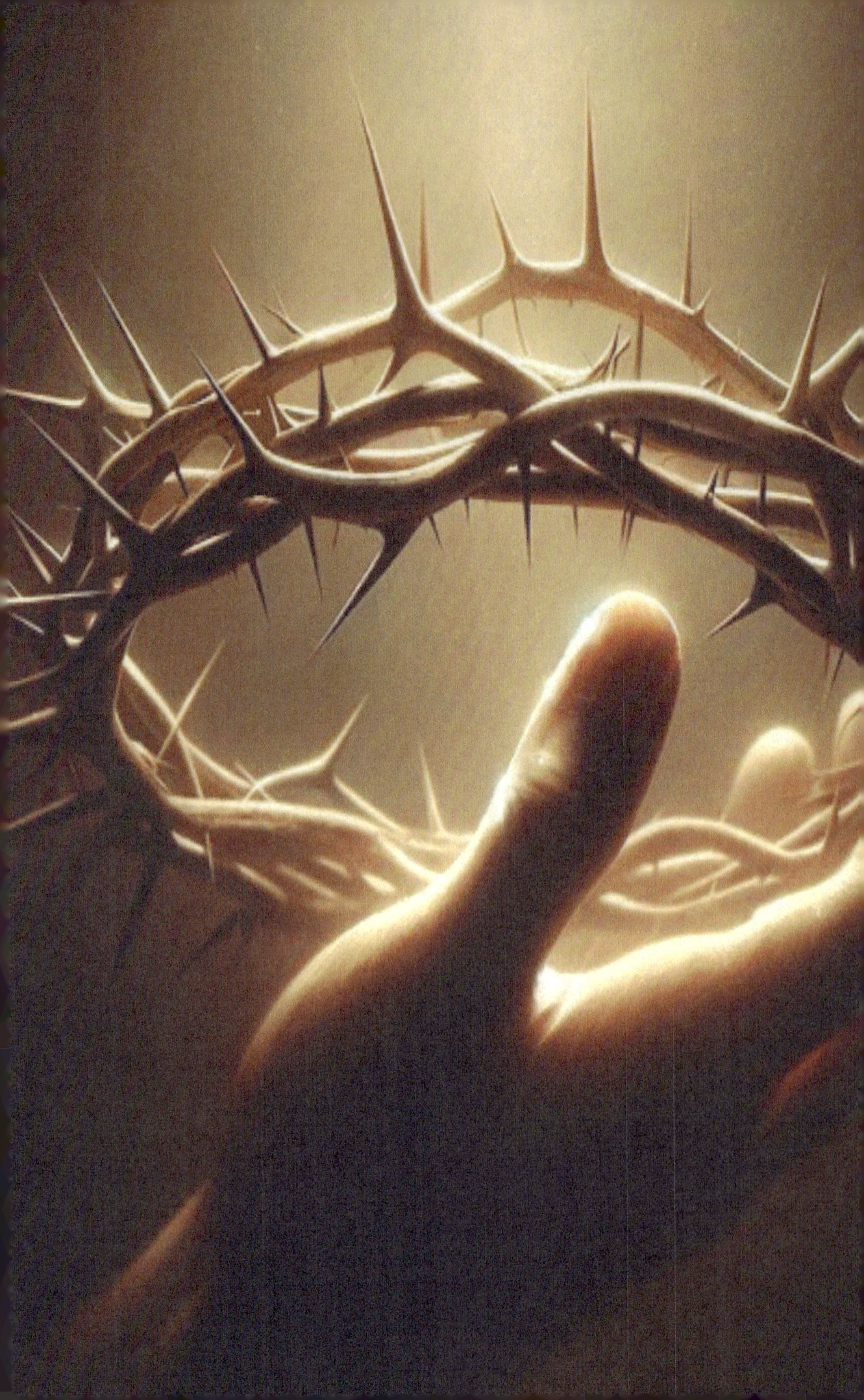

Echoes from the Heart

Crown of Thorns

In sorrow's hues, a visage worn,
Eyes deep as night, gaze forlorn.
Bearing not gold, but a crown of nails,
A silent tale where strength prevails.

Beneath the thorns, shadows lie,
Across features, strong and dry.
A testament of night and day,
Peace and pain in quiet sway.

Gray strokes whisper burdens borne,
Yet within, a light is worn.
Through the suffering, love shines bright,
Guiding all from endless night.

Each line etched tells a tale,
Of a spirit that does not fail.
Captured bold in time's long gaze,
A story told in muted praise.

For in this face, we find our own,
Shared pain in silence, strength has grown.
Through suffering, the light is shown,
A beauty from the trials known.

In every shadow, strength is sown,
A depth of love through pain has grown.
A figure bold in light and thorn,
A crown of sorrow, yet reborn.

The Lord's Mantle

In night's calm, under amber moon's glow,
Angelic whispers softly flow.
Gentle winds hum nature's tune,
As May flowers dance at noon.

Do we sense the angels near,
In breezes soft, so crystal clear?
Like blooms, can we rise and shine,
Washed in summer's rain divine?

Our voices rise like birds in flight,
Seeking truth in quiet light.
Do we reach for beauty's grace,
Striving in this earthly space?

Can we, like angels, rise above,
Embody peace, embrace pure love?
In our journey, hearts aligned,
Seeking God's embrace, entwined.

Soft as petals, love's sweet kiss,
Echoes God's eternal bliss.
In each step, with hope we climb,
To rest in grace, beyond all time.

May we strive, through joy and trial,
To sit beneath His watchful smile.
In life's dance, we seek to find,
Peace and grace for all mankind.

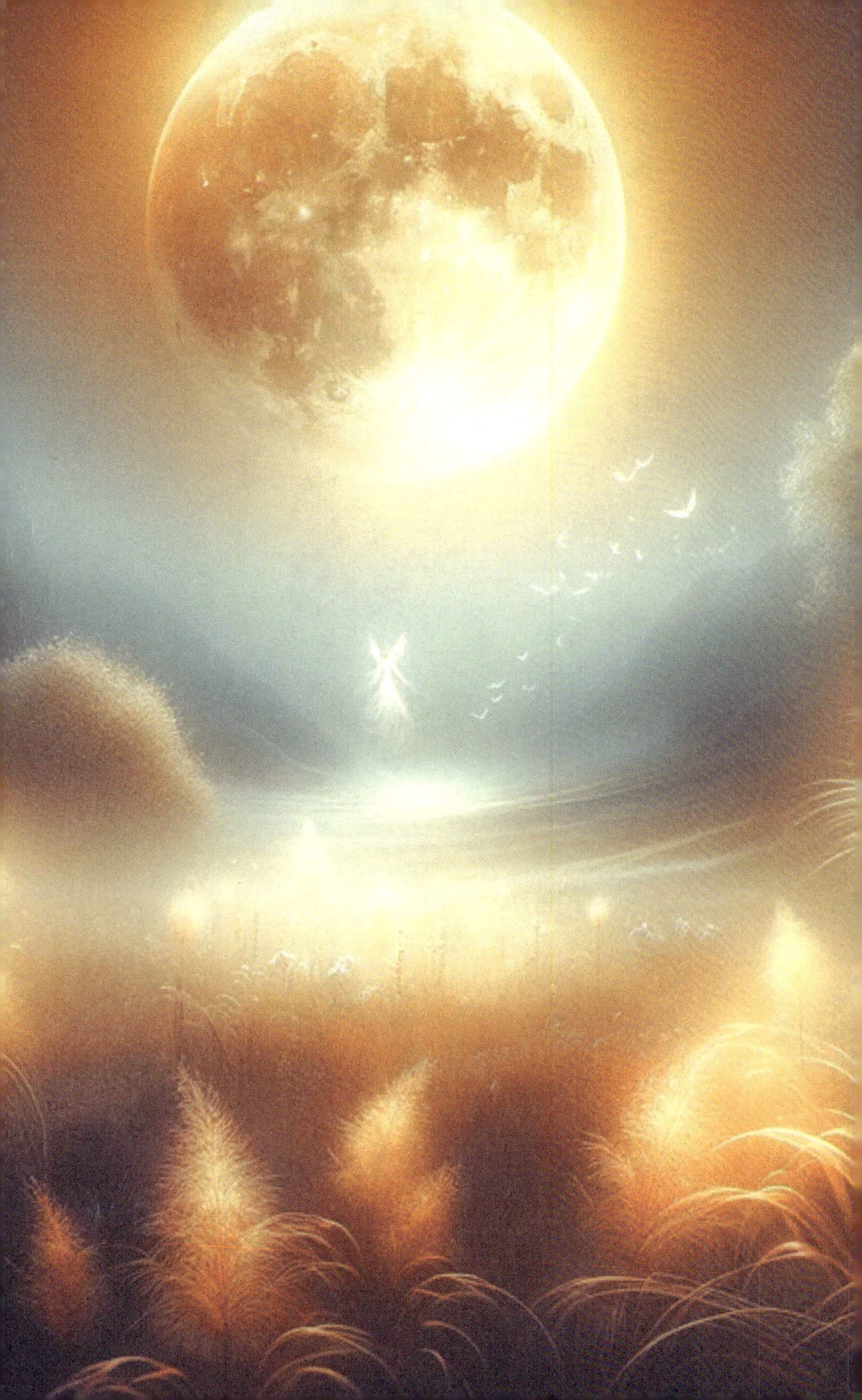

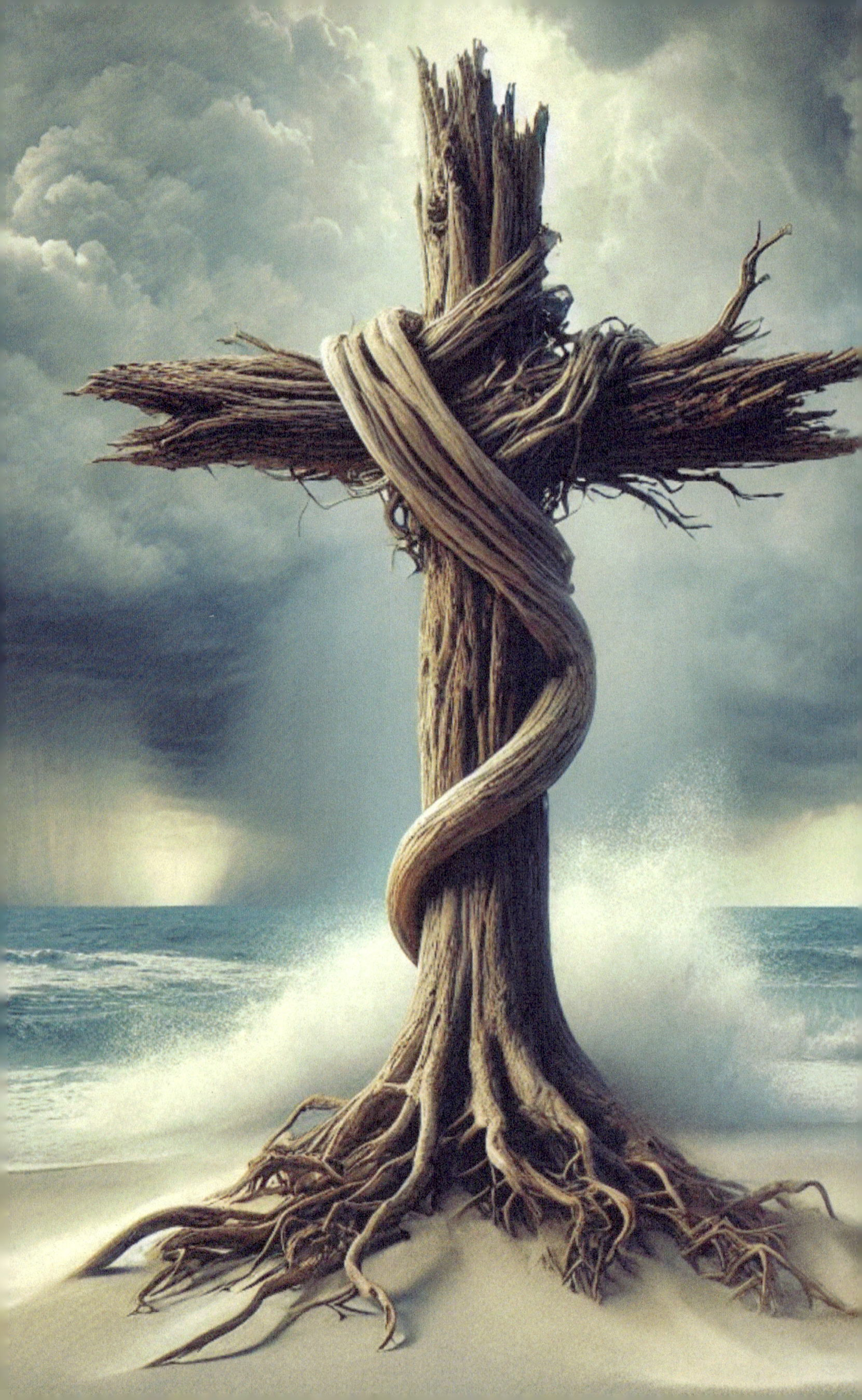

Echoes from the Heart

Faith Amidst the Fury

Where storms brew and skies roar,
Faith stands firm on the shore.
Like a sentinel in the surge,
Resisting the gale's fierce urge.

Thunder cracks, lightning strikes,
Yet faith holds through the night.
Rooted deep, unmoved by fear,
Unseen strength keeps it clear.

Winds howl, sand takes flight,
Faith burns bright in the fight.
Not just wood, but fire within,
A force that stands, where storms begin.

Amid chaos, where fear peaks,
Faith speaks the courage we seek.
Every bolt, every violent shake,
Shows how faith will never break.

Waves reach, but never clasp,
Faith eludes their futile grasp.
In the storm's heart, strength is taught,
Faith stands tall, cannot be caught.

Let the skies rage, oceans roar,
Faith endures forevermore.
In life's worst storms, let truth reside:
Faith rises as fears subside..

Always Believe

In the realm of possibility,
Where dreams take flight,
Anticipation's sweet decree,
In the darkest of night.

With stars above, the sky so vast,
Hope sparks in every heart,
As future's die is truly cast,
In this eternal art.

Infinite paths before our eyes,
Each step a new chance,
To seek the grandest prize,
In life's thrilling dance.

So, always believe, my friend,
In something wondrous, grand,
For when your faith won't bend,
You'll hold life's golden strand.

In moments of doubt, so cold and grim,
Find strength in your soul's hymn,
For in your heart lies a hidden gem,
Guiding you to victory's brim.

In your journey, under the moon's gleam,
Embrace each challenge, each stream,
For in the end, as you follow your dream,
You'll awaken in your own supreme beam.

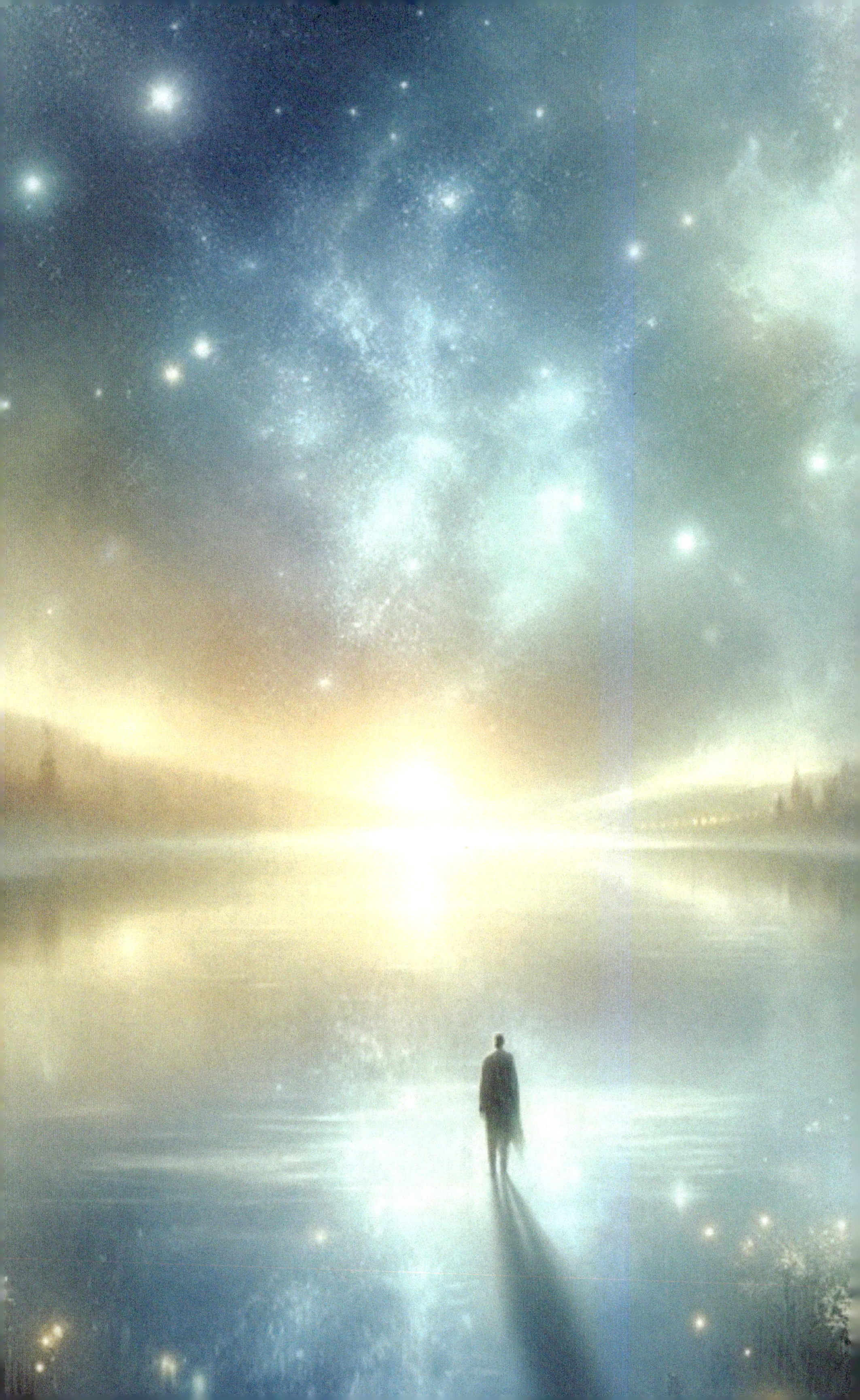

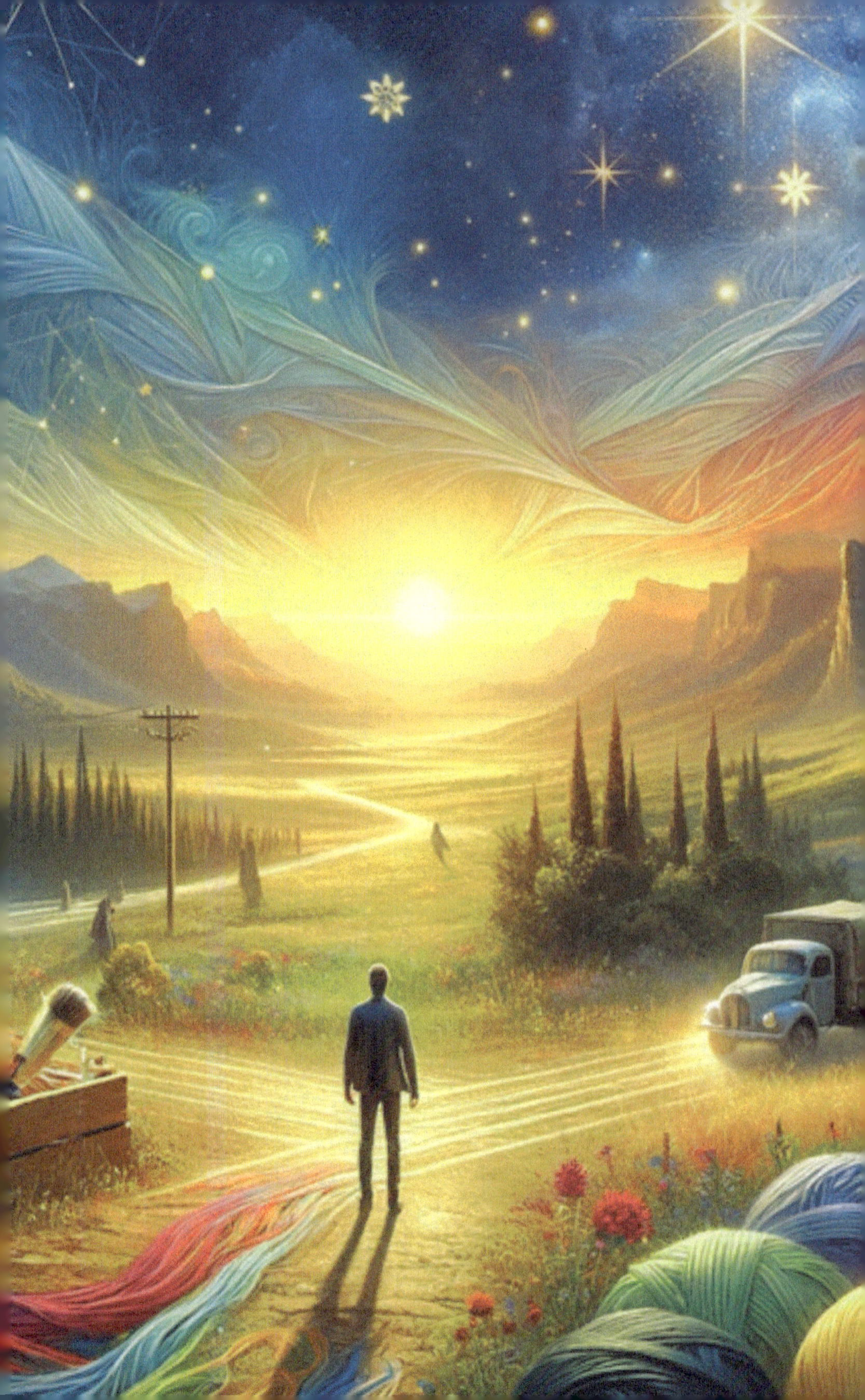

Echoes from the Heart

Build Your Own Testimony

In this world of endless wonder,
Where paths diverge and dreams take flight,
Craft your tale, let your spirit ponder,
Build your own testimony, ignite the light.

See the world with open eyes,
Beyond the horizon, where the secrets dwell,
Amidst the stars that grace the skies,
Forge your story, let it swell.

As rivers carve the land below,
Through trials, your strength will grow.
In moments vast or still and small,
Your story builds with every fall.

In the tapestry of life, we weave,
Each thread unique, a vibrant hue,
With every choice, we choose to believe,
In the power of dreams, both old and new.

Embrace the journey, both near and far,
In each moment, a chapter to explore,
With courage and faith, you'll raise the bar,
Build your own testimony, forevermore.

So, as you tread this path unknown,
Remember, the world is your canvas, your stage,
With each step you take, seeds are sown,
In the story of your life, turn the page.

Echoes from the Heart

ABOUT THE AUTHOR

Scott J. Lucius comes from the quiet countryside of rural Ohio, where he grew up with his siblings, learning life's lessons from his dedicated father. His father's simple but powerful advice, "Work hard and play harder," left a lasting impression on Scott, teaching him the value of both dedication and enjoyment in life.

Scott's educational path was diverse and lengthy, spanning 15 years. He explored various fields, including computer science, management information systems, art, literature, and social work. During these years, his love for poetry grew silently, waiting for the right time to emerge. It wasn't until he retired from a notable career in technology that Scott fully embraced his passion for writing.

He is a family-oriented person and a loyal friend, finding great happiness in these close relationships. An avid traveler, Scott loves to experience the world, gathering inspiration from his journeys for his creative endeavors.

As a poet and storyteller, Scott has a special talent for capturing the complexities of human emotions. His works, influenced by his rich literary background and a deep appreciation for nature, speak to those seeking meaningful and genuine expressions. When not writing, Scott enjoys the tranquility of Santa Fe, New Mexico, drawing inspiration from its picturesque landscapes and the simple beauty of daily life.

PHOTOGRAPH & PAINTINGS COPYRIGHTS

[i] Tarnoff, Laura. (2023). *Sunset* [Photograph]. Private collection of the artist, Santa Fe, New Mexico.

[ii] Wing, Kirsten. (2023). *Turtle Beach* [Photograph]. Private collection of the artist, Santa Fe, New Mexico.

[iii] Vos, Tina. (2023). *Waterwheel* [Photograph]. Private collection of the artist, Greenville, Michigan.

[iv] Tarnoff, Laura. (2023). *Lion* [Painting: Oil on Canvas]. Private collection. Santa Fe, New Mexico. Contact: outsideinartstudios@gmail.com. Prints available at [URL]: https://fineartamerica.com/featured/lion-laura-tarnoff.html.

[v] Vos, Tina. (2011). *Memorial* [Photograph]. Private collection of the artist, Greenville, Michigan.

[vi] Lowry, Ashley. (2023). *Marblehead* [Photograph]. Private collection of the artist, Tiffin, Ohio.

All other images and photographs are the original creations of the author, Scott J. Lucius, in 2024.